# PRAISE FOR *HAVE WE MET?*

"Baker's heart-wrenching and addictive debut follows a twenty-seven-year-old Black woman as she learns to regain hope and trust in the wake of her best friend's death . . . Baker shines in engaging portrayals of friendships old and new. Readers are in for a treat."

—*Publishers Weekly*

"Baker's debut is funny, steamy, and heartwarming all at once . . . A great read that's perfect for those with reunions on the horizon."

—*Booklist*

"*Have We Met?* by Camille Baker is as much a story about the lasting power of friendship as it is a charming rom-com."

—POPSUGAR

"A fun and current read, Baker's debut about a modern woman finding her place in the world is sure to satisfy. Perfect for those longing for this decade's *Sex and the City*."

—Liz Talley, *USA Today* bestselling author

"*Have We Met?* is the perfect blend of fantasy, fun, and hope, with a cast of characters who will make you believe in soul mates and remind you that the love stories we write are the ones we get to read over and over. Camille Baker's debut novel is a true delight!"

—Denise Williams, author of *How to Fail at Flirting*

# THE Moment WE MET

# ALSO BY CAMILLE BAKER

*Have We Met?*

# THE *Moment* WE MET

*a novel*

## CAMILLE BAKER

LAKE UNION
PUBLISHING

Text copyright © 2022 by Camille Baker
All rights reserved.

Published by Lake Union Publishing, Seattle

www.apub.com

Amazon, the Amazon logo, and Lake Union Publishing are trademarks of Amazon.com, Inc., or its affiliates.

ISBN-13: 9781542033633
ISBN-10: 1542033632

Cover design by Philip Pascuzzo

Cover illustration by Tyler Mishá Barnett

Printed in the United States of America

*To William, Ashleigh, Joclyn,*
*and anyone who understands the unique pain of*
*maternal loss. I see you. I ache with you.*

# CHAPTER ONE

Rejections are tiny deaths, sharp and inevitable. I take an hour, sometimes several, to compile my business hopes and dreams into easily digestible pages. *Believe in me,* I beseech of them in the allotted space. *Approve me for this grant.* Then, a month or so later, I'm met with a short note of condolences. The bright side: much like death, it's possible to become numb to rejection.

I quickly scan the latest one and file it in a folder labeled "Hateration." On to the next. Rather, back to the work I'd been engrossed in for hours before this email snapped me out of my trance. I minimize my personal email account containing birthday messages from various retailers and pull back up the report I'd been reviewing. Margie forwarded it to me a few minutes past four, with a request to send back my edits before the team meeting tomorrow morning. I knew by the end of the first page, riddled with my markups, it would take me a few hours. I don't know who to be more upset with—Margie or myself—for being online until 8:00 p.m. so often my coworkers now take it for granted.

My eyes start to glaze over, and I consider making a quick cup of coffee, thus committing to working late. My phone chimes, which means someone has tripped the security camera. I don't bother pulling up the feed, since a neighbor from 1A usually arrives around this time.

Black tea, I decide, and rise to my feet. Enough caffeine to give me a boost, but not so much that I'll be seeing spreadsheets behind my eyelids when I try to sleep later tonight. As I'm in midstretch, the intercom system buzzes. Instead of using the system to ask who it is, I pick up my phone. Sure enough, there are a couple of notifications with the pertinent information. The buzz is nothing more than a courtesy warning, because the heavy footsteps of my grandma and aunt Clara have already started to ascend the stairs. I open my door, waiting with a hand on my hip for them to come into view.

Clara is first, her shoulder-length twists pulled up into a haphazard bun that highlights her supple, golden-brown skin. Despite her coat, I bet her legs are freezing with the thin, billowy pants she's wearing. When she sees me, she pauses, mouth open in a *gotcha* smile and arms outstretched. She has a wine bottle in one hand, a tote bag in the other. She covers the last steps and wraps me in a hug, her familiar scent of verbena and shea butter soothing me in a way the best mug of tea could never.

Grandma is slower moving, this flight of stairs the top reason she'd cite for why I can count on my fingers how many times she's visited in the four years I've lived here.

"I don't understand why Vette couldn't have given you the first-floor unit," she says as she makes it to the landing, then adds, "Happy birthday, baby."

I give her a hug and decide there's no need to point out yet again that Auntie Yvette, who works in real estate, didn't *give* me this condo. I lease it. At a price much lower than she could get for it, but still.

Clara abandons the stuff she brought on the dining table and scans the room. Her eyes snag on my laptop, open and waiting for me to return to the couch.

"Told you she'd still be working," Clara snitches to Grandma, who tsks as she lowers herself to the couch and reaches for the remote. "I like this," Clara says, touching my hair. It's in two simple french braids on either side of my head, connecting in the back. The style is mostly functional. One less thing to worry about as I hurry out of bed and to the office in the morning.

"Are you ready to party?" Clara asks with a little jig.

I wince. "I just need five more minutes."

She drops her head to the side, understanding my five minutes of working time translates to roughly half an hour. She fishes in her cross-body purse and pulls out a small floral-patterned box where she keeps her stash. "I'll be on the patio," she says.

Clara is Grandma's youngest child and only seven years older than me. In my teenage years, I racked up comparisons to Clara, mostly from Grandma when she was upset with me. It wasn't the most effective insult, since I idolized her.

I grab a bottle of water for Grandma and sit on the couch with her, bringing my work laptop back in front of me. By pure will I get back into a workflow, catching errors and remedying them as deftly as possible. I don't check how much time has passed until Clara returns and sits on the middle couch cushion, her grassy scent annoying Grandma.

"You smoke more reefer than I ever did." She scrunches her nose.

"Well, you always did want more for us," Clara says. Before I can react, she reaches over and takes my laptop from me. She closes it with an audible snap on her lap. "Time's up. This is a sad way to bring in your thirtieth."

I've had that same thought the entire day. In the morning, I'd planned to carve some time out of my workday to do something just for me: take a walk up to my favorite café, go to the local bakery for a *pączki* . . . But short-notice meetings got added to my schedule and slashed those plans. I tried not to let it bother me. February is typically busy for my job, so I've gotten used to properly celebrating my birthday when I can. Some years, it's not until weeks later.

I don't protest Clara's strong-arming. We relocate to the dining table, where Clara pulls out a small cake and numerical candles.

She lights them, and I allow them to duet Stevie Wonder's "Happy Birthday" song. I feign making a wish and then extinguish the flames.

Since my adolescence, I've never been able to think of a wish fast enough for birthday cakes. When a family member would demand a wish from me, their faces stretched with glee, my mind would go blank. Or a thought of my parents would surface, and in the seconds it took for my brain to dismiss it as a possibility, the moment would be gone. I knew people expected me to get on with it and deliver their slices of cake with a simple saliva-speckled blow over the tops of the candles. Eventually, instead of trying to think up a wish, I'd started counting to three and moving it along.

"What did you wish for?" Clara lifts a knowing brow. She's well aware of my dried-up wishing well.

"For you to leave soon so I can send off this dumb report."

Clara scoffs. "Uninspired."

"Clara drove us, so we're not going anywhere with her under the influence," Grandma says.

We get slices of cake as I open the presents they brought. Clara gives a mix of gift cards to my favorite stores. Grandma presents an antique box of recipe cards. I scan a few of them and realize they're her own recipes, evident from measurements like "a good amount" and "a couple spoonfuls."

"There's one more thing," Grandma says. She reaches into her purse and pulls out a bound fabric-covered notebook, then slides it across the table toward me. The small baby shoes pictured on the front give me pause.

"Please don't tell me this is a plea for great-grandchildren," I say.

Both Clara and Grandma laugh at that idea more than necessary.

"Do you remember Vonette?" Grandma asks. I shake my head, running my finger along the worn edges of the cover. "Your mom's cousin. They were close."

Cousin Vonnie. I spent many afternoons at her house as a child. She and my mom hung out in the den, the only room with a television. I was always peeved at that, because they did more gabbing than watching, and I was sure I'd appreciate the television more than they did. Instead, I had to find something else to occupy myself with. I signal my belated recognition with a nod.

"We ran into each other last week over there on Torrence. She recognized me, of course; I wouldn't have looked twice at the girl." I steel my gaze so it doesn't accidentally slip skyward. "She asked about you and said she had something she thought you might like." Grandma gestures toward the notebook. "Your mom didn't keep a diary, but the doctor convinced her to do a pregnancy journal. This was one of the many things Vonette got her greedy hands on."

Clara swallows the bite of cake in her mouth and clears her throat. "Anyway, it's nice that she thought to share it with you."

The potential of its contents grows like ivy in my brain. My mom's words, her thoughts and feelings from the pregnancy that ultimately claimed her life. I can pull up images, whether real or imagined I'm not sure, of that time. Dad calling me over to place my small hands on the taut skin of Mom's belly. Taking advantage of Mom's exhaustion and playing Nintendo longer than normally allowed. But try as I might, I can't recall any conversations about it. Did she look forward to growing our small family? Was she worried at all? Might these questions be answered in the pages of the journal, or will I open it and be disappointed by belly measurements and notes on cravings?

"I'll take a look at it later." I put it in the bag along with my gifts. We're silent for a moment, and I can't stop my eyes from flicking to my laptop on the coffee table.

"No," Clara says. She obviously knows me too well. "I'm getting us wine. No more working."

"It's either finish up now or wake up early." I absently rub at a knot in my shoulder. The options sound bleak to my own ears.

Grandma tuts. "How many birthdays are you going to spend like this? It's not right."

Clara puts a glass in front of me and pours from the newly opened bottle. I don't even wait for it to breathe before taking a sip. This is far from what twenty-year-old me had in mind for my life. My younger self lived almost haughtily, prioritizing anything that made me happy. Whatever it took to veer my mind away from the grief. My mom and dad used to go overboard celebrating my birthdays. Grandma tried to carry on that tradition, finding small ways to make the day special for me. Sometimes she'd let me play hooky from school and we'd spend the day running errands and baking treats.

"Next year," I vow, "I'll be off for my birthday. On vacation, even!"

"Only way that's happening is if you quit," Clara says.

"That can be arranged," Grandma says.

Clara snaps her fingers and points at Grandma, her head bouncing up and down. She riffles through my work bag and pulls out the writing pad and pen I keep there for jotting down notes during meetings. "We're going to write your resignation letter, and you can hand it in when you're ready."

Clara narrates as she scrawls the opening lines. "What to say to the job that has sucked the soul out of me? Well, for starters, I wholeheartedly quit."

"All right, so I won't be handing this version in."

"I'm taking artistic liberties. You can edit it later, whenever you get around to using it."

"Make sure you list every single shitty thing they've done," Grandma says, letting her petty flag fly.

Clara starts with some of the most egregious stories I've told her, like when another manager quit so they "redistributed" her projects but gave the bulk of them to me. Or the time I went on a long-overdue vacation and my boss had the nerve to make an underhanded comment about me not responding to flagged emails while I was out. Grandma chimes in with her top hits, and once they've both run out of anecdotes, they turn to me. The top reasons to quit that come to mind aren't the huge injustices, though. They're the annoyances that have accumulated over the years to make me absolutely miserable every time I pull into the parking garage.

Whenever they say they're providing breakfast, it's only bagels. How our department always comes in last place for the company-wide step challenge. Whenever we have a family- and dog- friendly team-building event, without fail, Margie tells me I should "get one of my own," as if I have any spare time for that responsibility. How most people don't cover their food in the microwave so by the time I go to warm up my late lunch, it looks like a spaghetti-sauce crime scene. I rattle them off and Clara keeps up, the pen scratching against the paper, until my points become so ridiculous the two of us are gasping with laughter as Grandma just shakes her head.

I might not be able to ever give this letter to Margie as is, but it was therapeutic. And listing out all the reasons to quit this job makes me wonder, *What are the reasons to stay?* Other than a paycheck, I'm hard pressed to find any. If I'm going to keep my promise to myself to be free on my next birthday, I have to figure out an exit plan.

# CHAPTER TWO

When my alarm jerks me awake, the first thing I'm aware of is Clara's form pressed against my side. A wandering person by nature, even in sleep her body doesn't know how to stay still. I have a foggy memory of waking when she climbed into bed with me hours after I'd made sure the guest room was prepared for Grandma and left blankets on the couch for Clara, in case she stayed up late writing articles for the local news outlet like she normally did.

This is only the first of a series of three alarms, but I push myself up anyway with the thought of the work I left unfinished driving me upright. Clara shifts over, away from my movement.

"Whereyougoing?" Her words run together, muffled by the pillow.

"To work."

"But we quit."

"Yes, in spirit. Unfortunately, that doesn't count as far as my boss is concerned."

Clara is already gently snoring again by the time I finish speaking. She's been tuning out whenever I talk about work lately, so certain I'm hanging on to a period of my life that should have ended months ago. Easy for her to say. The moment she became burnt out from traveling for work, she was offered a position covering cultural and art events in the Chicago area. I hurry through my morning routine, all the while making mental notes of things I need to do, including making a new batch of face soap. Once, I couldn't find enough people to thrust my natural-soap creations upon. But between the start of busy season and losing a few members of our team, my stock has run out.

My work bag isn't packed like I usually ensure it is before bed, so I run around and collect my dead laptop from the kitchen table, my notes from the couch, and a slew of other items. I make a quick cup of coffee, transfer it into a travel mug, and am out the door.

The short drive from my condo to the office is something to be both appreciated and rued. I'm the first one of my team to arrive, but I don't bother turning on the overhead lights. By the end of the day, I'll have a headache from the combination of the fluorescent bulbs and staring at my screen.

I work for a half hour alone before my closest friend here, Chris, makes it in. His cubicle is right behind mine, so I turn to greet him.

"Thought you said you weren't showing up before nine today," I say.

"Yeah, yeah."

This is our routine. At the end of every workday, Chris promises he's not going to be in until after nine the following day. It's always a lie. We tend to show up around eight to "get ahead of the day," an impossible attempt. He once told me, "I'm serious; I'm not going to be in until late tomorrow. I'm having dental surgery in the morning." When I got there the next day at eight fifteen and he was already in his seat with a numbed jaw, I didn't blink an eye.

Our team meeting is at nine thirty. Margie admitted to scheduling them in this time slot because she's of a mind that if she gave us an extra half hour before having to convene and be sociable, we'd squander it. Better to cap our squandering at thirty minutes.

Chris and I head over together, carrying our laptops and first mugs of coffee for the day. It's mostly a status meeting detailing in what areas we're most behind for the audit for our company, Medical Innovative Lab. Chris and I have a notepad between our setups at the long table, where we slyly jot down out-of-context notes to make each other laugh. He's left handed, so it works out perfectly if we sit on the correct sides.

When I'd interviewed to work in MIL's accounting department, I honestly was excited to work with an ever-changing industry. But over the course of the years I've been here, my workload has increased in tandem with the company's sprawling sectors.

"Tiwanda, is there anything you want to add regarding the Home Devices product line?"

Chris immediately starts jotting a note down that I'm sure will be something along the lines of "Sharing is caring, Tee." I hadn't been paying close enough attention to be sure I successfully avoid repeating something that was already said, so I keep it broad.

"I'll be following up directly with my team, but in general, I think we're making incredible progress with an unreasonably tight deadline."

There's a short pause before Margie huffs, "Well, it's our busiest season, so not unreasonable by my standards. Stick around a bit longer and you'll see some things to put it in perspective." She pairs her words with a phony little laugh before moving on to the final point on the agenda.

I glance over at Chris's and my shared notepad. "Ooh burn," he's written.

Margie's dig does char my insides more than it normally would. It could be my recent birthday, or all the negative thoughts Clara brought to the surface with the resignation she penned last night. Tension is present in every inch of my body—from my clenched jaw to the phantom weight on my chest to even my toes flexing in my shoes to deter an outward response.

I've been here for seven years. Sure, it pales in comparison to the umpteenth year Margie is on, but I still have a valid perspective. It's not that she believes I don't, but that she picks and chooses when it's relevant. She trusted my *perspective* just fine when it came to assigning me as lead on multiple projects. But when I so much as hint at the strenuous workload, she dismisses me.

Chris's pen taps absently on the notepad, drawing my attention to the newest line: "Breathe."

Margie brings the meeting to a close, and I haven't heard anything she's said since her response to me. I pack my laptop bag carelessly, standing even as I continue to reach for the notepad to stash it away. When I lift it from the table, a piece of paper comes fluttering out. Chris picks it up from the floor.

"What's this?" he asks as he holds it out to me.

It's folded like an envelope, all the writing facing inside. On the outside in Clara's handwriting are the words "To whom it may concern." I take it from Chris and run my finger along the corner.

"A reminder," I say.

Margie appears at my side. "Let's have a quick chat in my office before you get back to it." She turns and exits the room without awaiting confirmation. I exchange a peeved look with Chris before following behind her.

The plush chairs across from Margie's wooden desk are the one consolation of spending so much time in her office. I've always enjoyed her organization, and the large window behind her that faces toward Lake Michigan, though the water isn't in sight. Even the few pictures she has of her family are nice, a reminder that like all of us here, she is more than this job.

"I understand this line of work asks a lot of us. It requires tenacity and grit. As a leader, I expect you to be more encouraging for the associates. Bemoaning the tasks at hand doesn't get them done."

She's right, in a way. A few busy seasons ago, I probably wouldn't have complained about being overcapacity at an all-team meeting. I would've bitten my tongue, put in more hours so the associates under me wouldn't hate their lives and quit on us mid–busy season, and suggested hiring more personnel on all levels. Which Margie would tell me HR would never approve.

The soft crinkle of paper reminds me I still have my faux resignation letter in my hand. My heartbeat speeds up as I look down at the faint lines of ink that made it through the paper.

"Well?" Margie asks impatiently.

I ignore her and unfold my letter, smoothing it open on my lap so that it's hidden from view. Scanning the list, I nod my head to myself.

"I think I quit." I blink up at Margie. The confusion I feel is reflected in her face. Part of me is surprised the words made it out.

She scoffs. "What are you saying? No you don't. You're just frustrated, as I am too. But you can handle this. You've earned the highest bonus payout level the past few years for a reason."

I could go along with her, agree that I don't actually quit. But when I open my mouth to do just that, my throat tightens against the attempt to take it back. Logic tells me that if I did, Margie would be watching me closer than ever, worrying I'm a flight risk. That, I could deal with. My heart thrums painfully in my chest, and my stomach churns with a hopeful uncertainty. The thought of backtracking, returning to my desk, and continuing my day as if I hadn't been on the brink of freedom makes me physically ill. I haven't planned for what comes next, not concretely at least, but maybe now is the time for me to jump in feetfirst. The head stuff—overthinking, second-guessing myself—that can follow me in.

"I can handle it, but I don't want to anymore. I do, Margie. I wholeheartedly quit."

# CHAPTER THREE

There's a buzz from my condo's intercom system, but I'm not surprised, since moments ago, my location tracker app informed me that both Elise and Cory are here. I have two location-sharing networks—one for my family, and another for my core friend group with Elise, Cory, and my cousin Corinne. I have notifications on for when anyone arrives at my home location, mainly to get a heads-up to know I'll need to buzz them up. In this case, I'm happy for the ambush warning.

It has barely been forty-eight hours since my last morning at work. Since then, I've been tallying all the necessary tasks to launch my business, Bathe in Chocolate. I have three weeks of vacation MIL will pay out, pushing my official end date. Three weeks to form an actionable plan to turn my pipe dreams into a reality. The handful of grant program rejections cast a doubtful light, but I can't afford to let that deter me. There once was a time when I lived like I was owed happiness, because of all the loss I'd endured. It's time to get that version of me back.

There are two things I love making more than any pastry I learned how to bake during my two years at Jon Wills Culinary Institute: chocolate and bar soap. My pastry school curriculum included an intensive half-semester study of chocolate. I fell so in love I imagined finding a job working at a confectionery, making chocolate and fudge before the sun rose. Or finding an apprenticeship in Europe, like so many of the pastry chefs I met throughout my time in school.

When my plans changed, it wasn't momentous. In my younger years, I deconstructed and re-formed them into something closer to what I truly desired without a second thought. I considered it a natural process and didn't allow myself to stand in the way of it. By graduation from pastry school, I had landed on the plan to transfer to a university. I'd major in accounting to put myself in a position to succeed at running my own business. As I got older, that natural evolution of life plans started to slow. I stopped following whims and instead started meticulously planning the path to my dreams. Planning can sneakily transform into deferment if not vigilant, and I was not.

I buzz Elise and Cory up without saying anything through the intercom. Upon opening the door, I listen to their steps trudge up to my second-floor suite. Elise takes the lead, pausing to dramatically sweep her eyes over the pajama set I'm still wearing. She continues up the last steps, ditches her snow boots, and saunters past me and into the living room. Cory follows.

"She called me here for backup," he explains on his way in, pulling off the beanie stretched over his locs.

I shake my head and rebolt the door behind them.

"I quit my job," I blurt out.

Neither Cory nor Elise feigns surprise. I frown at them.

Elise holds up her phone, then tosses it on the couch so she can take off her coat. She's of average height but carries the same stage presence she has in theater to her everyday life. Her recently cut hair brushes her collarbone and the tattoo there as she speaks. "You haven't left in days. When you didn't return my calls, I rang the office assistant's line. It was unlikely you forgot your phone at home, but worth a shot. Imagine my surprise when she informed me you no longer work there."

I sigh, knowing I gave her the means to track my location so there's only myself to blame for not being able to hold on to this secret a little longer.

"Congratulations," Cory says. "Should we . . . celebrate?"

Before my unceremonious resignation, I imagined this elusive moment would be cause for celebration. But jumping into the quitting abyss like this only fills me with an anxiety that makes it impossible to rejoice. I shake my head and collapse onto the couch between them. "Technically, I'm still on their payroll for three more weeks. I'm trying to figure out my next steps in that time. We can revisit celebrating then."

"Tee, this is a good thing," Elise says.

"I know, just keep reminding me when things inevitably go wrong."

"The problem with many of us is we assume when things don't go our way, it's wrong."

I let my head fall onto Cory's shoulder. This is why I didn't rush to tell Elise. She might be my best friend, but sometimes I need to not consider silver linings and fate. Sometimes I need to wallow in self-doubt just to figure out how to rise from its depths, victorious.

Cory jostles me off his shoulder and stands.

"Where are you going?" I whine, missing his quiet comfort.

He's heading toward the kitchen. "Looking for the chocolate I'm sure you stress-made at some point. Oh, here we go." He locates the container of caramel-and-pecan-filled bonbons and shakes it in my direction before taking a few and replacing it in the fridge. "Does you quitting mean it's time to start your business? The baking class thing?"

I nod, but his description is a bit off. "Think those boozy guided painting places, or cooking classes. But it would offer two options: making a customizable batch of chocolate bonbons, or making your own bars of natural soap. With or without wine involved. It could be for birthday parties, couples' nights . . ."

"Bachelorette activities, friend outings, school field trips, teen nights," Elise adds, enthusiasm dripping off each subsequent idea.

Cory settles back down on the couch beside me. "Chocolate and soap. That's an odd mix."

Whenever I first explain my idea in full to people, their faces often scrunch up at the incongruence. Cory is no exception, though he's known I've wanted to own a business for as long as I've known him. The first time we sat down for tutoring together and he asked me my major, I'd told him, "I'm only here so I can't blame never owning my own bakery on failing chemistry."

A general bakery was the tentative plan then. But the longer time stretched following my completion of pastry school, the more I realized I missed the chocolate component most of all. Sometimes I'll get a craving for a specific cake, or a torte with caramelized pears, but on those occurrences, I make it and move on. Chocolate is the only constant.

A random, splotchy breakout all over my chest and back during a particularly stressful finals week drove me to make my own soap from natural ingredients. The science of it, measurements, and attention to temperature reminded me of chocolate. With chocolate there are various potential additives and combinations to make each batch to your preference. It's the same with soap. Even using molds to shape the final product reminded me of chocolate. Once it worked to clear up my skin, I was hooked. So, chocolate and soap it is.

"Have you made either with me?"

Cory visually racks his brain, his gaze swiveling longer than it should take for him to find the answer, because I can recall a handful of times he's made himself scarce after I'd invited him to join me and Elise. "No," he finally answers.

"Then you wouldn't know, would you?" He exchanges a worried look with Elise. I huff and apologize for being snippy. "Sorry, I just feel like I'm flailing here. I know you're trying to help. I'd call it Bathe in Chocolate, and the setup for the kitchen would work perfectly for both."

"Just to be clear, I don't doubt you," Cory says.

I put my arm around his shoulders. I know this. None of my closest friends would doubt me; neither would Clara or Grandma. It's nice and all, but it doesn't help me feel better or more prepared. It makes me feel like if I fail, which any new business is liable to, I would blindside them all.

My phone vibrates on the side table nearest to Elise. She picks it up and passes it to me. I glance at the screen and tilt it for Cory to see the picture of his girlfriend, my cousin Corinne.

"Did y'all tell her to call for backup?" I ask as I answer the phone and press the speaker button. Before I can utter a formal greeting, Corinne's breathless voice, slightly muddled with the upbeat voices of her coworkers, reverberates throughout the living room.

"Have you checked your email?" she asks.

"This morning," I answer, already reaching for my tablet, spurred on by the anxiousness in her voice.

"Girl, check it again! The EMBERS Foundation selected who's moving on to the next round. Finance for the Fam was picked for the nonprofit side!"

"That's great, babe," Cory says beside me. I toss my phone in his lap for him to continue his praise while I pull up my inbox. Corinne encouraged me to apply for this program last year for the small-business focus. Elise leans into my side as the screen refreshes and new bold-font emails populate on top. The one from EMBERS Foundation's new grant program stands out among them. For a moment, I remember all the rejections I have accumulated in my folder and fear this one will join the ranks. Only one way to find out. I tap on it, Elise practically in my lap at this point. She jumps up and yells after only possibly reading as far as the first word in the email following the header: Congratulations!

# CHAPTER FOUR

I wave off Cory when he starts to open his driver's door as I approach the car with my suitcase. He hits the unlock button instead, and I haul my bag into the trunk and scoot into the back seat behind Corinne, who helpfully shifts the passenger seat up to give me more legroom.

She twists to see me, excitement and nerves etched on her face. Her hair is styled in two kinky buns, and her deep-brown skin soaks up every bit of the rising sun. "Ready for this?"

"I have no choice but to be."

Cory joins Corinne's head in the space between their seats. "That's the same thing you used to say when I'd ask about your chem exams."

I grin, my own nerves receding just a bit. People remembering random things in connection to me is my love language. "It was true then, and it's true now," I respond. There are lots of things I've had to face without pondering my preparedness. I've found success in just assuming my capability, then focusing my energy on the tasks ahead. Go figure, when it was up to me to decide if I was ready to launch my business, I postponed it for years.

In the month since I was accepted into the EMBERS—Empowering Marginalized Business Entrepreneurs Reparation Syndicate—Foundation grant program, I've been busy. I've fine-tuned my business plan, made profiles on a couple of commercial real estate websites, and even submitted the paperwork required to make Bathe in Chocolate a legal entity. In putting a menu together, I've made so many batches of chocolate and bar soap that my friends and family have begun to politely decline my offerings. And of course, I've obsessed over the grant website in preparation for this weekend.

Of all the grants I applied to, EMBERS Foundation's is not my favorite. If I advance to the next round, it comes with a mentorship. I'm sure the mentors will have great connections and experience, but I've already accumulated contacts from my pastry school days. Not to be all Scrooge McDuck about it, but the financial backing is what I'm after. However, getting selected into the mentorship round comes with triple the $5,000 I've already been granted. So I can deal with a mentor bothering me—ahem—*checking in* with me every week or so if it comes with cash.

This weekend is a conference for networking, strengthening ideas, and surviving a panel review of my business plan that will likely decide my fate. Those I face act as an advisory committee to pass their observations along to the board with the power to determine who advances to the mentorship round.

We arrive at Midway Airport an hour before our scheduled takeoff and get our bags checked in and through security without holdup. Aisha, Corinne's coworker, waits for us in the seating area near the gate. The program covered travel expenses to Cleveland for up to two people involved with the business or nonprofit. They also gave everyone the option of attending virtually. The thought of doing such an important panel remotely made the nauseated feeling I get whenever I feel things slipping out of my control swirl in my gut.

Aisha and Corinne fall into talk of their nonprofit organization, and I pull up the bookmarked grant site on my tablet. I swipe through the website pages, my eyes inattentively scanning the information since I've seen it so many times before. There's the mission statement explaining the tri-city involvement of Chicago, Cleveland, and Detroit. The nonprofits and small businesses have separate sections. The mentorship tab usually has a short blurb about how some of the brightest entrepreneurs and investors have been gathered to mentor the first crop of mentees. But now, after taking a long moment to load on the free airport Wi-Fi, two rows of pictures are there, twenty in all. Beside each professional headshot is their hyperlinked name and title.

I nudge Corinne's shoulder. "The mentor list is up."

"Let me see." She starts to reach over to take my tablet, but I stiff-arm her. I'm nice enough to tilt it so she can easily see as I navigate. The first one listed is Kelsey Johnson. The link opens to her website. She's based in Cleveland and is the co-owner of a home decor line now carried in major retail stores. The second one I click on is a nonprofit consultant with lots of experience. When I don't stay on his website long enough to read every word, Corinne gives up and uses her phone to continue fawning over the possibility of having access to his expertise.

I make my way through the ten mentors designated for small businesses until it's time to board. On the plane, I get settled in a window seat near Corinne and Aisha, stash my gadgets away on airplane mode, and pull out my mom's pregnancy journal. I'm not even halfway through it. I haven't figured out if my pace is all I can handle or if I'm rationing out these new pieces of my mom.

Today's entry is the four-month mark. The deeper I get into it, the more words I see crammed into the allocated spaces. While the beginning pages had one-word responses to some prompts, now her scrawled answers demand more space. According to the entry, she's finally started showing. My mom writes about how I seem to fall asleep nestled into her side more, my head resting between her growing belly and bosoms. I don't remember that, though I'm able to picture it as I peer out the little rectangular window at the fluffy white clouds and pristine blue sky.

I've loved planes for as long as I can remember, even when I used to get the worst earaches as a child. Once, my dad, along with a flight attendant, tried a number of things to help my aching ears. Gum, little cups to put over my ears, instructions to pinch my nose and seal my lips before forcibly pushing air against the airways, and finally distraction with a wings pin. My mom was still alive then, and she sat on my other side, rolling her eyes as Dad doted on me.

The number of childhood memories from the years after my mom's death but before my dad's, which I call "the in-between years," are plenty. Before that, not so much. That's what sucks the most about losing my mom that early. That event rocked my world, struck me so hard it's like it activated my memory. It was the most important thing that had happened to me so far, and I organize a lot of events in terms of whether they happened before or after she died. Most things are after.

What I remember most about my mom is how solid she felt when I sat beside her. Where my dad was a big softy, ready to give me whatever I wanted if I asked sweetly, my mom was more tempered. More careful. Later, I learned from my aunt that they'd waited eight years to try having another child because it took her that long to decide she wanted to do it again. My dad had always wanted me to have siblings, like he experienced, but had to wait for my mom to agree.

I often imagine how much guilt my dad carried in those in-between years. If that, along with family genetics, is the reason his heart gave out at such a young age. Or maybe I, a somber daughter prone to random breakdowns as I came to grips with how to recalibrate after losing someone who'd been such a constant force in my life, took a toll on him.

I look across the aisle at Corinne, who's fast asleep in her seat, her head drooping comically slowly to the side. It's the sight I need to reel in the tears building behind my eyes at the thought of child me. I had a lot of uncertainties about my life and people's ability to stay with me, no matter how much they wanted to. I suppose that's why I'm attached to Chicago. Anything I can do to keep those I love close to me.

We hit the landing strip with a jolt, and my heart thumps to awareness in my chest. Corinne snaps up, ready to bolt. I shake my head and grab my phone to turn off airplane mode. When it struggles to find a signal, I abandon it and ready my backpack to exit the plane.

Eagerness radiates from the three of us as we walk to baggage claim. I volunteer to order us a rideshare once we're only waiting for Aisha's bag but find that my phone still doesn't have any bars denoting service.

"What's up?" Corinne asks in response to my frustrated grunt.

"Phone's acting up."

"I can order the ride." She pulls her phone out of her pocket while I try in vain to get mine functioning. I might just need to get out into the open air. Aisha spots her bag, and we go outside to meet our driver.

I take the front seat while Corinne and Aisha slide into the back. Aisha takes the lead to hold a conversation with our driver while I wait for my phone to find a bar or two as we increase our distance from the airport. All at once, the bars appear, showing full strength. The moment I sink back into my seat, my home page is reduced to a single app, a white icon with a pink *M* breaking up the monotony. The familiarity causes my nose to twitch.

I click the icon before allowing panic to overtake me. The colors are the same, but the design is different. It might not be what I think it is, or fear it is, based on the queasy feeling burrowing in my gut. After seconds that drag on, it finally opens.

*Welcome to Met 2.0, Tiwanda.*

I'm going to kick my cousin's ass.

# CHAPTER FIVE

Met first appeared on Corinne's phone a year ago. Within the span of months, it claimed she had met her soul mate somewhere along the line of her twenty-seven years, and then proceeded to send four missed connections her way, leaving her to riddle out who it was. It was entertaining, if not unnecessarily convoluted. And apparently, it's transferable.

Once Corinne finished her tryst with Met, it offered her the option to share it with someone. Here it is nine months later, and Met finally made good on its promise. I stare at the question on the screen—"Have you met your soul mate?"—and ponder how best to exact my revenge against Corinne. I'm in the hotel room she's sharing with Aisha, waiting for her to get Elise on the line before allowing the app to reveal the answer.

When Corinne was subjected to this app, Elise and I were along with her every step of the way. Was I somewhat indifferent to the turmoil she faced as she went on dates with other people while falling for Cory? Sure, but I was in the midst of a particularly busy auditing season. I don't deserve this.

After giving Elise a rapid-fire summary, Corinne pushes her phone in front of my face. Elise screams when she sees me, more delighted with this news than when I quit my job.

"This is amazing! I can't believe it!"

"This is *not* amazing. You know I don't like people that much."

"Yes, I know. But . . . okay, okay." She lifts herself up from the bed she's in. She must be at Devin's place since I don't recognize the color-fully patterned headboard. "Hear me out, Tee. This isn't like that one time I challenged you to try a dating app for a week."

"Which I completed."

"Yeah and deleted it as soon as the seventh day was done—whatever. Met is different. One, it has a direct connection with kismet. Both Corinne and I are examples of that."

"I don't think you hooking up with Devin, a match sent for Corinne, was Met's goal."

Elise narrows her eyes and opens her mouth to retort but rethinks entertaining the argument I'm clearly looking for. "We'll agree to disagree."

"It's just . . ." I throw an accusatory glare at Corinne and snatch the phone from her to hold it myself. She retreats to her suitcase to hang up her panel outfit. "This is the worst time to have to deal with this."

This weekend was supposed to be for me to focus on my business and do everything I can to be selected for the next phase of the program. There's too much on the line for me to be sidetracked with a person from my past who Met thinks could be my soul mate.

"Sorry to break it to you, babe, but there's really no good time for love foolishness."

I let myself fall into the armchair in the corner, leaning uncomfortably against my backpack like an overturned turtle. "This will be the biggest waste of time. There's literally no one I've met worth sending my way again."

Even as the words leave my lips, one person springs to the forefront of my mind. We were the definition of bad timing. Mainly because I was oblivious to his flirtation. He'd been my unicorn, proof that it was possible for me to lust after a person in earnest and wonder what it'd be like to call him mine. Unfortunately, those feelings came *after* he'd moved on to another woman.

"How would you know?" Elise stares me down. "When do you give anyone a chance?"

"Wow, tell me how you really feel."

She grimaces but doesn't take her words back. "I'm just saying, Met managed with Corinne and Cory acting dumb as hell."

"Hey!" Corinne shouts from across the room. Elise doesn't acknowledge her.

"Surely it would send you people you could actually form a connection with. No matter what that looks like for you."

Like usual, Elise knows what to say to break down my defenses, at least until I can strategize how to rebuild them again. When we first met at a summer intern mixer, her outlook on life fascinated me. She doesn't get bogged down by things because she has radical faith that everything will work out. And I've been in her life long enough to see that the things that matter tend to.

I lift my upper body enough to unhook my arms from my backpack straps. When I bring my own phone to my face, it automatically unlocks to Met, awaiting my decision. Corinne, perhaps sensing my intent, comes to stand behind my shoulder. Aisha sits in front of us on the bed, curious after all the commotion.

*Have you met your soul mate?* My two options are separated in two circles. *Reveal the answer* in sky blue. *I don't want to know* in pale red. White outlines appear around each option, circling them in never-ending loops.

"Met got an upgrade," Corinne says.

"I want to see the phone, not your faces," Elise complains.

I hand Corinne back her phone so she can train it on my phone's screen. Without further delay, I press the blue circle. It's what we're all standing around for.

A diagonal timeline numbered to thirty pops up. The colors on the screen, mostly hot pink and white, swirl as Met pretends to puzzle out the answer.

*No.*

*Oh.* My heart shudders to a stop, then reboots with a jolt. I wasn't expecting that. What's the point of Met appearing on my phone if not to tell me I've met my soul mate somewhere along the line? Amid the disappointment is a potent relief. Finally, proof that I haven't failed along the way. Bad timing wasn't so bad after all. There wasn't a mystery person I'd brushed off after making a quick assessment based on my lack of attraction. I told Elise no one I'd met on that dating app was worth my time, and I'd been right. No secret soul mate there. None, because there's a slim chance of me having one of those in the first place.

"Well, this round of Met was handled quickly. I gotta say, I admire its efficiency."

"Tilt the phone a bit, Corinne," Elise says. "There! Press the info button in the corner."

I do, and up pops a short list of options containing more Met guidance than Corinne received.

*Met 2.0*
*New Features*
*Boost Option*

The boost option was the only thing included in Corinne's Met experience. Activating the boost sent people she'd met before into her path again. It provided her a second chance to make the connection she'd missed. This shouldn't apply to my situation. I select it.

*Boost Option: Send your soul mate? Activating this boost will cause you to meet four people. As part of our upgrade aimed at improved transparency, Met will alert you upon meeting a match. It's up to you to determine which is your soul mate.*

As soon as I've finished reading the blurb, my next two options populate at the bottom of the screen, shifting the boost description up to make room.

*No thanks, I'll pass.*
*Yes, I'm ready.*

It's accompanied by a two-minute countdown for me to claim the offer. So much for me waiting until I'm safely away from the conference to press the button that'll detonate my peace.

Corinne and Elise chat animatedly, curious about what else has changed with the upgrade. Meanwhile, I'm stuck staring at the absurd options. Knowing myself as well as I like to think I do, it would be satisfying to press no. But doubt wheedles its way into my brain, dissuading me. What if Elise has a point and I have cocooned myself with my understanding of my particular shade of gray sexuality and stopped giving others—and myself—due diligence? The swiftness of this self-doubt exposes weakness. I can't confidently pass on this offer, not when I now have an uncertain voice in my head. Perhaps it's due to the conceptions of romance I've ingested as a bystander, but the voice says that for someone like me, with tepid attraction, this might be the only chance I have at finding romantic love. Maybe I'll try it and realize it really isn't for me, but I have to at least do that much.

Amid Corinne and Elise's continued conversation as the countdown drops to under a minute, I make my decision.

# CHAPTER SIX

Before accepting Met's boost, I probably should've given a second thought to the sheer number of people I'd have to meet here. Many of the attendees arrive in the check-in area along with us. There's a mix of pairs and singles, the loners striking up conversation with anyone in the vicinity. I'm happy to have Aisha and Corinne as buffers. As we make our way to the front of the line, I realize there's no finessing my way out of meeting one of the volunteers working the table. Unless . . .

"You mind grabbing my packet too? Thanks," I say to Corinne as I start to fall behind her and Aisha on their march to the check-in table.

Corinne stops short, her face clouded by my request. "I can't check in for you. What's—" Her expression clears and she smiles menacingly, sauntering up closer to me. Her forehead barely comes up to my chin. "That's your plan? You think you can just avoid meeting people?"

"Obviously not forever; that's the whole point of me opting to do this boost anyway. Just until after this conference. I really need to be about my business this weekend, and I'd rather your app friend leave me alone until we get back home."

Her head tilts to the side. "You know what I think?"

"I'd prefer not to."

She ignores me and barrels ahead. The more time we spend around each other, the more we feel like sisters rather than cousins.

She's definitely giving me pesky-younger-sister-who-borrows-my-hair-supplies-and-never-returns-them vibes. "Met had a reason for picking now to follow through on my share request. There's someone you're supposed to meet here."

I pull out my phone with enough intent to lure Corinne into asking me what I'm doing. "Adding you to my list of things I don't have time for," I say with a smug smile.

She rolls her eyes. "I'll just give you one tip, as someone who has been through this. It's best to go with the flow. If I could go back and tell myself one thing before it all started, it would be to trust the process and have fun with it."

She smiles up at me earnestly as if she's just shared the most insightful philosophy.

"Why wouldn't you just tell your past self you'd met Cory before and he's the one?"

Though the realization that would be the better approach is clear on her face, she recovers, dismisses me with a flippant head shake, and turns her back on me. "Check in so we can go get lunch, ho."

Met is dormant throughout check-in and the entire first-day itinerary. At the welcome meeting, a few members of the foundation's board take turns welcoming us. Donnell Tate, who spearheaded this grant program, expresses his sheer enthusiasm at the ingenuity gathered in the room. I'm seated beside my cousin and Aisha, with their nonprofit addressing financial inequities, and a sister duo making renewable energy accessible to apartment living. My business idea has always been special to me, but it's nice to be held in such high esteem.

The first two days of the conference are designated for workshops focused on honing our business plans and helping each other discover new ideas to develop our companies further. Some of the mentors joined for the weekend, either as presenters or panelists or just for networking purposes. The nonprofits' schedule is similar to that of small businesses, but I'll be separate from Corinne and Aisha for the most part. The final day is reserved for panel interviews.

After the welcome meeting, we separate according to our individual schedules. In the workshop, I'm put in a group with two other businesses, including an interior decorating pair from Chicago. They're Deaf, which makes me regret not having enough time to join the community ASL class with Cory, but the interpreter remedies language barriers. We brainstorm expansion possibilities for each of our businesses. One great suggestion for Bathe in Chocolate is selling chocolate-making kits for those who want a DIY experience at home. I fill pages of notes from the discussion. The second half of the workshop focuses on market research. We all hop on our laptops and tablets and analyze the performances of similar businesses in our fields that we consider competitors. Then we regroup and discuss how to differentiate.

Our presenter dismisses us with enough time for me to drop my things off in my room before dinner. In the dining hall, Corinne and Aisha are already seated at a table with another pair of nonprofit owners. I drop into the vacant chair beside Aisha. Some of the mentors sit among the participants, spread around different tables. So far of the list of twenty, I've only matched five faces with the mentor headshots posted on the website.

There's a pitcher of water and a basket of warm bread on each round table, so I pour a glass and use the metal tongs to choose a soft piece of ciabatta bread. In pastry school, we had a full semester focused solely on baking different types of breads. I'll never in my life eat as much bread as I did over the course of those sixteen weeks. As I slather butter across my piece, my mouth waters at the thought of the garlic spread Chef used to whip up for us. One of my closest friends in pastry school took a liking to bread. Now she makes it to her heart's content, managing the bakery at a local grocery store.

"Tiwanda," Aisha emphasizes in a way that implies it isn't her first time. "Did you hear what we were talking about? Lots of us are going to that bar and games hangout place a few blocks away. Should be fun."

"The first workshop starts at eight tomorrow morning." I eat another bite of bread.

Corinne leans over Aisha. "It's networking, and we don't have to stay long."

I agree to go, since despite my urge to put my blinders on and secure the funds, I don't want to miss out on any part of this experience. When dinner finishes, we separate to our rooms to change out of business-casual clothing and meet back in the lobby with a group of nearly twenty people walking to the bar together.

Our destination is on the fourth floor of a commercial building that houses a variety of retail and restaurant businesses. It's a busy place. There's a semi-secluded bar area for those who might not want to be bothered with the bells and whistles, but no one in our group heads in that direction. Some break off to snag a bowling lane, a few head toward the virtual-reality games section, and I go with the group drifting toward the pool tables.

In this section, there are ample high seats at tables with bar service. The entire place has dimmed lighting for the nighttime hours, but each lawn-green setup has an extra light hanging overhead that makes the place less of a vampire den. It also helps Corinne chat with Victor and Yazmin, the interior decorating pair from my earlier group, in sign language. The bit of sign I've learned to better converse with my cousin, Corrine's brother, is enough for me to catch some familiar signs but not enough to piece together the meaning. I eventually give up and chat with Aisha.

Networking would be a lot more enjoyable if the threat of Met weren't hanging over each interaction. Thankfully as the drinks flow, people stop formally introducing themselves and just skip to chatting about whatever. I'm not sure if Met agrees, but from where I stand, you haven't met someone if you don't at the very least know their name.

Aisha and I team up to play a game of pool against Victor and Yazmin. Corinne sits at a nearby high table speaking with the same non-profit pair who sat with us at dinner. During my off turns, I join them at the table, sipping on my Long Island iced tea and keeping an eye on the clock. I hit the red striped ball in, followed by the yellow, then completely miss my next target. When I retreat to the table, Corinne and the pair's focus is elsewhere—on a table situated on the opposite side of our area.

"Kassie is in love." Corinne lifts her chin toward the table.

There are three people sitting there, two men and one woman. They all look attraction worthy, so it's not obvious which one she's referring to. The woman has a mass of curly hair pulled up with a patterned scarf. One man is pale brown, with buzz-cut hair. From this distance I can't tell for sure, but I imagine his face is freckled. The last guy is massive in comparison to the other two. His posture as he idly chats is enviable. I have to always remind myself to sit up straight, and usually not until my fatigued muscles alert me to my ergonomic errors. He turns a bit at the same time the slowly alternating overhead neon lights switch from blue to yellow, basking his deep-brown skin in a sunny glow. It also highlights the sharp edge up of the low fade haircut he sports. With his wry grin at something the other guy says, it hits me.

"They're mentors," I tell the table. They turn to me.

"I didn't see her during the welcome or dinner. I would have noticed her," Kassie says, cluing me in to which of the three has her attention.

I take out my phone and pull up the browser window I haven't closed and probably won't for at least the rest of the weekend. It's even already on the page I need. First, I spot the light-skinned guy; the freckles I assumed were imagined was actually me remembering how he looks with adequate lighting in a close-up shot. I hold it out to Corinne and company.

Kassie reaches out to swipe down until she finds the matching photo of her crush. "She's from my city!" Detroit, she means. She hops off the stool, running her fingers through her black pencil-straight hair.

"What are you doing?" her nonprofit partner, Ren, asks with a growing smile on their face, already suspecting the answer.

Kassie gives us a challenging smile. "Going over to meet her—well, all of them. They're mentors, we're potential mentees. This is my perfect in. Y'all coming with me?"

Corinne shrugs and stands, along with Ren. I throw another glance their table's way, and for the first time since Met, I have the urge to meet someone new.

"Nah, my turn is coming up," I say, stifling that urge.

Corinne's eyes sparkle with mirth before she follows them over. I watch as they all awkwardly descend on the trio's previously peaceful conversation. Kassie makes the introduction, gesturing back over to where I sit, seemingly to explain where they came from. As three pairs of mentors' eyes swing my way, I hurriedly refocus on my phone, scrolling down the list of mentors until I find the final one.

Benoit Sabi. He's based in Philadelphia, which isn't one of the cities involved in the program. He started working in investment banking post graduating college, leveraged his experience there to get hired at a venture capitalist firm, then turned that into becoming an investor in businesses located in vulnerable communities. Aisha interrupts my research when it's my turn, and I pull myself away from whatever hole I'm tiptoeing around.

Even after draining another striped ball, we lose, thanks to Aisha's novice status and partially due to my loss of focus. I used to pride myself on my ability to compartmentalize. That ended the semester before I graduated with my business degree. That time was a mess of final exams and interviewing for full-time accounting-adjacent jobs, though I really wanted to be baking somewhere. When I spoke to Grandma about how I was "handling everything like normal," she (rudely) pointed out that although I may pack my feelings into boxes, I then climb atop them and try to carry out business as usual. Meanwhile, the boxes shake underneath me from the force of my suppressed feelings, affecting every move I make.

Sometimes I consider not readily experiencing romantic feelings as my saving grace, because I already have more than my fair share of emotions. Imagine what would happen if I threw that in the mix.

Corinne, Kassie, and Ren are back at the table when Aisha and I rejoin them as losers. They fill us in on meeting the three mentors. The trio made it in town after dinner, which is why they came here to eat, but will be present throughout the rest of the weekend.

Many of the other program participants seem poised to stay here for hours on end. Some are at nearby tables; a group of six takes up one of the bowling lanes. I spot more familiar faces playing with the gigantic Jenga set. I decide to head out anyway and decline Corinne's offer to walk back with me. It's Friday night, and there should be plenty of people out along the well-lit walk back to the hotel.

My long legs cover the short distance in no time. My mom used to hurry me and my dad along, telling us to "Walk with a purpose!" and it has stuck with me to this day. Dad was an inch shorter than Mom, and he walked like he had all the time in the world, moseying from one place to another, abiding only by his own clock.

I arrive in the lobby at the same time as a raucous group. They crowd inside a single elevator. I wait for the door to close on their sardine formation and the number above it to tick to the second floor, then push to call another lift.

It arrives just as another set of footsteps taps against the polished tiles toward the elevator bank. I step in and press the sixth floor for myself as the person follows me in. I look up to ask which floor they'd like, but the question dies on my tongue as I recognize Benoit from the website. This close, my neck tilted up, his size is even more intimidating.

"Twelve, please."

His words stop me from staring. I press the button for his floor. The doors take forever to start closing, and once they do, I see another group approaching, led by a screechy brunette who yells, "Hold that!" I reach down and press the arrows facing toward each other repeatedly. Benoit makes a startled, cough-like sound on the other side of the elevator but makes no move to sacrifice his arm to trigger the detector and stop it from closing.

When the doors seal shut, I let out a sigh of relief. But my triumph is dashed when we don't move upward, and the door pings open again. I blink up at the number one, confused.

"Got it!" Someone sounds awfully pleased with himself.

"Thank you," the brunette says as she, along with a friend, and the man who caught it and his two companions board the lift. She touches his shoulder, which turns into a lean of support as she starts to lose her balance. I shuffle to the back corner, Benoit taking up the other one. Our gazes catch. I'm sure he sees just how annoyed I am at losing this round of elevator roulette.

He's adorably trying to make himself smaller for the newcomers, or maybe trying to keep space between himself and the drunker of the two women, who leans against the side of the compartment. The guy who was able to catch the door breaks the silence to ask his friends about tomorrow's workshop. I hadn't placed them as participants.

"You all here for the EMBERS conference?" Benoit asks.

I look over at him again, and although the question must be aimed at the guy clearly speaking about a morning workshop, his focus is on me.

"Yeah." The guy perks up and turns around to Benoit. I face forward and stare at the progression of increasing floor numbers as they make introductions. When it reaches floor six, the hallway lights outside the elevator welcome me like a beacon. They make room for me to leave, and I don't look back.

# CHAPTER SEVEN

Anticipation for the first full day of the conference has me awake an hour early. I use the time to go downstairs for the free breakfast. Corinne hasn't responded to my text, so I assume she and Aisha are still fast asleep. I get a table for myself and work on light edits to my business plan while I eat and sip on lemon tea.

Ten minutes before the first workshop is to begin and I'm clearing my table, Corinne and Aisha hustle into the dining area to grab pastries and fruit.

"Late night?" I ask near Corinne's ear. She jumps, nearly dropping her blueberry muffin.

"We left not even an hour after you. I just underestimated how much time Aisha takes in the bathroom."

"Same for you!" Aisha counters.

Corinne shoves a couple of bottles of orange juice in my arms to serve as her human purse, and we make our way up the escalator to the second floor, where all conference rooms are located. I walk them to their assigned room to learn about measuring the impact of their nonprofit, as the presentation title screen promises. Once I unload their goods, I find my room and use the next five minutes to mentally prepare for the long day ahead.

There are three two-hour workshops on my schedule. While last night's workshop was a good overview on business placement, today's workshops are a deep dive into viability. We discuss financial projections and experiment with various software. I regret not paying more attention in my undergrad marketing class when I'm tasked with finding ways to drum up and retain clientele. The workshop focusing on logistics and management has me second-guessing my decision to run this solo at the outset.

Between the end of the last workshop and dinner, we have a couple of hours to grapple with all the information thrown at us and prepare for tomorrow's panels. There's space for us to cowork, with four rotating "on-call" mentors available to help with any questions or just generally chat. I occupy a table with Victor and Yazmin.

My focus, since logistics is fresh in my mind, is figuring out my suppliers. I study the bios of the four mentors here. None of them are Benoit, though I've seen him floating around between workshops. He's hard to miss. That's probably why he's always deep in conversation with a small posse of participants, or another mentor.

I end up consulting Terry, who looks over the suppliers I'm considering and gives me which one they would go with from the information. They also advise how to approach all options for bulk discount opportunities. Then I can evaluate and choose one or a custom mix using multiple suppliers. I entered this program with money in mind, but if I had Terry for a mentor, that would be beneficial.

The panel schedule is posted and emailed to us after dinner. They had to consider everyone's departure plans before setting it up. I'm not surprised I'm placed in the final slot, since my flight doesn't leave until the evening. Though Corinne and Aisha are on the same flight, they manage to get a morning time.

I have breakfast with them and wish them luck before holing up in my room for the few hours I have left before checkout. We still have access to the shared spaces and conference rooms not being used for panel meetings, so I relocate to a secluded corner postlunch. I study my business plan as if it's not my own personal brainchild. This panel will not catch me heels down. The number of people in the large room dwindles as more finish their panels and leave to return home. Corinne and Aisha try to coax me down to the lobby bar, where they're unwinding with other attendees, but I stay put until it's finally time for my panel.

There's a small waiting area set up outside the four meeting rooms in use. A pair is already sitting, their quiet, nervous energy reaching out to stoke what I'd tamped down by focusing on the mechanics of walking over here. I sit away from them and turn my phone setting to Do Not Disturb. Two other people arrive and join the wait club. I wish I knew who would be on my panel. I could better prepare if I knew what their angles would likely be.

A volunteer comes out of the leftmost room promptly at two forty-five and calls for the duo. They hurry over and disappear behind the door. The next door that opens is on the right side, and my breath hitches before the volunteer consults the printed list in hand. "Tiwanda Harris?"

I acknowledge her and force myself to slowly gather my bearings before making a move toward that door. A person rushes when they're running behind. If I start now, the entire panel will feel like I'm playing catch-up. This is my business idea. My baby that I've nurtured for seven years. I'm the expert here. No matter what happens, their decision won't negate my belief in this idea, my belief in myself. It may take a few months for me to figure out another route to make it happen, but it will happen.

The rectangular table in the room has enough space for twelve people to sit comfortably around the perimeter, but all extra seats are removed except four on one side and two on the other. The volunteer extends an arm toward the side with fewer chairs, opposite of where two panelists are already seated. They pause their conversation to greet me and let me know the other two panelists will return shortly.

I recognize both of them. One is Donnell Tate, the founder of the program, who welcomed us all the first day. His presence causes the pace of my heartbeat to increase a notch. The other is a consultant I've seen around all weekend. She has short salt-and-pepper curly hair and a shrewd gaze. I get settled in my seat and place my bag in the second chair. As I take out my tablet and notebook to have all my business plans and financial reports at my fingertips, the second entrance opens. I don't even attempt to hide my eagerness.

The first to enter is Terry, and I press my lips together to resist outwardly celebrating. But when the final panelist follows them in, my tablet slips from my hand and thumps on the table. I have the attention of all four now, including Benoit Sabi. Thankfully, there's no recognition there. True as it might be, I don't want him labeling me as a ruthless woman who didn't want to be packed in an elevator with drunk strangers. He carries a drink in either hand and passes one to the lone woman on the panel, then takes his seat in the rightmost chair. He sighs, not loud enough to be heard but obvious in the rapid rise of his chest followed by a slow deflation. As he starts to navigate the tablet propped in front of him, I refocus on my own device and flip to a blank page in my notebook.

The founder, Donnell, sitting on the left side, kicks off the meeting. "How was the weekend for you?"

The informal start catches me off guard, but I follow his lead. "Great. Every workshop showed me something I didn't know, despite majoring in business."

"What focus?"

"Accounting."

"That'll be helpful." I nod my agreement. "Ready?" He checks for the go-ahead from each of the other panelists. "We've introduced ourselves a dozen times today, but let's do one last round for Miss Harris, who we've already read so much about through her business plan."

He gives the spiel about himself but keeps it short, knowing even if I hadn't already done my research, I would have seen him at the welcome meeting. Next is Tricia Ibrahim. She primarily works as a business consultant, after stepping away from the day-to-day operations of the multiple service-focused businesses she owns.

"Nice to see you again," Terry says. "You already know I work mostly with restaurants and own several around the Cleveland area, blah blah." They wink at me and take a sip of their purplish drink. The introduction line passes right along to Benoit.

"We haven't met yet. I'm Ben. I invest in businesses."

"Seriously?" Terry says. "That's what you've whittled it down to?"

Ben shrugs and appears to be smiling, though his lips barely move. "The long version, then. I started off in investment banking, then joined a firm that invests in nascent businesses. Now I'm narrowing my focus to Black-owned businesses."

Though I know all of this from his bio, I'm happy Terry made him continue. In the elevator, I didn't notice how his soft baritone voice faded the background noise to a hush.

The surrounding quiet is interrupted by a high-pitched ping, followed by a shimmery flourish of stair-stepped notes. I go stock-still, not even sparing a look to the chair where my phone is stashed in my bag.

"You want to go ahead and silence your phone before we begin?" Donnell asks.

"It already is." I realize the truth isn't the best response here the moment after it leaves my lips. Donnell and Terry frown at me while Tricia, bless her soul, checks her own phone. I try to keep it moving. "Nice to meet you all." I make eye contact with each of them in turn. Ben assesses me with a cool removal that makes me aware of each hair follicle on my forearms.

Donnell takes pity on me and says, "Let's hear your pitch."

Of course, I have it memorized. "My business is called Bathe in Chocolate. It's a service-oriented business that provides a fun alternative for get-togethers of all occasions. It combines my love of making chocolate and soap, two things that are both necessities in life."

Tricia chuckles. "I agree. From your business plan, I get the sense you have a clear vision of where you fit in the market."

More compliments are given. Donnell calls Bathe in Chocolate "definitely unique." Terry says it's "one of the more promising ideas." There are questions too, but most of the panelists just ask me to expand on something from my business plan. Ben attentively takes notes but doesn't jump in with any questions of his own. Not until Tricia says, "I really like this one. It's something my daughters would take me to. Lots of fun. Any concerns?" She looks over at the other panelists.

Ben looks up from his tablet, the direct attention alerting me of his intent to speak. "With so many party-focused establishments out there, how do you plan to break in and grab some of that market share?"

"Through sheer will," I say. He stares at me impassively, my attempt at being chummy falling flat. "I studied other new businesses in the space. It seems many parents are eager for a new way to celebrate."

"Sure, I went to a paint night. Once. A few years ago. How do you get people to come back regularly? Before they wait so long that your business shuts down?"

*Ouch.* Just the thought of that potential swift failure makes my chest hot. And has me adopting a straight-spined, defensive posture.

"I don't need the person who books the event to come back monthly, or even yearly. I just need them to bring five to ten of their closest friends, and one or two of those friends to think, *Wow, this would be a great idea for . . . whoever.*"

Terry and Tricia nod, but Ben is unmoved. "While Bathe in Chocolate is one of the more spirited ideas here, the uncertainty of customers still gives me pause."

"Word of mouth isn't easily predictable."

"I agree; that's why your financial projections are almost worthless to me."

My lips turn down, but I nod. "As you can see, it includes a low estimate as well. That's the best I can do. Now I plan to focus my energy on anything that will help me get people in the door. Trust me, no one feels more pressure to deliver on that end than I do."

"This isn't the type of business I normally invest in." Ben is still looking at me, but it's like he's assessing a spreadsheet floating in front of his face, invisible to the rest of us in the room. "I've seen lots of similar businesses fail over the years. In the event of an economic recession, this activity expense would be one of the first cut in many family and personal budgets."

If we were on an episode of *Shark Tank*, this is the point where he would harshly say, "I'm out," and sit back to see if the other panelists have enough sense to follow suit. I respond as if he's done just that.

"Thank you for your assessment," I say with a phony smile. Then I shift my head away from him to the other panelists.

Terry throws me a life vest. "It's similar to restaurants in that there's little room for failure the first year. People come in and don't enjoy one entrée from a three-page menu and vow to never return." They shrug, all their years of experience evident in the flippant movement. "It comes with the territory."

"These concerns aren't unique to your business," Donnell assures me. "Every business is founded on hopes and plans. Then you launch and see if it takes off or blows up in your face."

"Beautiful analogy," I say.

"I do my best. One thing we can all agree on is that we are rooting for your success. This business can bring people together in a new way."

They close the meeting with an overview of the next steps. Immediately following my departure, they'll combine and send off their notes. Then the board will deliberate over the following week, and everyone should be notified if they're moving on to the next round within two weeks. As I exit the room, the relief of tension is instantaneous. I would feel good about how it all went if Bitter Ben hadn't undone most of the glowing praise. It's only then that the knowledge I gained at the very beginning of the meeting resurfaces. Benoit is my first Met match.

# CHAPTER EIGHT

"One down!" Corinne says as she holds her cocktail glass up. Aisha follows suit, and I begrudgingly clink my glass against both of theirs.

I'd rather humor her excitement over Met than obsess over everything that went wrong in my panel. The interactions with Ben aside, my brain is now attempting to turn all the positive parts sour. Maybe they were feigning excitement. Maybe all the panelists had the doubts Ben expressed but pitied me enough to not speak them aloud. *Nope, try again.* After the number of counseling sessions I was forced to attend through my teenage years, the correction comes easily. This entire weekend was filled with business professionals providing honest feedback and guidance. They wouldn't start withholding the truth now.

As soon as I left the panel, I picked up my suitcase and hightailed it to the hotel bar. The majority of attendees are long gone, but a handful remain, scattered about. We plan to head to the airport in about fifteen minutes, once we finish the last of our drinks.

"Maybe you should try to get a feel for Ben, before we leave," Corinne says out of the blue.

"I think I got plenty of feels from the panel. It was spiky."

"You're sure it's a no? You wouldn't want to ask him anything else if you could?"

"If I don't get chosen to move on to the next round, I will forever associate his face with my failure. So no. I would prefer not to see him again."

Corinne flashes her teeth in a grimace, looking over my shoulder. I turn and there is Ben, settling into a seat at the far end of the bar with Tricia. She quickly orders something from the bartender and walks toward the lobby bathrooms, leaving Ben alone for the moment.

Aisha stands, also needing to use the bathroom before we depart.

"Wait, I'll go with you," Corinne says. She hesitates. "Unless you changed your mind and need a wingwoman."

"No, go. This is Met's throwaway. I'll watch our bags."

They leave and I intercept a bartender to settle our tab. All the while, I attempt to ignore Ben. He sits right at the edge of my peripheral and at the forefront of my most hostile thoughts. I don't need his approval for my business to succeed, that much I'm sure of. But in the moment of his criticism, I was too focused on appealing to the other panelists who could override his judgment and help me advance to the next round to properly give him a piece of my mind. Not that he deserves it.

I finish off my drink and glare at him as I mull it over. Screw it. The conference is over. I've been sitting here long enough that I can safely assume every point he shared has already been documented and forwarded to the board. Surely he wouldn't send an addendum for me asking a few innocent, clarifying questions. This is the last time I'll see him, and Met has inconveniently decided to begin my list of matches with his name. I can settle a couple of things tonight and be done.

Ben doesn't look over until I'm scooting out the bar chair.

"Uh, Tiwanda." He successfully fishes the depths of his mind for my name and nods as if proud of himself.

I get settled in my new seat, my entire body turned to face him. "Are you interested in me?"

His brown eyes narrow, but the confusion clears in an instant. "In your business?"

"God, no. The answer to that has been well established." My tone is sharper than it should be for someone who is unaffected by the lack of imagination of this investor. His mouth parts, and I push on before he can derail my agenda. "In me." I wave my hands down my body when words to expand don't immediately come. "In dating me. Or having your way with me, that sort of thing."

Ben's eyes widen as he replies with an emphatic "No." He casts a glance around us. "I'm sorry, did I—"

I continue, relieving him from needlessly going down that road. "It's fine. We're on the same page. Like—" I slash my arm in front of me and shake my head a bit. "No. Just needed to check that off for . . . reasons."

The barkeep returns with the drinks Ben and Tricia ordered. He thanks her and takes a long draw from the glass. I use this opportunity to get this done without interruption.

"Anyway, I mostly came over here to point out your blind spot. Sure, you know the market, financial projections, ROI ratios, et cetera. What you *don't* know is how to valuate experiences, and spotting trends, and . . . pretty much everything my business is about. So."

He replaces his drink on the coaster. "Okay."

"Okay." I stand, my mission completed. "It was . . . *something*, meeting you. Have a safe trip home."

Corinne and Aisha return from the bathroom as I'm attempting the slowest dramatic exit ever, wheeling all three of our suitcases toward the sliding doors. Together, we leave for the airport, and alone, I sit with my head leaning against the rounded corners of the airplane window, my mom's words as reading material.

# CHAPTER NINE

After weeks of crawling my way through my mom's journal, it takes mere days after I return from Cleveland to finish it. I'm nestled on the couch as I read the final pages. It's a strange feeling, holding new words in my hands, new thoughts. The fact that it was written and immortalized decades ago is unimportant. Death has a way of dismissing the linear time constraint of the living.

I press my finger into the sharp corner of the business card I found wedged into the pages. It belongs to Cousin Vonnie, the woman who passed this along to me. On the back side, her cell phone number is written in blue ink. I know it wasn't left behind by mistake. Assuming she's read it, Vonnie is the only person who'd understand what I'm feeling. I dial the number. She answers just as I expect to hear a voice mail greeting.

"Did you know my mom didn't want to have another child?" I ask.

There's a pregnant pause and then, "Tiwanda. I'm glad you called. One second." In the background there's movement. After the sound of a door clicking, she's back on the line. "I did know. I remember the moment she told me she'd changed her mind."

"Dad pressured her."

"I tend to use the word *persuade*. Or *convince*. She became excited about it a few months in."

I'd picked up on that. The excitement was laced with trepidation, though, about how a new baby would affect our lives. More specifically, how it would affect *my* life.

"Listen, I'd love to see you. I knew when I passed that journal along to you it might cause you to revert to that space, of remembering what you lost. But there's a lot of people on this side of the family who miss you, Tiwanda."

Miss me? The lack of outreach from them says otherwise. "We can meet up."

"We're having a small get-together for my uncle's birthday next weekend. Everyone would love to see you."

Before I can hedge this group reunion and negotiate for a more intimate situation, there's an uptick in noise in her background. She speaks away from the phone for a few muddled sentences before returning for a hurried goodbye. "I have to run. I'll text you the details."

I sigh and drop the phone into my lap. That conversation did nothing to ease the unrest in my spirit. Though, I think as I pick up my phone and navigate to my bookmarked recipes, it's not just the journal at the root of this. For too many years, my life navigated around my job. Now that I'm free of that, and taking a break from planning Bathe in Chocolate pending results of the grant program, I've been listless. The extensive tally of things I'd do if I worked less fell to the wayside the moment it became plausible.

My phone chirps as a Met notification interrupts my recipe scrolling. I haven't opened the app since Cleveland, and I haven't been at risk of bumping into any new matches from my couch.

*Get the most out of Met! Ask me a question.*

I frown at the screen. This isn't something Corinne had when Met was meddling around in her life. Since it doesn't give me the option to dismiss the nudge, I open the app.

*Ask Met any question. Limit one per day.*

*Any* question? That seems way too simple. I sit up a little straighter on the couch. My thumbs twitch as I attempt to strategize. After a moment, I give up and start typing the first question that comes to mind. Even if it's fruitless, I get another go at asking a question tomorrow.

Is this worth my time?

A pink spinning pinwheel pops up as Met riddles out the answer. It comforts me that it has to think about it.

> *It depends on you. Met provides options with soul mate potential but doesn't force your actions. Above all, Met prioritizes choice.*

There's another pinwheel as I process this information. All through-out Corinne's go with Met, I wondered what it meant to meet your soul mate. Does it mean you're supposed to be with that person from now until indefinitely? Or that you'd eventually end up with them, even if it takes a few decades? Or that maybe you're not even supposed to be together in this lifetime? Now that Met is in my hands, I'm unsure I'll handle it correctly.

> *Met can tell you that it's an opportunity for you to explore romantic connections in a way you've never experienced. Maybe you'll decide you're happier without the hassle of romantic love. So the question for you, Tiwanda, is this: Is knowing worth your time?*

"Doubt it," I answer aloud. I exit the app and instead pull up my friends' location map. Corinne is in the office. Elise is out, en route somewhere downtown. Cory is at Corinne's place. I give him a call, confirm he's done with physical therapy appointments for the day, and tell him I'm going to swing by and pick him up soon. Because it dawns on me that something I've wanted for years is now finally attainable.

~

Cory slides into my passenger seat, bringing his smoky vanilla scent with him. I shift gears as he buckles up. Lately, he spends more time at Corinne's place than his own. His lease is up at the end of the summer, and even though he hasn't overtly said so, I know he is loath to renew it when he hardly uses his apartment.

"Have you told Corinne you want to move in together?" The quick way he opens his mouth is all I need to know to shut him down. "Don't bullshit me. I know you."

He sighs. "It's just more efficient. You can appreciate that."

"I do. It's just the logistics of sharing a one-bedroom apartment that freak me out. What do you do when you need your space?"

"We have work; isn't that enough time apart?"

"No," I panic-whisper. He laughs and shakes his head at me.

"Where are we going?" Cory asks, checking out the GPS.

"To see a dog about a bone." He casts a side-eye at me. "Seriously. Well, to see Animal Care and Control about a dog. I'm ready to share my life and space with another being."

I park in the animal shelter's visitor lot, and we hop out and walk toward the signs pointing us to the adoption event in progress. When a flyer advertising this event first showed up on the corkboard beside the condos' mailboxes, I paid it little mind. Now, the twenty-five-dollar adoption of any cat or dog, shots and fees included, feels like it was always meant for me. If only Margie knew my ability to take her dog ownership advice was contingent on me being free from her management. On my list of things to keep me occupied during this break, a dog ranks higher than a romantic interest for sure.

I sign in, and they lead us to the area where the dogs are housed. Though I admire cats' independence and survival skills, I'm allergic to their dander.

"I can't believe you want a housemate," Cory mutters.

I ignore him. The volunteer explains how most people came early in the day to get first dibs on the animals. There are eleven dogs left, but I eliminate five right off the bat based on their size. I want one that'll take up as little of my space as possible. The volunteer asks me which one I'd like to meet so she can take it out of its prison chamber, and I survey the bunch. They whine and bark at the proximity of freedom. All except one.

"This is Penelope," the handler says as she opens the cage for the small dog. She doesn't come barreling out. She barely lifts her head to acknowledge she's being summoned. "She's a Yorkie mix, five years old, and she's pretty chill until she's not."

"What?" Cory startles at the turn of the end of that statement, but I'm unperturbed. I could be described the same way in some circles.

The handler finally manages to coax Penelope out of her cage. I squat closer to her level. The woman releases her with a little pat. "Go say hi, Pen." Penelope takes two little steps toward me, then bolts to the door. Cory jumps out of her way instead of blocking the path like someone with enough sense would do. The handler goes running after her.

I get off the ground and push Cory's shoulder. "Why didn't you try to stop her? You were right there."

"You heard what the lady said. I don't want to know how that dog is when she's not chill."

I laugh upon seeing that a second volunteer has joined the chase, calling after Penelope. There's a flash of brown-and-black fluff. "I think we're seeing it now."

From what I could tell in the cage, Penelope's fur is black at the top half of her face and head, an even mix of black and brown on her body, and light brown on her underside. The doors leading outside must be secured, because Penelope rounds the corner and hauls ass back toward us. She comes to a skidding stop at my feet and jumps up onto her hind legs, her front paws only coming up to my shins. I stoop down again and pet her tiny head.

"I get it," I confide to her. The volunteers come walking up to us, panting. "She's the one," I say to the handler who mistakenly let her run free.

"Thank you, Jesus."

# CHAPTER TEN

Penelope quickly makes herself at home in my condo. When Cory helped me haul her upstairs, along with the bags of supplies we stopped for along the way, she bounded inside as swiftly as when she tried to make her escape. We watched her zoom off the accumulated energy of captivity with open-mouthed awe. Then, she hopped on the doggy bed I set up in the corner and made herself comfortable. In the days since, we've established a meal and walking schedule and fallen into a companionable shared living arrangement.

I pack her into her travel kennel, battling just a bit of resistance, then carry her down to the car for our first appointment with the vet. I took a referral from my former work bestie, Chris. It's where he takes all three of his dogs. Every holiday they're photographed in new doggy outfits, so I trust his judgment.

It's a small but well-kept clinic. After checking in with the vet assistant managing the front desk, I find a seat. A sleepy pit bull waits with her human in the corner, and across from me, a man fills out paperwork while his cat hisses from the carrier. Through the mesh, I can see Pen regarding the cat with a judgmental glare. We're shepherded to a room in the back by a vet tech named Sue before anything can be instigated.

Sue checks Penelope's vitals and does a careful external examination with gloved hands. She's gentle, and Pen doesn't put up a fuss.

"She looks good, just a bit underweight."

"They said she wasn't a consistent eater, but she's been doing good the past few days."

Sue nods while scribing notes in a tablet. "The shelter environment can be stressful. I think a bit of stability and a less busy environment will do her good." She strokes the top of Pen's head. "Dr. Pace will be in shortly to speak with you."

Once the door clicks shut, Pen becomes anxious on the examination bed. Her nails scratch against the paper covering as she shuffles around, peeking over the edge. I stand to comfort her. She settles a bit at my touch. Between making sure I have everything a good dog owner needs and reading article upon article of dog-training tips, I've finally evaded the haunting of father capitalism. Meaning, the unsettling feeling when I'm lounging around that there is something I'm meant to be doing—an email that needs responding, a report that needs prepping, an alarm that needs setting. I think tending to Penelope will be good for me too.

There's a double knock on the door before it opens.

"Penelope?" Dr. Pace says as if he's genuinely expecting her to answer.

I can feel her freeze underneath my fingertips for a moment before she leaps off the bed. My instinct is to try and catch her in midair, but thankfully my outreach is empty handed. I probably would have caused her to get hurt. Dr. Pace swiftly shuts the door, trapping Penelope in the room with us. She still zooms around in the limited space before tucking herself behind my legs.

"She was good with Sue, so it must be you," I say.

Dr. Pace throws a humored glance my way before stooping down. "Penelope," he says in a sure tone. "Come over and let me take a look at you before you make your mom replace me. Come on. Give a brother a chance." The conspiratorial way he looks up at me from under his long eyelashes convinces me to throw him a bone.

I bend and scoop Penelope up. From her meetings with my friends, I know her preferred way to meet humans is being held in my arms. I'm guessing she appreciates the level playing field. As it happens, Dr. Pace is about my height when he stands again.

He holds out his hand for Pen to sniff and then cautiously pets her. "Now we're talking," he says. "Want to try putting her back on the bed again? I'll sit."

He rolls a chair over as I place her back down. Penelope plops into a lying position like a petulant child but behaves as he does his own brief examination, including checking her teeth. Once he's done, he discards his gloves.

"Now that I've met Penelope, hi, I'm Elliot. Only the animals have to call me Dr. Pace. Chris referred you?"

He extends his hand toward me. "Tiwanda," I say as I clasp his hand in mine. When the triumphant Met jingle sounds before I can expand upon my connection to Chris, I just sigh. Because of course Met would want to throw this young, successful veterinarian into the mix. And now that Met has pointed him out, I guess he is good looking. Illustrious brown skin, high cheekbones, and pronounced eyes; but what really sets him apart is the confidence.

"Do you need to get that?"

I notice I'm still holding his hand and release it. "No, sorry. I got distracted." At this explanation, he smirks as he pushes off to roll over and collect the tablet. He asks additional questions about Pen's home behavior and our routine, and then we're done.

"Penelope is all good. We'll email you our food and vitamin suggestions along with health insurance options. Assuming no incidents, we suggest annual exams. But since she's underweight, I'd like to see how she's doing in six months." He turns to Pen. "So, Penelope, my new friend, I'll see you then."

"Six months, got it."

"Tia will get you set up for an appointment, and we'll send reminders." He reaches into his scrubs breast pocket. "Here's our card and . . ." He pulls out a pen and scribbles on the back side. "If any emergencies arise, you can text me on my cell. I know any friend of Chris is cool."

I thank him and tuck the card into my purse. "Come on, Pen." I get her situated back in the travel carrier, much to her dismay. "We'll be home soon," I tell her.

Elliot opens the door for me but pauses halfway. "Tiwanda?" I meet his gaze. "It can be tough, adoptees adjusting. Feel free to update me on how Pen is getting along. And you too."

"Sure," I say, because I figure it's the fastest way to escape this dubious come-on. Met could have me imagining his flirtation. He gives me a broad grin and finishes pulling the door open.

As soon as I get in the car, I pull out my phone.

Pen's veterinarian? I type in the Ask Met chat window. This is very inconvenient.

> *Quite the contrary. I'd call it matching with a purpose. Met meets you where you are; how much more convenient can it get?*

That night, we have Penelope's puppy shower. Cory and Corinne show up with dog toys and treats. Though Elise enters with "I can't believe we're celebrating your dog when you skipped your whole thirtieth," she supplies the doggy cake and ice cream.

"I didn't skip it, I just postponed it. I'll probably do something next month sometime."

Clara brings just herself, which is more than can be expected since the only animals she has attempted to care for was a pair of fish that somehow became one under her watch. We catch each other up on our weeks for a bit while Penelope stays tucked in her corner bed, avoiding the foot traffic.

"Oh, I met another match today," I say as I'm riffling through a kitchen drawer in search of candles. Clara and Cory are in deep conversation about natural remedies at the dining room table, but both Elise and Corinne are nearby. They snap to attention.

When I don't elaborate, Elise waves an impatient hand. "Details!"

"He's Pen's vet. Nice guy, I guess. But isn't it weird to like animals that much?"

"Yes," Clara says emphatically before turning back to Cory and finishing her sentence.

"Did you try to make conversation?" Elise asks.

"Ask him out?" Corinne presses.

"Noooo." I stretch out the word like if I just hold it long enough, they'll forget the matter at hand. It doesn't work. "I wasn't attracted to him that way."

Corinne looks to Elise, clearly in search of someone else who shares her frustration. "Don't you think you might as well give everyone a chance? This is the second match you've dismissed. Ben, now Elliot. There are only two left."

"So either one of those two will inspire me, or else I'll go about my life none the lesser." I successfully find the pack of candles and toss them on the counter.

Corinne mumbles something mostly unintelligible, but I'm certain the word *waste* is uttered, so I surmise the rest.

"Maybe it is a waste, but I didn't ask you to send me this stupid app in the first place." The music playing from the television becomes extra loud as everyone quiets. "So maybe understand that I'm not feeling *super extra grateful* about all of this."

"I didn't ask for it either," she counters. "But at least I actually figured out how to use it for my benefit. And look how it turned out." She bobs her head toward Cory, who's now tuned in to our conversation.

"Yeah? And how does it feel knowing your true soul mate could be Elise's partner?" It's a petty dig, since Elise's partner, Devin, was also one of Corinne's Met matches.

"Hey," Elise complains. Cory's sharp frown almost makes me laugh, though seconds later I regret being facetious. He, of all my friends, doesn't seem to expect anything from me as far as Met is concerned.

"Can we just give Pen her cake now?" I say.

At this point, that's all any of us wants to do if it means it'll get us one step closer to ending this night. I carry a confused Penelope over, and we sing "Happy Found-day" at double speed. Once I sit her on the floor along with her cake, she drags it back over to her bed.

Everyone leaves shortly after. Corinne doesn't make eye contact as she tells me goodbye. Elise hugs me tighter and promises to call tomorrow. When I'm alone with only the sounds of Penelope's gentle snoring and the slosh of water from my dishwashing, Met chirps at me. As if it hasn't had enough presence in my life today. I take my time finishing up the dishes and wiping down the counters and dining room table before checking it.

*Met Tip: Even wrong steps can lead to new right ones.*

So Met also thinks I'm already making mistakes. But at least it hasn't given up on me yet. Giving up on myself, though, that's another problem entirely. I give Grandma a call. She routinely stays up until midnight, and with her busy activity schedule, this is the best hour to reach her. Whenever I speak to Grandma, I feel foolish for thinking I have so much figured out. About life and about myself. She exemplifies a promise of continual exploration that I find comforting. Even though we just recap our days and don't discuss my debacle directly, I hang up the phone call with more resolve.

I can't go through Met's rigmarole with my friends looking over my shoulder, criticizing me. I know they love me, but I need to do this myself. It's the only way I'll have the room to take chances, probably screw everything up, but possibly discover something new about myself. And, I'm going to text Elliot.

I find his business card in my purse, but the displayed time on my bedside alarm makes me pause. I'm going to text Elliot *tomorrow*. When it's not presumed thinking-about-a-roll-in-the-hay-with-a-vet hours. He probably doesn't even work with horses. I'm pretty sure they require specialists. Doggy-style-with-a-vet hours, then. I'll reach out to him in the acceptable humans-sharing-casual-communication window.

# CHAPTER ELEVEN

I text Elliot after Penelope's breakfast. It's neutral, focusing mostly on how good Pen did in yesterday's group setting. I expect him to respond with general pleasantries and that will be it for the conversation, but a line of communication would be opened. That's not what happens. The pleasantries come: That's great to hear! But then he asks about how I'm doing adjusting to caring for an animal. Now I've found myself in a full-blown text conversation squeezed into the pockets of time Elliot has between appointments.

Elliot: Does Penelope have dog friends? Maybe she'd get along with mine.

I glance up across the street at the sound of a yapping dog. The owner tugs the Chihuahua's leash, but it's completely overcome at the sight of Penelope. Pen continues to sniff her bush.

Me: I get the vibe she's not here to make friends.

Elliot: That makes two of us.

My brain flips through the possible meanings of that until a follow-up text appears.

Elliot: I take hour lunches so I can let my dog out of the house for a bit. I'll send you the address of the park, just in case. It'd be nice to see you.

It's not like I have anything better to do.

The dog park is a spacious, enclosed area, and not too crowded on a weekday. I easily spot Elliot, tossing a toy for his dog in a game of fetch. We try to facilitate a meeting between his German shepherd, Kyro, and Penelope, but the moment I sit Penelope down, she bounds away from all three of us and finds an isolated place in the shade. Once Kyro stops immediately returning the toy to Elliot, we take a seat on a bench.

"I'm interested in getting to know you," Elliot says.

I appreciate his directness. If the people whose advances I'd unknowingly brushed off over the years would've had this approach, I could have . . . well, *knowingly* brushed off their advances.

"I can tell you all there is to know about me right now."

Elliot's lips turn up as he observes me like I'm a walking, talking riddle. "I strongly doubt that."

"Enough that you won't be interested anymore. At least not in that way."

His eyebrows arch a bit, but he maintains his cool resolve. When Kyro returns with his ball, Elliot bends over to pick it up by the least slobbery part and launches it away again. Penelope still lounges in the shade provided by a tree. "Okay, shoot."

"First and foremost, I don't do relationships. Never have."

Surprise sends a quick shock through Elliot's features, but his eyes almost immediately soften. Oh no. He's absolutely a relationship guy. Only that could cause that flash of pity across his face, as if he thinks I'm missing out on something he cherishes.

"You've had bad experiences?" he asks.

"Not really. I just don't . . . understand them? No." I pause, clench my hand into a fist on my lap, release it, and try again. "I recognize a good pairing when I see one. So I get it, for other people. But it wouldn't work for me."

"How are you so sure?"

"Long-term, life-merging things freak me out. The thought of sharing anything less than a five-bedroom, two-story house with a partner makes me want to crawl out of my skin. Anything less and we'd bump into each other every two steps."

"I think some couples *enjoy* bumping into each other, but keep going." The smile playing along his lips gives the illusion of safety. If he thinks this is amusing, then we can laugh about it together, and I can strike him off my list as efficiently as I did with Ben.

"I hate PDA. When I see people holding hands, I just know someone isn't walking their preferred pace. And how annoying is that? I think if someone kissed me in public, I'd either freeze or throw up, and I don't want to take the chance and find out which one."

His eyes have a skeptical squint to them, but he's still following along with slight bounces of his head, not making the sign for the holy cross. So I give him even more of me.

"I don't have crushes. When I see someone objectively attractive, my brain finds or makes up a list of no fewer than five things that could be wrong with them, thus obliterating any attraction that might have been there. You, for example, probably smell like a zoo more often than not. Your confidence is dangerously close to crossing the line to cockiness. You seem to be having a hard time believing everything I'm saying, so it probably means you don't believe women."

"Whoa," Elliot says, cutting me off on number three. Finally, the reaction I expected. He should be bowing out in three . . . two . . . one . . . "I'm going to focus most on the fact that since you have this list at the ready, you find me attractive." He flashes me a smile. "But also, I shower after work, or after the gym if I have the energy to make it there. I am confident, and I have the doctorate degree to back it up. I think you like it. And yes, I believe women, and I believe you. Everything you're saying."

"Oh. Well. As you should."

"I'm guessing you never give your rejects the chance to refute your list?"

"Rejects?"

"Surely many have tried to get at you, so I imagine you leave a long line of rejects in your wake." I laugh, shaking my head. "Yeah you do. And I'm seeing how it happens. Getting the authentic experience."

"I've actually never had this conversation. It's never needed. They flirt, I ignore it, and they move on. It's quite easy not to date, if you don't go looking for it."

When Kyro returns, Elliot takes a bowl and water canteen from his bag to pour him a drink. I didn't think to bring water for Pen, not that she exerted much energy to require it, but I did stash some of her treats in my pocket. "Pen," I call to her. "Come here." She lifts her head an inch but ultimately stays put. Brat.

"My last two relationships were with women I met on Tinder, so you might have a point there," Elliot says. "I haven't tried to shoot my shot in person since . . . undergrad maybe?"

"Wow. Sorry to ruin the art of spontaneously hitting on women forever for you."

He laughs under his breath. "I don't think you have." He looks at me, his eyes intense for a moment. "We should go on a date."

I gape at him. "What about what we just discussed makes you think that's a good idea?"

He shrugs. "Because I like talking to you. And I want to do it some more. Take it from me, building a relationship is really that simple."

I force air from my nose. He doesn't get it. Guys like him never will. He probably started dating seriously in middle school and would've had a joint lunch account with his girlfriend if he could. "It's *not* that simple. We go out on a date, maybe have dinner, do an activity, but that's *all* we do. No touching, no kissing, no nothing. I don't get the signals to level it up on the romantic scale. It never feels right."

Elliot's nodding more thoughtfully this time. "That doesn't sound like a bad trade-off. I've gone on dates where the chemistry isn't there. It can still be a good time."

"But if you're looking for a relationship, then it's a waste."

"If it's time with you, it can't be a waste."

~

The email I've been waiting for arrives the following morning, sometime between putting long passion twists in my hair and texting back and forth with Elliot as he plans our date. The sight of the bolded "EMBERS Foundation Mentorship Round" in the subject line sends a tremor through my hands that makes it hard to click to open it. When I finally get my hand to cooperate, the email begins with the words, We are pleased to inform you that Bathe in Chocolate has been selected to advance to the mentorship round of the EMBERS Grant Program. I jump up from my couch, frightening Penelope awake from her nap.

With my advancement, I'll be awarded a $15,000 grant. After the completion of the three-month-long mentorship, a panel of judges will select five businesses to receive an additional $50,000 grant. *Holy shit.* I can hardly imagine such a boost. Even the $15K will be of great use.

The hyperlink at the end of the email routes to the website, which now includes a page for mentor-mentee pairings. "Terry, Terry, Terry," I mutter under my breath. They would be the best match for me, with their extensive knowledge of the food industry and suppliers. I scan the chart for my name. It's composed of three columns: business owner, city, mentor.

I find my name under the business-owner column, accompanied by a thumbnail-size picture they took of me during the headshot photo shoot held between workshop sessions. I'd pulled my braids back into a bun to hide the color on their tips right before the photo was snapped. City column, Chicago, of course. Mentor . . . Benoit Sabi.

*No.* I trace a line with my finger from my name to the mentor name, but the result doesn't change. I start to text my friend group chat the good—and not so good—news, until I remember how tense we left off last night. Then I pull my head out of my own ass long enough to realize I'm not the only one with a stake in this thing.

I navigate to the nonprofit mentorship round selections and search for a familiar name. I get to the end of the chart and work my way to the top again, eyes reading more carefully. Still, Corinne and Aisha's organization isn't listed. They weren't chosen to move forward. I dial Corinne's number, but it goes to voice mail after just a few rings.

~

Grandma steps onto her porch as I'm opening the back seat door to gather Penelope. "Congratulations, business owner!" she shouts. As I approach, she extends her arms to hug me until she spots the ball of fur I'm cradling and folds them against her chest.

"Now I know you did not bring a dog to my house," she says. "I told you: a picture was a good enough meeting."

I squeeze past her. Despite allowing me to have a dog as a child, thanks to my counselor advocating for it as a way to combat grief, Grandma hates them. She did a lot to support me in the five years leading up to high school graduation. She had my guidance counselor on speed dial. High school was a blur of various sports teams and clubs while my grades roiled like a stormy tide, but Grandma and the counselor adamantly made sure I didn't fall behind.

"How can you say no to this face?" I gently take Penelope under the chin and shake her little head.

Grandma doesn't crack a smile. "No."

I turn around to return to my car and come back with a blanket and the collapsed crate I had the foresight to bring for this exact reason. I get her set up in the corner facing the television for entertainment. She makes herself comfortable and doesn't protest being confined. Guess she understands this is Grandma's domain.

Grandma lives in a relatively new fifty-five-plus neighborhood. The modern, open layout is much different from the house I grew up visiting often and eventually lived in during my teenage years. Grandma didn't have a sentimental bone in her body when she decided to get rid of most of her old furniture and decor and "start fresh."

The sizzle of oil and the scent of freshly fried catfish fills the entire connected living room, dining area, and kitchen space. I join Grandma in the kitchen as she's monitoring the last batch. We spent so many years baking together, she doesn't even shoo me away as I pick up the lid of the pot on the back eye, fire turned all the way to low. I stir the spaghetti and replace the lid.

"Auntie Sharon?" I ask.

"Mhmmm. She left but the kids are in the guest room."

On cue, there's a loud thump against a wall. The hung pictures shake a bit. Grandma opens her mouth to reprimand them, but I cut in.

"I'll go check on them. Give the food a chance to cool off before I burn my tongue being greedy."

The guest room door is slightly ajar, and as I knock, it opens most of the way. The youngest, Xavier, has his video game system set up and is engrossed in a game. Still, he yells out a "Hi, Tiwanda!" and then explains to whoever he's connected with through his headset that he's talking to his cousin, not them. Ava gets up from her lounging spot on the bed to give me a hug, then returns to her phone. A football is on the floor, about halfway between Xavier and the wall shared with the living room. I'm guessing that's what caused the thump.

Xavier and Ava are the youngest of Auntie Sharon's children, inherited through marriage to Aunt Lola. She also has three adult children scattered around the Midwest from her previous marriage. When she met Lola a decade ago, the merging of their children was like a miniature sapphic Brady Bunch. I stay in the room for a bit, watching Xavier play and wheedling out tidbits of information about Ava's teenage life. Eventually, I pull out the big guns. I bring Penelope to her. She's instantly enamored, and Pen gets freedom from her carrier. I leave them together and return to the kitchen.

"I told Josie and Veola your good news," Grandma says. "They're all excited for you of course. Pulled up the website and everything."

"That's nice." I grab a plate and imagine them going through the trouble of navigating the internet just to see my little photo posted there. Grandma's grapevine network moves fast.

"You don't seem that excited."

I pull my eyebrows up in an attempt to look livelier. "No, I am. That money is going to be really helpful. It's just . . ." Going through mentorship hoops will be a waste of my time. I have to see Ben again, thus ruining my perfect tell-off-and-exit combo. He already emailed me, along with the three other people he's mentoring, to find a time for us all to meet next week. "Corinne wasn't selected, so I'm a bit sad for her," I settle on.

During the drive over here, I'd told Elise the same thing. She wasn't concerned in the slightest. "Better is in store for her," she said in the assured way only she can manage. Grandma manages an adequately trite expression.

"That's too bad." She pauses in sad commemoration for a few seconds, then abruptly moves on. "What else has been going on?"

"I spoke with Vonnie," I say. "She left her number in the journal."

"Oh?"

"We didn't speak long, but I'm going to go see her next week." I hop up to grab my phone. "She sent a couple pictures she came across." One is of me and her—I was only about seven years old at the time. Another is of her and my mom. It's slightly off-kilter and taken from a low enough angle to assume I was the amateur photographer. Grandma looks over both of them, lingering longer on the second one.

"That's the same outfit she wore when your daddy brought her to meet me for the first time."

I'm amazed at her memory. "Did you like her? Right away, I mean."

"Short answer, no."

I gawk at her. "What?"

"Well, don't look at me like that. You met your mother."

"I only knew her for eight years. What age were you when you finally felt like you knew your mom?"

My great-grandma lived long enough to hold me, though I have no memory of it. I just have a copy of the picture of me in her arms, Grandma sitting on one side and my dad sitting on the other. I don't know where my mom was. Maybe she was the designated photographer to capture the four generations.

"Well into adulthood," Grandma says with a sad smile. It's hard to admit, but only having someone for eight years, interacting with them only through the lens of a child, isn't enough to really know the person. My mom could've been a serial killer for all I know, and I'd be here, twenty-two years postmortem, on the news saying, "I would've never expected this from her. She always kept me clothed and fed. She made the best chicken pot pies out of the box."

"Within five minutes of her walking through the door, I knew she was pregnant. Could sense it."

"You didn't like her because she was pregnant out of wedlock? Didn't you have Auntie Yvette with another m—"

"Hush, we're not talking about me. Anyway, that wasn't it. I didn't like her because I didn't think she really loved my baby." *Huh.* I'd always considered my mom and dad a pinnacle example of marriage. In response to my obvious befuddlement, she elaborates. "Wendell had brought women to meet me only twice before. Both times, lovely women. Couldn't get enough of him. Doted on him, sucked up to me. It was Sharon's birthday, the whole family together, and your mom barely seemed to want to be there."

"So you didn't like her because she wasn't a sycophant?"

"Well. I'll start by saying I was wrong. I saw that in time. But I thought because she wasn't tripping over herself to fix his plate, and because she was fine with sitting alone and not right up under him, that it meant she was less in love with him."

Now that she mentions it, I have no memory of how my parents showed affection to one another. I'm sure there was at least hand holding . . . wasn't there? Yes, when I was in the middle, one hand in each of theirs. But just them two . . . I got nothing. My brain spins as I wonder what I might have subconsciously picked up from them about romantic relationships.

"Wait, how did you know she was pregnant? Was she far along?"

Grandma shakes her head. "It was your daddy. The panic in his eyes whenever he'd lost sight of her. Sure, he was in love with her, that much was clear. But it was something bigger. I knew he must've been in love with, well, you."

This makes me smile even as my heart contracts. I miss my dad so much. My mom . . . well. Sometimes I feel like I don't remember enough to miss her. Logically, I know there isn't some memory quota that has to be satisfied to justify missing a person. It's just that *miss* isn't the word I'd use to describe the discomforting sensation I get when I think of her. It's more of a longing. After all these years, I still actively ache for my mom and what could've been.

# CHAPTER TWELVE

The chill from the winter is carrying over into spring, typical for Chicago. Despite the vicissitude, it's my favorite season. Year after year, I spend these months happily checking the weather daily, drifting between the closet in the primary bedroom that holds most of my wardrobe and the office closet for my heavier winter gear.

On this cool evening in the final days of March, I dress in a cream sweater french tucked into olive-green, high-waisted pants, along with booties that give me an extra three inches. For important meetings at work, my outfit wasn't complete without heels. No better feeling than standing up at the end of the meeting and towering over those who tried to speak over me. It even trumps the intimidation my height and thick build inspired on the basketball court back in my youth.

Ben reserved a meeting room in the hotel he's staying at throughout the mentorship. It's in the South Loop, not far from Cory's apartment. I was tempted to leave my place early and stop by en route to drop off Penelope, but upon checking friends' locations saw Corinne is there. We've only communicated via group text since the puppy shower a week ago. She's congratulated me and I've sent my condolences to her, all in the confines of a phone screen with two other sets of eyes on the interaction. I really didn't want to have whatever conversation is awaiting us before my first mentee meeting. Penelope will be on her own for a few hours, as she probably prefers.

At the hotel, the lobby is bustling. The front desk staff directs me down a long hallway to the meeting rooms. I find our designated one empty, despite my best attempts at arriving right on time. The U-shaped table is set up with centered pitchers of water and tea and empty glasses on coasters in front of each of the six chairs. As I try to predict which seat Ben will occupy and pick the one farthest from it, someone approaches.

I clear the doorway and make way for the woman to enter. Since I've done my research, I already know she's Pilar Thomas. She looks like the picture on the website, though full size makes more of an impression. I have a very specific type of woman I'm attracted to, and I'm just now realizing Pilar is the embodiment of it. Breathtakingly beautiful with an edge to her looks that hints at the toughness underneath the surface. Her hair is slicked back into a low ponytail of fluffy, tight curls. She holds a blazer in the crook of her elbow, and the silky V-cut blouse she wears exposes the tip of a tattoo on her chest, right between her breasts.

"I'll show you a picture of the full thing if you're curious," she says.

I pull my eyes up as the warmth of embarrassment rushes to the back of my neck. Pilar tosses her blazer on the back of a chair and adjusts her blouse up a couple of inches. She takes her seat, and I move around the table to the chair across from her.

"Tiwanda, right? I'm Pilar. Your business sounds dope."

Before I can thank her and return the compliment, Met joins the conversation with its insistent melody. I glance at the screen.

*Third time's the charm?* ☺

I deposit my phone into my purse and bring my attention back to Pilar. "Pales in comparison to your hair supply store. I'll be in there weekly."

The rest of our group arrives together. Victor and Yazmin enter first. We greet each other like old friends.

*"Congratulations!"* Yazmin signs as she takes the seat to my right.

*"You too! Exciting!"*

Our interpreter sits across from them beside Pilar, and Ben takes the remaining seat between the interpreter and Victor. If Pilar and I were in opposite places, I could probably position myself just right to avoid being in his line of sight for most of the meeting. As it is, I have nowhere to hide, and Pilar squanders her seat, rolling around the edge of the table a bit to get into view.

"Apologies for being late; we were in the business center and lost track of time," Ben says, indicating Victor and Yazmin. His eyes sweep around the table. "How's it going?"

There's silence as the four of us exchange looks. "I'd say pretty great, since we're all here and $15K richer," Pilar ventures.

Yazmin, Victor, and I nod our agreement.

*"That, exactly,"* Victor adds.

Ben's lips pinch in an almost grin. "I'm excited to mentor you all over the next three months. Your business goals are impressive, and my job is to do everything I can to help them come to fruition."

His gaze pauses on me, and I can practically read his thoughts: *Except you, Tiwanda. Take your chocolate and soap and bathe in hell.* My eyes twitch as I resist the urge to roll them.

Before kicking off the meeting, we pause to look at the hotel's restaurant menu. Ben calls the group's orders in, referencing the small paper we passed around to jot them down. Then, he asks questions to get to know us, and for us to get to know each other. Though our three businesses aren't similar, Ben wants us to act as a cohort of sorts. That includes access to a coworking space the foundation is sponsoring for all mentees in each city.

"I know some of you might prefer the convenience of work-ing at home, but utilizing the coworking space also provides a good networking opportunity," Ben says. "It's not far from here. I'll try to be there two or three times a week."

Ben also proposes weekly one-on-one check-ins, either in person or remotely. Pilar, Yazmin, and Victor all enthusiastically agree to the weekly contact. My silence goes unnoticed. After all, I have the most availability. Pilar works full-time as an executive assistant. Yazmin is a massage therapist, and Victor a freelance tax accountant. They both transitioned to working part-time last year when they'd started earning enough money from interior decorating projects.

The food arrives, and the conversation ping-pongs between business matters and personal lives. Yazmin and Victor have been engaged for two years but are waiting until their business is officially launched before planning a wedding. Pilar's family moved from Puerto Rico to Chicago, her dad's hometown, when she was seven. Ben was born in Benin but grew up in Chicago and hasn't lived here since he went away for college. He's been in Philadelphia the past five years.

"Are you familiar with the Chicago economy?" I ask, surprising myself. This definitely should've been a snide question I kept inside my head. Despite my instant regret, his prolonged stare doesn't cause me to squirm or walk it back. I hold my ground with an expectant tilt of my head.

"Familiar enough to take on the responsibility of guiding three businesses, each in distinct business sectors." He breaks eye contact before continuing, "Tiwanda makes a good point. You should always interrogate information and advice. I'll be getting to know you all well and vice versa, and I want you to feel comfortable asking questions."

I watch in awe as Ben has the other mentees hanging on his every word as if he's the messiah sent to lead us to the $50,000 jackpot. Ben shares more about his career before he moved to Philly, during which he worked in NYC as an analyst for a venture capital firm. There, the workload was split by area. Ben's area included the Midwest. So yes, he is quite familiar with the Chicago economy and market. *Gag.*

We wrap up shortly after everyone finishes eating, setting up our first one-on-one meetings with Ben and exchanging phone numbers before leaving. I walk out with Pilar, after we discover we parked in the same direction.

"Ben seems legit," she says. It was her first time meeting him. She attended the conference virtually, and he wasn't on her panel. "Lots of connections—should be great to have him in our pocket."

"Yeah, if he supports your business concept," I say. Then I decide to tell her how my panel went, how I was sure I wasn't going to be selected because of all the contrarian comments he threw my way.

"Sheesh," she says after I finish my recap. "Sometimes you gotta say, 'Forget the haters.'"

"Yeah, and sometimes you say, 'Forget the haters,' and he ends up being your mentor for the next three months."

# CHAPTER THIRTEEN

Saturday afternoon, I pick up Clara and head to the address Cousin Vonnie sent for her uncle's eightieth birthday get-together. Yes, I enlisted backup instead of going into this only vaguely knowing one person. I imagine being a stranger among family is at the top-tier level of loneliness.

No matter how this goes, I can only stay for a maximum of two hours. Elliot and I settled on meeting up this evening for an event at the museum. I didn't want to plan anything following this family reunion of sorts, but it was the best overlap of availability between Elliot's and my schedules for the next week. So I'll show my face, chat with Vonnie, and leave with enough time to drop Clara back off. Having a time limit calms my nerves a bit.

"What are you thinking about?" Clara asks.

Clara is unaware of Met and my date with Elliot, and I'd like to keep it that way. I go with my first train of thought.

"Thinking how weird it's going to be seeing people for the first time in twenty years."

"That reminds me: my twenty-year high school reunion is coming up this year."

"Gonna go?"

She scoffs. "I see enough of their asses on social media to know I don't need to see them in person. Hmm. Maybe we should've started there with your mom's people. In an online safe space to gauge if Momma is right about them."

I ignore Grandma's clear influence on Clara and continue to our destination. We park curbside in front of a boarded-up house a few lots down, the best option available. I grab the lemon-glazed pound cake from the back seat before heading to the side gate, per Cousin Vonnie's instructions. If it were up to me, I would've brought the dozens of chocolate bonbons I stress-made throughout the week, but Clara shut that idea down.

"No one wants your experimental chocolates at a backyard barbecue," she'd said.

So now we're arriving with a more acceptable dessert offering. It seems wrong entering the backyard without someone welcoming us in. And even though music and laughter are audible, I have the illogical fear that we'll show up to the wrong family and not realize it until hours later.

We follow the stone pathway along the side of the house. The backyard is set up with two rectangular tables covered in gold plastic tablecloths. People sit around, chatting while they eat. The temperature is in the low seventies today and the sun is out, so it's perfect weather for a backyard barbecue. Four people sit at a separate square table, where one woman slaps down a domino and says, "Fifteen, count 'em."

"Food goes inside, honey," someone says in passing, pointing toward the back door.

I go to find a spot for the cake while Clara stays outside. There's plenty in the dessert section already. I move aside some store-bought platters and give my cake the space it deserves. With the blank note card and Sharpie packed in my purse, I scribble a description and a list of the allergens, then place it in front of the cake dish.

As I leave, the woman climbing the steps pauses and regards me from head to toe. "Little Wanda," she says.

The moniker, along with her familiar round face, clues me in. "Cousin Vonnie."

I move to the side of the narrow steps to make room for her to pass. "Were you going inside?"

"Just to find you. I saw you enter but was helping Tully with the grill. I'll introduce you to the family. You might remember some of them."

I don't remember any of them. Vonnie leads me around the backyard to speak with anyone of note. She personalizes the introduction based on the person. It's usually a variation of "Tiwanda is my baby cousin" or "She's Whitney's daughter," which always brings instant recognition. The resulting facial expressions weren't what I would expect, though. Not sad or pitying, but more like "You're the one we've heard stories about." The only person unreservedly happy to see me is the man of honor, my great-uncle.

After I meet an adequate number of people, Vonnie gets called to help with something, and I'm free to make a plate of food. I sit among a group of three whose familial connections I only vaguely remember. One is a cousin of Vonnie's also, so maybe my second cousin? Whatever. I'm just biding time until I have a chance to speak with Vonnie. I don't expect to feel an instant closeness. There's a burst of laughter from the dominoes table, where Clara now occupies one of the seats. She has her glass vaporizer in one hand and her three remaining dominoes in the other.

"You're Whitney's daughter, Von says?" The man posing the question sucks the last bit of meat off a rib bone.

"Yes."

The woman sitting beside him tilts her head to one side, eyes lingering on the parts of my body that can be seen above the table.

"Whitney was such a beauty. Always poised. Lit up every room."

"I remember," I say honestly.

"Mnmm. You look just like your daddy." The woman continues eating, either unaware of her shade or just excellent at throwing it.

Clara lasts three rounds of dominoes, and I, biding my time until Cousin Vonnie has a moment to talk, sample every dessert on the table.

Well, the homemade ones. I can confidently say mine is the best. Clara finds me at a table with my dessert plate as the sun starts to slip behind the neighboring houses.

"Why are you making your ranking pastries face?" she says.

I scoff. "I'm not. This is a family-friendly function." I glance at my watch, though I checked it only a few minutes ago. "We should probably head out," I say.

"How was your talk with Vonnie?"

"We haven't spoken, not really. She's been running around since we got here."

"Vonnie has always been a busybody—at least that's what Momma says."

"Grandma says lots of things. Anyway, I have somewhere to be, and I have to drop you back off. We can just go; I'll catch up with Vonnie later."

I look around to see where she is so I can at the very least say a goodbye, and find her turning on the last faux lantern as we start to lose daylight. The departure of sun carries the warmth away with it, and several people are packing up to leave.

As I approach, Von sees me and smiles. "I'm sorry I've been all over the place. Cherie was supposed to help me, and she came down sick this morning. But I'm all done now. Let's sit." She takes the lead toward a couple of nearby vacant seats. I turn and catch Clara's eye from across the yard. She makes a shooing gesture at me, so I follow Vonnie. Just a few minutes won't hurt. I can make up that time on the expressway.

"I'm sure it's been strange for you, being around so much family you don't know."

I nod, though "strange" simplifies it a bit. Her statement gives me permission to acknowledge what I've felt the past few hours. I was in performance mode before, smiling, reintroducing myself, laughing on the outskirts of conversations. But underneath the cheer is a steady current of betrayal. These people, my family, know all about my mother's death. Maybe a third of them seemed aware my dad followed suit mere years later. Why did no one make an effort to keep in contact with me, if they were as close to my mom as they make it seem?

"Thank you for the journal, by the way. Don't think I said that on the phone."

"I'm not sure it deserves thanks. When I ran into your grandmother, it just felt right. I hoped you'd find it comforting."

The wince that flashes across my face is involuntary. "I think I'm still digesting. I've been rereading parts of it."

"I've probably read it cover to cover once a year for a decade. Took me a while to crack it open after she'd passed on; then it became a sort of ritual."

"Hm." This small hum of observation has resentment underlying it. How nice for Vonnie that she had this journal to revisit all these years, to have a glimpse of what was going on in my mom's head during her final months. What claim do I have on my mother? I was born from her, yes, but what of the people, like Vonnie, who grew up alongside her for decades? I inhale a deep breath and with the exhale, try to release the anger that's trying to taint this reunion.

Vonnie is staring at me as I process this, her eyes slightly widened as they roam my face. I tuck a twisted lock of hair behind my ear under her scrutiny.

"Sorry it's just—I look at you and it hurts, not knowing you. I used to call you my baby. When Whitney died, I tried to help Wendell as much as I could, but he held you so close to his chest."

Those are the years I remember the most of my dad—just me and him. When I was a preteen, trudging through lingering grief but also desperate to hang out with my friends, he limited my outside hang time to one weekend out of the month. If I wanted to go see a movie or go to the mall with my friends, I had to pick my weekend wisely. Otherwise, I was spending time with my dad or convincing my best friend to chill with me at our house. If he needed someone to watch me, his go-to was

Grandma's house, where I'd follow Clara around as much as she would allow. There's not only one side at fault here.

"Then when Wendell died, I tried for custody, you know."

I nod. I remember multiple visits to the courthouse with Grandma and Auntie Sharon. Since I was thirteen, the judge took into consideration my wants. At that point, the separation between my mom's and dad's sides had already started to take place. I saw Vonnie maybe twice a year, compared to my weekly visits to my grandma and aunts. So I told the judge I'd rather go with Grandma. Apparently, Vonnie took that to mean a total rejection of her and the rest of my mom's family. But I was just a girl, clinging to some sense of normalcy.

I can't imagine what my life would look like if I'd spent my teenage years with Vonnie instead of Grandma. Maybe that version of me does exist in some alternate dimension.

Cousin Vonnie knows the milestones I've hit—high school and college graduations, getting a full-time job—because she's friends with Auntie Sharon and Auntie Yvette on Facebook. I fill her in on things that can't be found on social media, and she takes to everything with great interest. When I tell her about my business plans, she gives me the contact information for my cousin Grady, who works as a commercial Realtor.

Vonnie is the soon-to-be-retired director of a day care, divorced from her first husband, with no children of her own but with a steady boyfriend. Just as I start to feel there's potential here for mending what was left untended, Vonnie has to go help clean. I say goodbye to those I spoke to over the past few hours. They tell me, "Don't be a stranger," and I want to pointedly return the phrase, but I know it'll be up to me to keep contact. It's a responsibility I'm more than willing to share. Because once you become an adult, the onus is on you to heal from the tragedies of childhood. On one hand, it feels like getting the short end of the stick I didn't ask to break in the first place. On the other, it reminds me that even a shortened stick can be formed into a weapon against the things that have hurt me.

# CHAPTER FOURTEEN

Clara slides into the passenger seat with a take-home container of food as I stash my empty cake dish in the back seat. "That was a long chat," she says as she puts on her seat belt.

I glance at the time on the dash. There's no way I can drop Clara off at her condo and get to the museum in time. I'd be at least thirty minutes late, closer to an hour if traffic has any say.

"Maybe I should just cancel," I say aloud.

"I've noticed you haven't told me what you're in a rush to get to."

I sigh. "I have a date." Clara's mouth drops open. "With Penelope's vet," I finish before she can ask.

She shakes her head a bit, as if her innate lie detector went off. "You don't date."

"Exactly. I'm just going to cancel."

"If you would have told me about this truly random and possibly inappropriate date, I could have ordered a rideshare home. Or found a way home with one of your attractive cousins."

"Ew. You're related by proxy."

"Tell that to my libido."

I ignore Clara's antics and start composing a text to Elliot. Hopefully I can catch him before he's in transit. Clara grabs my arm.

"Wait, let's figure this out. You agreed to this date, so I'm already impressed with the guy. Where's it at?"

"The Museum of Science and Industry."

"Okay, so he's either a nerd or a try hard, but fine. I haven't been in a while; I'll just tag along and make myself scarce." I side-eye her. "You'll barely know I'm there."

Even if I believed in her ability to mind her business, this isn't an option. It isn't normal museum entrance hours, open to the public. "It's for a special exhibit preview. He got tickets in advance and everything."

Clara makes a face at me, completely unfazed. "Do you know who I am?"

Because I do, in fact, know who my aunt is, I delete my partially drafted text and replace it with **On my way!**, then head to the museum.

By the time we arrive, Clara has not only gotten her name added to the list but scored a QR code for free parking. We separate upon entry, Clara seeking out media colleagues while I find Elliot in the line to exchange our drink tickets for plastic flutes filled with a limited selection of alcoholic beverages.

Elliot starts to lift his arms and lean in but stops short and dips his head in greeting instead.

"Hugs are fine," I say. It's an understatement. Hugs are incredible. It's my favorite form of physical affection.

He grins and pulls me into his strong arms. I have to strike out the first con on my list because he does not, in fact, smell like a zoo. His scent is crisp and refreshing. It also makes me all too aware that I probably smell like barbecue smoke and bug repellent incense. I have a royal-blue blazer over the casual dress I wore to the party, but Elliot is taking the cocktail attire requirement more seriously. He looks good with his trim-fit slacks and a silky, royal-blue button-up. There's a paisley design woven into it with orange threads.

I select champagne, hoping it'll inject that bubbly, first-date feeling I've never experienced into my bloodstream. We float from table to table, sampling various hors d'oeuvres and exchanging stories of our weeks as we await the opening remarks.

Once they finally welcome us and briefly describe the vision behind the exhibition, we're allowed to leave the lobby area to go to the various rooms involved. I crane my neck around, trying to catch sight of Clara, but can't find her.

The new exhibit, in honor of Earth Day, focuses on modern green designs around the world and how they're transforming society. It's separated by continent, complete with replicas, some of which we can manipulate and play around with. Since most people flock elsewhere, we start in the North America section.

Clara was right in her assessment of Elliot's date choice. He's both a nerd and a try hard. It's a welcome combination. We crank handles to make a water-powered exhibit run, and try blowing against a sensor hard enough to trigger the wind turbine exhibit. In the Africa section, we strategically set up our solar panels based on the light bulb mimicking the sun's patterns, trying to catch enough light to fill our battery meter before the strangers we're competing with fill theirs. We lose, and despite my competitiveness, we're laughing the entire way. It makes me wish Elise, Corinne, and Cory were here. Wish that I were on speaking terms with Corinne in the first place.

"Ow," Elliot says as someone roughly bumps into his shoulder. "Excuse me," he says genuinely even though it wasn't his fault.

I'm so focused on him and if he's all right that I don't notice the person who ran into him until she turns around, twists swinging. Clara is not dressed in cocktail attire in the slightest, but she doesn't seem out of place, even in her thong sandals.

She avoids eye contact with me, which is inconvenient in my attempt to send a telepathic message reminding her of our agreement.

"No, excuse me, I wasn't looking where I was walking." She looks him up and down lasciviously. Elliot takes a step back. "I'm Tara." Clara extends her hand to him. I roll my eyes.

"Ah, Elliot." He fails to resist his manners and shakes her hand.

"Are you enjoying the exhibit?"

Elliot's shoulders relax at this question, probably figuring Clara works here or something.

"Oh yes." He takes another step backward and puts his arm around my back, but the contact is slight. It's clear it's for the sake of appearances, and he's sensitive to my aversion to PDA. "We are."

Clara's lips downturn as she nods, impressed. She looks at me for the first time. "Oh, I didn't realize you two were together. Is this your girlfriend?"

"I don't think it's your business?" The lilt at the end softens his words, but there's a mischievous glint in Clara's eyes that I know means she won't back down.

"Well, it is, because if she's not, I was going to ask if you'd want to grab a drink with me." She holds up drink tickets.

"Okay, no," I say, unable to entertain this charade anymore. I don't care if Elliot thinks I put her up to this. "Clara, enough."

"I think it's Tara," Elliot corrects me at the same time Clara does the same.

"You know, I didn't see it at first, but you two make a good-looking couple," Clara says. "Sorry for before. I don't pursue taken people. Only was a mistress twice before I knew nope, definitely not for me. So, how long have you been together?"

"Why are you like this?" I deadpan.

Elliot's hand finds its way to my arm and gives it a light squeeze before letting go. "Three years, almost."

My eyes bulge, but Clara flashes me a sly grin. "Oh yeah? That's sweet. I've never had a relationship that long." That part is true. "What's it like?"

"It's . . . good," Elliot says. He's obviously not a habitual liar, so that's a plus. Turning to me, he continues. "I still love learning new things about her. Three years, but it hasn't been nearly enough time."

Clara raises her eyebrows at me, a silent communication that should make it evident to Elliot that we know each other. But he's not paying attention because he's leaning toward me, turning his head so that his mouth is facing away from Clara. I feel the hush of his words against the shell of my ear when he says, "If I promise to let you set the pace as we walk away, can we level up to hand holding just for the duration of our escape?"

My surprised laugh is just a quick burst of air as I take Elliot's hand in mine. "We're leaving now," I say. Then I turn and lead us toward the Asia display. Surprisingly, holding hands isn't so bad when we're of similar heights and united in our mission to make a getaway.

# CHAPTER FIFTEEN

I proposed to do my first one-on-one meeting with Ben virtually, but he wants us all to see the shared working space the EMBERS Foundation is sponsoring for the duration of the mentorship, plus six months afterward. It's housed in a multistory building in Hyde Park. If the foundation isn't covering parking for us too, this might be the first and last time I make an appearance. Despite my seven-year routine of traveling to an office, I've been working on Bathe in Chocolate just fine from home.

The building has a Whole Foods on the street level, along with several other retail stores. I take the elevator up to the eleventh floor. The receptionist steers me in the direction of the meeting rooms, one of which Ben has reserved. It's a hip place, one of several coworking spaces that has popped up in the Chicago area in the past five years to encourage entrepreneurs to pool resources.

Ben's on the phone as I take the partially open door as an invitation to enter without knocking. He holds up a finger as he stands and wraps up his call.

"Have you had a chance to look around?" he asks me.

I hadn't intended to do much exploring since I don't plan on being here often. "No."

"Let's start with that, and then we can talk about Bic."

I blink at him, wondering why we're talking about pens.

"Bathe in Chocolate, I mean. I've been abbreviating it in my notes."

*Notes.* He probably has a list entitled, *Reasons BiC will fail.*

I follow Ben as he gives me a tour. There are small meeting rooms like the one we're in, but also conference rooms with the necessary technology for video calls. They have a few podcast recording studios. Perhaps most importantly, there's a huge space for simply working, with a variety of tables, couches, cozy seats, and even a few beanbags. They also have a small cubicle area for those who want a bit more privacy. There are about two dozen people scattered among the space. Some have headphones on and work in solitary. Others sit in small groups.

Then we tour the kitchen areas. There's one large kitchen, with four fridges and four microwaves for our use. It's stocked with free snacks.

"Coffee and tea are always free too," Ben says as I snag a bag of white-cheddar popcorn. "Unless you want something fancier, then there's a café on the first level."

Aside from the main kitchen, we check out the two break rooms. They have the aforementioned free coffee and tea, along with a water machine.

"Alkaline water. This is definitely worth leaving the comfort of my own home for," I say without inflection.

"It gives me a headache, but sure."

I don't bother clarifying my sarcasm. We walk back to the meeting room and sit across from each other at the round table. Ben opens his laptop. I didn't bring my iPad, or even scratch paper to jot notes down. Since I'm not staying to work here after the meeting, I figured I didn't need it. But as Ben glances at my empty side of the table, I realize I might have miscalculated the agenda of this meeting.

"First, I wanted to establish goals for the program's mentoring period. You can include longer-term goals if you want, but I think it's best to focus on what we can accomplish over the next three months."

I list them out on my fingers. My brain's biggest fault is that it tries to figure out ten problems at once, and then I find myself wasting time thinking about something not urgent, like class scheduling. To remedy that, I've memorized my short-term goals. "Find a shop location, choose my suppliers, and get an accountant-slash–all other business logistical things set up. Then get an intern to help with running classes."

Ben takes notes on his laptop. "Do you have a date in mind of when you'd like to launch?"

I can't entertain solidifying a launch date until I find the perfect location. "No. It's too dependent at the moment."

"Got it. For what it's worth, though, I think a good goal would be to launch in the fall."

"Not much," I breathe out the words with a sigh.

"What was that?"

"Ambitious," I say.

"Aren't you?" His eyebrows raise.

"I just want it done right, not necessarily fast."

"Every month you postpone is opportunity cost. By choosing to take your time, you lose out on potential—"

"I'm aware of the meaning, thanks. Those are my goals for these three months."

He studies my face for a moment, then gives me a singular nod. "I know a great commercial real estate agent in the area. I'll email you her info."

"Thanks, but I already have an agent searching for me." I reached out to my cousin Grady, the one Vonnie connected me with, and he's excited to work together to find the perfect space for Bathe in Chocolate.

"Okay." He consults his laptop. "Suppliers. I'm not sure of the major companies for culinary."

"It's fine, I know them. I just have to do more research on pricing."

"And the intern?"

"On that too." Chef Kim, my favorite from culinary school, said she'd be able to send me a few great candidates.

Ben leans back in his chair. "You've been busy since the conference."

"Well. I had good reason to think I'd be going about this on my own. So."

His eyebrows furrow but clear a moment later. "Any questions for me?"

I grab my purse and hang the long strap across my body. "Can I do our weekly check-ins by email?"

He surveys me from head to where my hand rests on my purse against my hip. "If you'd prefer it that way, Tiwanda, sure."

"Wonderful," I say, even though the exhausted manner in which he used my name is anything but.

~

"Hey, are you home? I'm in the area," Corinne says when I answer her call. She has easy access to check my location, which means she's really just asking permission to come. I give it to her, of course.

In the days since my meeting with Ben, all I can think about is his outrageous impression that I could be ready to launch by the fall. My cousin/Realtor sent me the first batch of properties he's found. After weeding out about half of them based on the pictures and specifications alone, he's getting us scheduled to visit the rest. If I found the right location for Bathe in Chocolate fast enough, maybe it wouldn't be so far-fetched. I can't lie, the thought of having those final months to start drumming up interest ahead of the first full calendar year is tempting.

When Corinne arrives, we greet each other with a stiffer hug than usual. "What brought you over this way?" I ask.

"A dentist appointment and my guilty conscience."

I meet her gaze and grin. "I'll pour us some moscato."

Corinne catches me up on the last few weeks of her life, details that weren't captured in the group text thread or the chats I've had with her mom. I express my regret in person that she wasn't picked to advance to the mentorship round of the program.

"I still won, because you got in," Corinne says. "Sorry I didn't make that clear these last weeks. I took it kind of hard."

"How's the rest of the team?"

"Oh." She blows a raspberry. "They're used to getting turned down for grants, so they were over it by the end of the day. We're working on a joint event with one of the nonprofits we met there, so it wasn't a total waste of time."

I give her the rundown on my progress with Bathe in Chocolate, and lack of progress in certain areas. It seems the cooldown walk I took earlier with Pen didn't totally defuse the tangled web of my frustrations and hopes, because it all comes spilling out of me. How tough it is finding a store, and how I fear the wrong location will kill my chances of longevity, and how I feel like the universe is punishing me for recklessly confronting Ben at that hotel lobby bar.

"So, Benoit the mentor," Corinne says with a sly grin. Of everything I said, *that's* what she chooses to latch on to. I wave a dismissive hand.

"He was forced to mentor me. I'm serious," I add at her cackle. "He thinks Bathe in Chocolate is super risky." I take a sip from my refilled glass. "I mean, truthfully, it is, but he tried to roast me on that panel. It was uncalled for."

"Key word: tried." We clink our glasses together. "Speaking of Met . . ."

"We weren't speaking of Met."

"We were speaking of Met by way of Ben." I sigh my defeat but let her continue. "I also wanted to apologize for . . . all of this. I mostly thought it would be entertaining if the share button actually worked, but I shouldn't have expected you to be, like, thankful for it."

I bump my shoulder with hers. "It's all right. Met helped me realize it's within my power to do nothing with the matches if I choose."

"It did?"

I nod.

Corinne seems to wrestle with herself a bit before asking, "Can I see what all it's said?"

"Sure." I reach for my phone immediately, not allowing my brain to cower at the vulnerability of some of the questions I've asked Met over the past few weeks. Corinne starts at the top of the Ask Met chain and slowly scrolls down. I pick at my cuticles and review a mental list of the bulk ingredients I'll need to order for BiC.

"Really, Tee?" Corinne holds my phone up to my face. Her finger is beside a question I asked over a week ago, as the last minutes of my day ticked away. In my haste not to waste a question, I'd asked, How do I delete this?

Met responded:

*Don't worry about it. I'll go when I'm ready.*

I shrug. "What? I've met three out of four now, and that's plenty."

Corinne shakes her head and continues her descent into my Ask Met correspondence. The way her eyes dissect the words, lips silently forming select phrases, makes me uneasy. It's as if I'm intruding on an intimate moment. When Met was on Corinne's phone, it had begun to feel like a friend to her. Specifically, her best friend, Joelle, who she'd lost tragically. We all carried the conviction that Joelle was guiding her somehow. But now that Met is on my phone, I can't say I've experienced the same feeling.

Finally, she hands the phone back to me, a little crease between her eyebrows.

"Any hidden meanings? Something I might've overlooked?"

She shakes her head. "No . . . it doesn't sound like Joelle at all."

91

# CHAPTER SIXTEEN

What's everyone up to? Pilar texts in the mentee group chat.

Since it includes Ben, I'm not inclined to share the depths of my entrepreneurial insecurities following the lackluster potential spaces I viewed. How can I feel like I have everything under control one moment and then like I'm winging everything and someone's going to call me out on it the next?

Instead of the bleak, I offer the group some good news. Spoke to the accountant Victor recommended. I officially have a business accountant!

Yazmin sends a picture of a ceramic vase she finished last week and already sold. She and Victor are working on updating their online shop to integrate it to a website also advertising their interior decorating services. Pilar says she's researching inventory systems, and her eyes are crossed looking at a spreadsheet of the running list of products she needs to order. But she mostly texted the group because she took the rest of the week off work to focus on her business and she's alone at the coworking space.

I stare at the text chain long enough for it to become blurry. I haven't been getting much done here today—maybe it would be worth it to change scenery and go to our vagabond office. Before I can change my mind, I send a quick text: I'll come keep you company.

She immediately sends out a GIF of a telenovela star gasping in Spanish. A rare Tiwanda sighting?

Yazmin chimes in with, I think that means good luck for seven years or something.

It's only been a couple of weeks since we gained access to the coworking space. I hadn't realized my absence was noticed. The group text is most frequently used by either Ben, Pilar, or Yazmin letting us all know when they're in the office to coordinate a coworking meetup.

I pack my laptop and fill Penelope's water bowl, and then I'm off. Pilar has set up shop in the main area on one of the comfy couches. She sports two french braids on either side of her head, complete with slicked edges. She looks up as I approach.

"Gotta say, I didn't believe you were serious." She pats the space beside her, the green emerald adorning her ring finger catching my eye. This is outrageous. Before Met, I wouldn't spare a second thought about her relationship status. Now I'm wondering who her partner is and if they're anything like me.

I grab one of the laptop trays kept within arm's reach of the couches and get set up. My focus for today is suppliers. I've narrowed it down to four companies, and I think I might need to use a combination of them. I email Terry, the mentor I met at the conference who had advised me on suppliers.

While we work, Pilar and I commiserate about the setbacks we're facing. My first-round bust of checking out properties and how it has the potential to delay my entire timeline. Pilar feeling like she simply doesn't have enough time in the day for all the things she must take into consideration.

After an hour, Pilar's smartwatch beeps. She glances at the notification as she presses the side button to dismiss it, then closes her computer.

"I have an appointment with someone who owns a natural hair care line," she explains. "She's letting me watch them make some products. Are you staying here much longer?"

I snap my laptop closed too. "Nope. Only came because your moping in the group text was distracting me. I'll go back to stressing out in the confines of my home office."

"Or," Pilar says, flashing me a mischievous grin, "you can take a break from the stress of it all and come with me."

We take one car to our destination, with Pilar driving and giving me the rundown. The hair care line is owned locally by a group of siblings—two sisters and one brother. It started out of one of their homes five years ago. They moved to renting a facility that could accommodate bigger batches almost two years ago. Pilar plans to have an entire section dedicated to locally sourced hair products, and they'll be one of the featured brands.

When we arrive, the younger sister greets us and gets us prepped with white long-sleeve lab jackets made of a lightweight fabric. We also get face masks, eye-protection glasses, and hairnets. Then she gives us a tour of the production area, where three people are working on prepping for the first batch they plan to make of leave-in conditioner. One of the people is her brother, the co-owner. The other two are employees they hired when they couldn't keep up with demand between the three of them.

Pilar and I stand as close as possible without getting in their way. Even though they fall into an easy rhythm, they're sure to check the measurement specification sheets posted at each station. The aroma is so potent I can smell the mixture through my face mask. With ingredients like macadamia nut oil, almond milk, and honey, it reminds me of a pastry.

They divvy up tasks—one person measuring, another operating the mixing machines, one readying the containers by applying the labels, and another filling and storing them appropriately. After two batches of the conditioner, they switch to a styling butter with a thicker consistency.

Once that single batch is whipped and packaged, the younger sister of the owners leads us back out to the office area. We take off our protective wear, and I listen as Pilar asks questions about their distribution and shelf life. I ask about their formulation process. It's not exactly the same as how I go about soapmaking, but we both use natural healing products.

"That was amazing," I tell Pilar once we're back in her car.

She nods emphatically. "At one point I considered launching my own hair product line. I make my own oil mixes and a shea butter–based moisturizer I live by. But I realized that's not really my niche. They were like chemists in there, exact with measurements and making sure the product is the same every time. I improvise. My real skill is organization. I love hair products, finding new ones and introducing them to people."

Sometimes what you're meant to do with a talent isn't straightforward. When deciding to attend pastry school, I envisioned myself owning a bakery or getting on one of those bake-off television shows. But now here I am, wanting to guide groups of strangers with either chocolate or soapmaking.

"Well, running your store will be a great use of that skill. Thanks for letting me tag along."

"Of course. I decided that since Victor and Yazmin have each other to lean on during this process, we have each other. Hope you're cool with that."

~

Elise comes over that evening to spend the night. We made these plans last week, though admittedly it slipped my mind until she called, asking what to bring. It's been a while since we've had a proper sleepover. I'm so excited to spend an extended amount of time with my best friend, I don't even tease her that the only reason she's here is because Devin is out of town visiting family in California.

We touch base on the website she's designing for my business, but for the most part we just enjoy holding space with each other. We order food, watch movies, and share inconsequential tidbits of our lives that require room and time to surface.

"When was your last audition?" I ask, realizing she hasn't mentioned any in a while.

"I don't know. I'm just waiting for the rehearsals for *Little Women* to start next week. I want to focus on wrapping that up. I sent in a few tapes for TV and film, though."

I frown a little. Elise usually has a steady stream of auditions set up. Even if she was cast in a play, she'd continue auditioning for upcoming plays too. So long as the rehearsals and performances didn't conflict, she was good to go. Maybe she's experiencing burnout.

Elise cuts into my speculative thoughts. "Can we take a moment and appreciate how amazing it is that we can do this in the middle of the week?"

It really is. I used to be MIA Monday through Friday afternoon. At random times, while working on Bathe in Chocolate, I glance at the clock and imagine what I'd be doing if I still worked at my old job. I've even texted Chris a few times to check in on him. He assured me it was still a shit show. Elise only shifted to freelance web design while she pursued her acting career a year ago. At the time, it seemed like she was so far ahead of me, taking the leap to attain her goals. I doubted I'd ever catch up.

"This might turn out to be a very expensive break, but I feel like it saved my life in a way?" I hadn't realized I was drowning until I was pulled out of the water, thanks to Grandma and Clara.

"Oh, it's much more than that. A break implies resuming what you left. Even if your business goes belly-up, there's no going back."

"That's reassuring, I guess." In the same way everyone's mutual impending death is.

"Mhmmm." Elise nods sincerely as she eats a bite of edible cookie dough. "So I'm thinking, it's about time we have your belated birthday-and-I-quit-my-job party."

I grunt. "Shouldn't we just wait until next year? Thirty-one is just as celebration worthy." I reach for the remote but pause, my hand stalling in midair. "If I were a number, it would be thirty-one. Intimidating if you read it the wrong way. And often left behind. I should do a dirty thirty-*first*."

Elise shakes her head. "I refute that. You're definitely a thirty. Curvaceous, and sneaks up on you while you're having fun."

My jaw goes slack. "What does that even mean?"

"You know how your romantic feelings are slow going?"

"No going most often, but yeah."

"I kind of think that's how your friendships go too. When we first met, I don't think either of us would have predicted how close we'd become, and that our summer internship acquaintance would turn into this." She waves her arm around at our setup, fortified by pillows, blankets, and a never-ending supply of snacks on my bed. "It subtly became one of my most important relationships. Like a sneak attack. Isn't that how it happened with Cory, and now with Corinne?"

I blink as I consider this. I've known Corinne since we were young because we're cousins, but we only recently became close friends. My friendship with Cory formed over a year of tutoring and running into each other from overlapping circles.

"Fine, I'm all the numbers," I concede.

"Guess you have to celebrate them all, then."

We spend the rest of the night throwing out party ideas that I can pull together quickly. The easiest solution would be a small party here at my condo, but I did that last year, and I'm over cleaning up after people once the party's over. If I go through the trouble of having a belated party, I'm going to enjoy it. Despite my reluctance, I know without a doubt my parents would be satisfied I'm living up to their high standards for birthday celebrations.

# CHAPTER SEVENTEEN

It's strange being back in the West Loop lunch rush crowd. This used to be my escape from the office for a half hour. Or if Chris was involved, the full hour. I arrive at the restaurant of choice first so I can snag us a table, then text both Chris and Elliot that I'm here.

Since Chris and Elliot are friends, and now so are Elliot and I, it made sense for us all to get together. Elliot says he's parking, and Chris is leaving the office, which is about a five-minute walk from here.

"Tiwanda?"

I look up, not knowing which past coworker I expect spotted me. But when I see *his* face, I stiffen. He is a past coworker, but from nearly five years ago.

"Sorry, I was sitting over there with some friends from work when I saw you come in. Can I?" He pulls out the seat across from me and lowers himself into it even as I'm unable to do more than blink at him in my current state of shock.

In this moment, I understand the jolt Corinne experienced each time Met sent her someone from her past. Because here in the flesh is the only person who came to mind when Met first appeared on my phone and I assumed I'd be subjected to a similar song and dance. Elise and I refer to him as my unicorn, the first person I'd had a serious crush on. Not a fleeting crush, but one that nestled into my mind. Once that happened, it wasn't a matter of not sensing when to level up. It was wanting to be on all the levels at once.

I pull my shoulders back and lengthen my posture. "Tobias. It's been a while."

He nods emphatically. "Are you still at MIL?"

"Not anymore."

"Good. I was worried you'd retire there."

My eyes narrow. Tobias knew I wanted to start my own business. Back then, I was even more adamant about it than in the months leading up to my departure. We were close. Along with Chris, he was one of my best work buddies. It had been Chris who pointed out that what I took as Tobias being friendly was flirtation. For months, I denied and ignored it. Long story short, by the time I registered I wanted him in a romantic way, he'd already moved on to pursue someone who reciprocated his feelings in a better-aligned time frame.

Thinking about it still makes my insides boil with embarrassment. And maybe a little bit of fury. That end-of-year holiday office party and just enough drinks to lose my inhibition. It wasn't until after we ran off to his place, undressed each other in frenzied disbelief, touched and licked to a quick release, that he told me I was too late. The thing he had with this other woman, it wasn't official yet, but it was heading in that direction, and I wasn't enough to stop it.

"Hey." Elliot's voice is like a brief brush against sandpaper as he slides into the seat beside me. He gives me a side hug and leaves his arm on the back of my chair when he pulls away. I don't miss the way Tobias sizes him up.

"This is an old coworker," I tell Elliot. It's the best introduction I can muster up. Elliot nods slowly, his lips upturned in the neutral-friendly position people with customer-facing jobs tend to perfect. The calculating way his eyes roam my face gives him away, though.

"Tobias." He adds his name himself and reaches across the table to shake Elliot's hand.

Elliot grasps it briefly. "Dr. Pace. It's good y'all had a chance to catch up." Then, turning to me, he adds, "Are you ready to order?"

The dismissal is effective. Tobias pushes back from the table to stand. "Maybe I'll see you around, Tee. I want to hear about what you're doing now that you escaped M-I-Hell."

I give a purposefully fake hiccup of a laugh at our old inside joke. "Maybe."

"Do you still have my number?" He begins to reach for the phone-shaped bulge in his pocket.

Pressing my lips together, I shake my head absently. "Probably not."

Tobias stops his pursuit of his phone as the blunt delivery of my words lands. "All right. I'll leave you to your lunch. Ordering it, I mean. The wraps here are really good."

He retreats to a table across the restaurant. Elliot removes his hand from my chair, smoothly using it to pull up the menu on his phone instead.

"I feel like protective asshole is a level up we didn't agree to, so I'm sorry if I guessed wrong and that wasn't the energy you needed."

I snake my hand under the table and place it on his thigh. "It actually was. Thank you."

Without breaking eye contact, he swaps his phone to his other side and covers my hand with his own. "Anytime."

"This looks cozy."

Chris's voice breaks me from my Elliot-induced trance. I scramble out of my chair to give him a hug strong enough to make up for the months I haven't seen him. He's the only person I miss from my old job. My best memories there involve him, most of them of us making the best out of shared misery.

"Just ran into your best friend," I say as I lift my chin in the direction of Tobias's table.

Chris is already frowning as he turns toward where Tobias is surreptitiously glancing over at us.

"For fuck's sake," Chris mumbles. There was side choosing when Tobias and I stopped talking to each other altogether after that holiday party half a decade ago. Chris made the obvious choice. "Wow, so today is a double blast from my past."

"Hey, I'm not your past!" I protest.

"I wasn't so sure until you set this up. You up and quit one day. No warning. I think it was a Wednesday. Who quits on a Wednesday?"

He has a point, so after we place our orders, I give him the floor to rant as much as he wants about the past two months of work. I sympathize appropriately and hide my childish relief that he doesn't care much for my replacement.

Once Chris can't extend his lunch break any further, we leave together. Chris takes off to the right, back toward the office. Elliot and I walk toward where I'm parked to the left. I hold up my hand in offering.

"Level up?"

He interlaces his fingers with mine, but after a few steps loosens his hold on me. "We don't have to, you know. If you don't like it."

"I know. But I like you." I also like how my words catch him off guard. His surprise morphs into a haughty grin. He was right. I am into the cock-fidence.

"I like you too, Tiwanda. We can find our own ways of leveling up. How about . . ." Elliot puts his arm around my lower back instead. It jostles a bit as we walk, but he keeps it in place. "Better or worse?"

"Definitely worse."

He laughs and lets his arm fall back to his side. "The search continues."

Returning home after lunch instead of to the office with Chris is the reassurance I need that this was the right career move for me. I scan my inbox for the fourth time today. No one told me starting my own business was going to be 80 percent checking my email at the outset. Tuesday is my designated day to send my weekly update to Ben, with a concise bulleted list of my progress. I sent it before leaving to meet

Elliot and Chris for lunch, so his response is waiting for me. He's consistent. Quick responses within a couple of hours, reiterating he's here if I need anything. I don't, so I'll keep trekking along until next week's check-in. It's a perfect arrangement.

Along with Ben's email, Terry responded only minutes ago to my message regarding suppliers. I scan the couple of sentences they composed and reach for my phone to dial the number shared with me.

"You're quick," Terry answers.

We spend the next forty-five minutes of their day off hashing out my supplier vexations. They boot up their laptop to do quick secondary research on the companies I'm considering. By the end of the call, I've decided on which companies I'll use for my initial order, one of which is a personal favorite of Terry's.

"Thank you," I say. "I'm excited to not think about this until it's time to place the orders."

"That's the only reason I get anything done—so I can free up brain space. Let me know if you run into any other problems."

I hang up and instantly register how much this singular problem had been weighing me down. It's like that for me. The collective weight on my shoulders becomes so massive I can't distinguish how much each worry is contributing until it's separated from the rest by elimination. With this relief, I get a glimpse of what awaits me when I get Bathe in Chocolate up and running. Maybe this mentorship is worth more than its monetary value after all. Just a little bit.

# CHAPTER EIGHTEEN

I make my return to the coworking space to meet Pilar. It's early evening, and I arrive with the rush of people putting in entrepreneurial work after their day jobs. Pilar is at a small circular table today, which I take to mean she's really taking care of business.

"Oh, great," she says as I pull out a chair. She holds up her phone and angles the camera so we're both on-screen for the picture. "I'm trying to convince Yazmin and Victor to come work here so we can have a proper mentee team reunion."

It's been a month since our introductory group meeting and I haven't seen Yaz or Vic. In Ben's latest email, he mentioned wanting to have a group outing, so we'll reunite sooner or later. Yazmin replies back with a picture of a love seat they're reupholstering with a striking gold fabric.

"What have you been working on?" Pilar asks.

"Honestly, planning my party is taking up half of my brain. The other half is still stumped on kitchen spaces."

Corinne found a cabin rental on the lake that also offers fun activities like horseback riding and canoes. It sleeps up to fourteen people, which feels like a good, controlled size to me. The properties I saw with Grady last week were both okay, nothing special. And neither inspired me enough to want to pour the money into it to make it special. I'm hopeful we're getting closer, though. It's nice working with Grady, bonding over our love for the city, pinpointing exactly how we're related, and expanding my connection with that side of my family beyond Vonnie.

"What party, and why don't I know about it already?"

I share my tentative plans and explain the delay from my birthday and surprise self-employment months ago.

"There's always reason for a good party." She gasps. "You should invite the whole team, since it's part job-quitting celebration."

"Once I get confirmation on the dates, I'll text the chat," I promise.

Pilar's phone rings before she can do more than a little happy jig in her chair.

"It's my boo. Hold on, we've been trying to catch each other all day."

I nod and shift my focus to my laptop as if I'm not about to eavesdrop the hell out of her conversation. Sometimes I forget Pilar is a Met match. It's been easy around her since the beginning, as if Met isn't involved at all.

Her side of the conversation isn't juicy. It's mostly hums of engagement, low laughter, and a couple of quick lines about how her workday went. She ends with, "Okay, my love. See you tomorrow." Her voice is soft and sweet, completely transformed from the normal speaking voice she uses with everyone. It makes me . . . not jealous, exactly. Curious.

"That was your . . . ?"

"My partner," she says with a smitten grin. "We've been together four years." She holds her left hand up, stroking the underside of her ring with her thumb. "Commitment ring. She hasn't gotten me down the aisle yet."

Since I'm not a home-wrecker, or a home-starter, for that matter, their lack of a certificate affirming their union is negligible. For all intents and purposes, Pilar has met her soul mate. Which raises the question: How many can we have?

"Got something against it?" I ask.

Her head tilts to the side, gaze drifting into space. "Honestly"—she steadies herself with both elbows on the table—"my motto has been we'll do it after I get my business up and running, however long that takes. We already live together, so what's the rush? To me, marriage feels like locking in what you have. But I know this isn't our final form. I don't want to essentially trap us. We should have—no, I *need* to have freedom to redefine our relationship without the confines of marriage. No matter how imagined they are."

I nod, considering telling her to also beware of the tax implications marriage can have but decide against it. "I guess some people do associate marriage with steadiness, but it's obviously not the case since so many fail."

"Tiwanda," she gasps. "Are you a Cynical Cindy?"

"I'm a Realistic . . . Reba."

She shakes her head in a way that makes me think she's gearing up to read me like a book. But then she looks up at something over my shoulder, and her smile grows.

"Hey! You didn't say you were coming in today."

Pilar holds out her fist, and I turn, craning my neck as Ben half-heartedly returns her fist bump.

"I was in the area. Tiwanda, can you spare a minute? I'd like to touch base with you."

With me? Everything about this feels off in a way that makes my heart beat a nervous rhythm. His sudden appearance, the jogger pants that look out of place on him, though lots of people here wear comfortable lounge clothes. But the biggest reason my brain hits a snag is that he seems hell-bent on speaking with me when I thought our weekly email check-ins have been going perfectly. They're succinct and save me unnecessary travel. Guess Benoit doesn't agree.

I wave a hand to the empty seat at the table.

"There's a meeting room available, so we can take it in there."

Pilar and I share a look that confirms I'm not the only one who thinks this is strange. She offers to watch my things, so I stand and follow Ben to one of the small meeting rooms.

The moment we're both seated, he asks, "Are you running into any issues? With BiC?"

My lips turn down as my head starts to shake reflexively. "Nope."

He runs his thumbnail across his bottom lip. "No roadblocks?"

"Nothing I'm not handling."

He nods, his eyes trained just above my head. When he lowers his gaze and regards me again, his face is wiped free of emotion.

"Are you familiar with how mentorships work?"

"Yeah, I think so." I nod emphatically. "There's men involved and they build boats, a.k.a. ships."

He stares at me blankly, the only way he seems capable of, then sighs. "That was a pedantic question."

"Yes."

"I apologize. I'm just not understanding why I can't get more than 'I'm handling it' from you, when apparently you do need help sometimes but just prefer to go to other mentors in the program."

*Oh.* My assuredness slides back into place as the catalyst for this meeting is revealed.

"I went to a person I'd connected with during the conference who has a shit ton of experience with suppliers. I wasn't aware that was discouraged."

"It's not." His concessions send a trickle of warmth through me.

"Do you have some secret extensive knowledge of suppliers I didn't know about?"

"I do not."

The corners of my lips turn up, but it isn't a smile—it's the acknowledgment of winning with such a sound argument. Silence stretches between us as I wait for Ben to close the meeting. He doesn't.

"We have mentor group calls every two weeks. Terry shared how impressed they were with you."

*Glad someone is,* I think.

Ben continues. "I've been trying to meet you where you're comfortable, make this mentorship work around your life and preferences. But if I'm honest, it hasn't been ideal. More than that, I think it's doing you a disservice."

"I'll be honest with you too. Mentors are nice and all, but I entered this program specifically with funding in mind."

"That's understandable, but I don't see why you wouldn't want to take advantage of every resource along the way."

My gaze travels sporadically around the room, in an admittedly dramatic display of thinking. "Since Terry is a resource, I'm going to assume you mean yourself."

"Well, yes. But also the resources I could connect you to. If you had disclosed your issue with suppliers in your check-in email, fine, I probably would have put you in touch with Terry." He lifts a defiant hand in response to my triumphant smile. "So imagine having access to the perfect person to help you through whatever problem you have, every time. That's what I can do."

I can't deny how enticing this offer is. I'm not sure how this conversation quickly turned into Ben pitching himself to become my mentor in a true capacity, but he seems sincere in his desire to help me.

"Why are you mentoring me?" He allows an infinitesimal squint of his eyes. "I mean, did they force you to take me on?"

"The board chooses who advances, but the prospective mentor has to agree. They want to make sure we feel confident guiding the business."

"So you just said, 'Why the hell not?' and accepted me?"

His lips pull up enough to definitely fall into the classification of a smile. "More like, if I don't mentor you, I'd see BiC—Bathe in

Chocolate—become a wildly successful franchise and regret not being a part of it for the rest of my life."

My mouth drops open. "I don't want to franchise," I say.

"I'd like to talk with you about that. Maybe a few years from now."

My insides contract with a laugh that gets trapped.

"So you don't hate my business?"

His eyebrows furrow, genuinely confused. It's the most emotion I've seen on his face so far. "Why would you think that?"

"Do you not remember the panel?" *And afterward.* "You dragged me for filth."

"As if I could. You had an answer for every concern I threw at you. I don't tend to have confidence often enough to invest in the service industry. Yields low profits, and unreliable on top of that. People are flaky when it comes to such things."

"Please, go on. I love hearing about how susceptible my business is to failure."

"Like I said, I don't *tend* to."

"Well, you should know, I was bullshitting everything I said on the panel. So."

He laughs, and the unexpected sound has my shoulders rolling back just a bit even as he seems to relax.

"I only gave you the drawbacks I noticed for BiC, so we're even."

I tilt my head and hesitate for just a moment before deciding to just ask. "Why did you withhold the good stuff?"

"It's not that I withheld it. The other panelists covered it. No need to harp on what's already known. It's a unique business idea, you know exactly where you could fit in the market, and you're an asset in yourself. Your business knowledge is at the level I wish all aspiring entrepreneurs were at before opening their businesses."

"Oh."

He lets my one-syllable response linger between us for an elongated moment before saying, "Just so we're on the same page, I have full belief in Bathe in Chocolate and am not mentoring you out of spite."

I take a deep breath. This won't be so bad. I'll let Ben help occasionally. Surely I can handle that. It might even lead to quicker solutions.

"Well. Sorry I accosted you after the panel," I say to the table between us. "Hopefully no issues come up. But if they do, I'll let you know. So you can perform your mentor duties. Since you practically begged."

"All right." Ben stands.

"It was touching, if not a tad embarrassing," I say, still seated.

"Okay, get out, meeting adjourned."

Grinning, I rise from my chair and walk through the door he holds open for me.

"One last thing," he says before I get too far. "I'd like to have our check-in meetings face-to-face, whenever possible. It's been working well for the other three, and the board encourages it."

That quickly erases the grin from my face.

# CHAPTER NINETEEN

Grandma takes off her seat belt and adjusts the ruffles on her blouse.

"I don't see why I have to be here," she huffs under her breath.

"You don't," Clara says from the back seat. "It's an invitation, not an order."

"It'll be fun," I say before Grandma can launch into her thought process behind accepting this invitation to Cousin Vonnie's retirement dinner. I'd already heard it once, and it involved a healthy dose of pride and not letting Vonette have the upper hand for extending the olive branch.

We leave the car and enter the restaurant. The hostess directs us to the private room, where half the seats are filled. A quick scan of the room confirms Vonnie hasn't arrived yet.

"Tiwanda?" a woman nearly my height asks. She walks over from the balloon bundle she was in the process of turning so that the word *CONGRATS* is visible. "I'm your cousin Cherie. Glad you made it." She greets me with a hug. I introduce Clara and Grandma and wonder if I imagine the tightness in Cherie's smile as she shakes Grandma's hand.

"Did I meet you at the barbecue a few weeks ago?" Clara asks.

Cherie shakes her head as she relieves me of my gift bag. "Supposed to, but I was sick as a dog. Poor Von had to run the whole party herself.

Tonight's my chance to make it up to her. Thirty-five years, isn't that something?"

She shows us to our spots at the table, marked with our names handwritten on little place cards. The long table has twelve chairs on each side, and we're surprisingly placed near the middle. I thought for sure we'd be squeezed at the end. I check the name in front of the empty chair to my left—Vonette. Clara is across from me, and Grandma is to her right. Hopefully that's enough distance to obscure her disdain from the person of honor.

The table fills over the next fifteen minutes, until finally Vonnie arrives wearing a beautiful gold dress that matches the black-and-gold decor. Cherie quickly hits play on her phone, and a Mary J. Blige song plays over the speaker. The table follows her lead and applauds Vonnie's entrance, her boyfriend standing to the side as she does a few twirls for the photographer.

Once the last few standing settle in their seats, the waitstaff descends to start collecting drink orders beyond the water already on the table. For the first hour, everything goes smoothly. Conversations overlap at the table, and in our position it's easy to slip in and out of them at our leisure. On one side I have Vonnie and her past coworkers sharing their favorite teaching stories. On the other are some cousins I just met, whose conversation is mostly a mix of family gossip, politics, and sports. Grandma does well, though she only actively listens to Vonnie's work stories if forced—i.e., everyone at the table has tuned in and there are no other conversations to choose instead.

When the retirement cake is served, I'm in a relaxed state. We made it. After nearly two decades of family beef, we sat at a long table and broke bread together. Jesus would be proud. Judas would be shaking in his sandals. Sure, my older aunts harbor more of a grudge than Clara, but they'll follow Grandma's lead if she closes the rift. For once, I'm feeling like that's a real possibility.

"So where have you been all these years?"

This question comes as I'm contentedly eating my slice of carrot cake. The woman asking is a cousin who earlier said she remembered me from when I was a child. I slowly finish my bite, buying time to figure out how to answer the question.

"Here, mostly. I lived in Michigan for a bit, and I tag along with Clara for travel as much as I can, but mostly here. I live in the West Loop now."

"Bougie," she says appreciatively.

"Bougie aunt," I amend.

"Wait, you've been in Chicago?" Someone else hops in the conversation from farther down the table. I think his name is Kenny, but I haven't had a chance to speak to him. "Why am I just now meeting you?"

It dawns on me that everyone doesn't know my story. I'm not sure if I'm grateful for Vonnie giving me the chance to just be a newfound cousin, or disappointed that I'm largely unknown to them.

"Tiwanda was stashed away from us," Vonnie says in a joking tone.

Grandma's sharp head movement signals she either doesn't pick up or care about Vonnie's tone.

"Oh, is *that* how you say it went?" she asks.

"Let's not get into it," Clara says. Her attempt to quell the conversation is barely heard because Vonnie turns as if Grandma never said anything and addresses Kenny.

"After they got custody, they acted like Tiwanda only had one side of the family. But we're here to remedy that. Let bygones be bygones and enjoy the time we have left."

I'm grateful for Vonnie's attempt to turn it into a bright note. Grandma is not.

She picks up the cloth napkin from her lap, tosses it over her half-eaten cake, and says, "Honey, it's time to retire your lies like you're retiring your career."

The table goes quiet except for Cherie's daughter's disbelieving "I know she lying" from the end of the table. The waiter, who'd come to collect some emptied plates, retreats from the room with only two dishes.

"Whitney loved your son, but she would have never wanted Tiwanda to be raised by you." Though Vonnie's words aren't directed at me, I feel the vicarious sting of them. After Grandma's recent reveal that she and my mom didn't get along, I can't help but think there's some truth to it.

Grandma stands, grabbing her purse hanging from the back of the chair. Clara shovels her last bite of cake into her mouth and stands with her, ready for whatever power exit must be coming. I'm driving, so they can't go without me, but I don't want to further this divide, and immediately standing would do just that.

"Doesn't matter. That girl right there dealt with more than her fair share, only for you to come and force her through a baseless custody battle." Her fierce gaze flicks to me before going back to Vonnie. "She's a persevering, intelligent young woman. That's thanks to Wendell, and thanks to Whitney, but it's also thanks to me."

Grandma power-struts out of the room. Clara takes two steps to follow her, then remembers the retirement card in her purse we'd stopped to pick up along the way. She fishes it out and hands it to Vonnie.

"This is from both of us," she says with a wince. Then she mimes turning keys in the ignition to me, which is a pointless attempt at discretion since everyone sees me pass them off to her over the table.

I round the group for quick, awkward goodbyes. The next time I meet with Vonnie, I'm going to make sure it's just the two of us.

Five minutes into our car ride away from the restaurant, I realize I'm not sure if my silent fuming is having any effect on Grandma, who appears to be engaging in some silent fuming of her own. I sigh.

"So what if Mom preferred me with her side of the family?" I say. "Dad wanted the same." And he was the last parent standing, so he prevailed.

"Bullshit," Grandma says. "Even when both Whitney and Wendell were alive, you all spent more time with us than them. She wouldn't want to separate you from us."

Regardless of if that's true, I know she surely wouldn't want me separated from her side of the family either. "You did say you didn't like my mom much. That's probably what Vonnie was talking about."

She swats my theory away. "That was in the beginning. She just took some warming up to, that's all. We got along just fine down the road."

I check the rearview mirror for Clara's reaction. She seems to agree with that claim.

"In fact, I remember the exact moment I decided I liked her. It wasn't until after you were born."

"That means you were at odds her whole pregnancy with me? Nine months to warm up?"

"About two years, more like it, when you were starting to walk. You were a late developer. I just knew you weren't meant to have any siblings because you took your sweet time hitting any of the quote-unquote milestones." She pauses with a sad sigh. If her thoughts went where mine did, it's at the striking irony that maybe she was right, since both my sibling and my mom didn't make it when my parents tried for another.

"You'd been trying to stand up on your own for some time, your chubby legs wobbling before falling on your behind again. You fell so many times, we'd stopped watching you. Your dad had run out to get something from the store. So it was just me and your mom, both of us minding our own business."

"Wait, where was I?" Clara interjects from the back seat.

"I don't know, were you in town?"

"I had to be what, seven or eight years old? I wasn't traveling then, Momma."

"Well, you've been gone a lot, how am I supposed to know? Anyway. Me, you, your mom, and *maybe* Clara is there. I was going between watching television and checking on the food. Whitney was sitting at the table keeping one eye on the book she was reading and the other on you. My house wasn't babyproofed, and she was paranoid bringing you over there. As if I hadn't raised four children in that house without incident."

"There was that one time Yvette fell off the bed and bust her head open on that sharp corner of the side table," Clara says.

"Hush up; that wouldn't have happened if she wasn't jumping on the bed in the first place. An-y-way," she drags out each syllable. "You stood up this one time, no different than any of the others, but for whatever reason, both of us happened to look right at you in that moment. Maybe it was divine timing, or a tick of determination we picked up on peripherally, but you didn't fall down immediately. Instead, you took one shaky step, and then another. On the third, I said we should stop you, so your daddy could see it.

"Whitney turned to me, her face as mean as I ever did see it, and said, 'I will not. All the mess she'll have to deal with in this world. You think I'm ever going to be the one to stand in her way?' By the time she finished her little grandstand, you'd fallen already. But it stuck with me. After I got over being spoken to so rudely, I realized I kind of liked the girl."

Clara and I exchange a look through the mirror, but neither of us comes up with anything to say. Goose bumps cover my arms, and I redirect the AC vents to a neutral space. How do you respond to a story like that? Nothing adequate, so I simply sit with the knowledge of the fierce protection my mom had over me, and for a moment I feel it as potently as if it's cast over me even now.

# CHAPTER TWENTY

I've had some disastrous pastry moments from Baking While Upset. Bread that refused to rise, a simple birthday cake that stuck to the pan so much icing couldn't fix it, you name it. Graduating from pastry school didn't make me the perfect pastry chef, but it did make me astute at figuring out what went wrong. My forensic skills aside, I've stopped attempting to bake my feelings out. Instead, I make chocolate.

To get it tempered just right, it requires constant movement. So do I. We're a perfect match. I stir and track the temperature, removing and replacing it over the double boiler accordingly. By the time the dark chocolate morsels I started with become a smooth, shiny liquid, thoughts of Grady dropping me have been banished to the back of my mind.

"I'm no longer confident I can serve your needs" were his exact words. So formal, like he'd copied and pasted it into the email. I'd hoped our joint effort in finding a home for Bathe in Chocolate was the beginning of a new relationship with a cousin from my mom's side. An additional string tying me to her. I'm seeing now just how little weight it held for Grady. With Vonnie's retirement dinner ending in flames and now this, I'm starting to question if it's meant for me to reconnect with my family. Maybe the two sides never fit together, and now that I've been engulfed by one side, I don't fit the other either.

Even after all the batches of chocolate I've tempered, I still test a drop on wax paper and sit it in the fridge to harden. After a minute I take it out and snap it in half. It makes a clean, satisfying break. Moving with culinary-level quickness now, I pour the chocolate into the polycarbonate molds, then drip the excess back into the bowl, scrape the surface clean, then sit it in the fridge. Once that hardens some, I pipe a bit of guava jam I found at the market into each hole, then follow it with ganache. Finally, I finish up with ladling more chocolate to provide the base of the bonbon. Another scraping, and back in the fridge it goes. I feel the loss of having a task greater than the accomplishment of creation.

But then I glance at the clock and realize I have half an hour before my video call with Ben. It's our first official one-on-one check-in, and the tension in my shoulders and neck as I clean the kitchen feels suspiciously like nerves. I don't know how to be with Ben, now that we've reached common ground.

I log in to the meeting right on time. Ben looks up, slightly surprised.

"Good afternoon," he says.

"Hi." We stare at each other so long I check that my internet hasn't dropped. Maybe we both are unsure of how to proceed. "How do you usually start these things?"

The question kicks Ben into gear. "Pretty casually. Catch up on each other's day. Talk about the weather."

"Okay. I at most need a light jacket when I take my dog out in the mornings, so that's good enough weather for me. And I made chocolate today."

A smile teases the corners of his lips. "That's on par with what I pictured you did all day, working from home."

"What?" It's part a response to the absurdity and part incredulity that he imagines what I'm up to in the first place.

"Figuring out different chocolate recipes and soap formulas."

"Not quite. I don't need to go full-blown test kitchen. For the most part, people who come to my classes will decide the flavors they want themselves. And I'll provide suggestions as needed."

"Gotcha." He lowers his head as he writes a note.

"Uh, how has your day been so far?" Conversing with him minus hostility is still clunky, but I'll get there.

He glances up like he's checking it's still me asking and not some random intruder who upon entry decided not to rob me blind but instead took over my business call for me. He's silent for a moment as he seems to consider his day.

"It was okay. Got everything moved into my new apartment. I'll be back in Chicago the day after tomorrow."

I smile and nod. Him being in Philly for part of the week was great timing for me to avoid having this meeting in person.

"You're ready to start talking business already, aren't you?"

I'm not surprised he picked up that I'd exhausted all my small-talk topics, but I am surprised that he called me out on it.

"Please," I say.

He has a lot of questions for me. Questions that make me aware of just how little I was giving him in my weekly check-in emails. And not just logistical ones. Interspersed between inquiries about estimated sunk costs and possible hours of operation, he asks questions like, "What do you envision for your business one year post opening?" It took me a minute to answer that one. I've been so focused on getting in position to launch that I hadn't thought that far ahead.

Finally, he asks the question I knew would come up. "You mentioned in your last email that you were going to see more properties with your Realtor. How did that go?"

His eyebrows are drawing together before I even open my mouth to answer, because I can't prevent all the frustration I tried to drown in chocolate from showing on my face.

"Not great," I say. "Neither was right. Then my Realtor kind of dropped me. I wasn't worth the hassle. My own cousin. I didn't know him until a month ago, but still."

He's frowning now. "For future reference, any crises should be prioritized at the beginning of our meetings." His face gets closer to the camera. When his eyes start moving across the screen, I assume he's pulled up another window on his end. "How long have you been without a Realtor?"

"Since this morning. I wasn't keeping it from you. I just figured since we had this meeting scheduled anyway, it could wait."

He shakes his head as he begins typing something. "Is this an issue that negatively affects your business?"

"Not in the long run hopefully, but in the moment? Yes."

"And did it upset you?"

This question is unexpectedly tender. "Yes," I say.

"Then it warrants immediate notification. You can email me, or text me. I know this is new for you, and you seem to prefer as little contact as possible—"

"It's not that. You were moving today and out of the city. I was just being considerate."

He somehow manages to scrutinize me through a camera lens. "So you didn't try to solve this problem yourself by finding another Realtor?"

I draw my bottom lip into my mouth.

"How many?"

"Three," I admit. I'd contacted three potential Realtors before I decided to busy myself with chocolate instead of desperate emails. "One responded already and said they would be back in town in two weeks. Still waiting on the other two."

"Don't. I emailed my Realtor friend, same one I had in mind for you before. I copied you on an introduction email. It should be in your inbox."

"Oh." I had completely forgotten his earlier offer to help with this. I was so sure Grady would lead me to the right location for my shop. "Thank you."

He interlaces his fingers and places them on the tabletop in front of him. "That wasn't so bad, was it?"

"Are you kidding? The worst."

The following week, my new commercial real estate agent, Robin, texts me and Ben that she's two minutes away. We're viewing four different properties, and she prefers carpooling to streamline everything. Ben offered to tag along, and though every inch of me screamed "I got it from here," I couldn't get the words out. Not after he saved my ass. It won't be unbearable having his perspective.

I don't know much about Robin, but I already have a good feeling. In this initial batch, she sent five properties, and I eliminated only one, which she'd already flagged as a long shot. The four we're going to see today all meet my requirements—minimum square footage, enough space for parties, a large kitchen, and minimal repairs and updates needed.

Though Ben has a good four inches on me, when Robin arrives, he heads straight to the back seat of her SUV, angling his knees diagonally to fit.

We start with the farthest location, so we can work our way back toward my condo. Robin and I chat on the way there, while Ben mostly keeps quiet. She asks about his family, and he answers in a vague way that seems intentional. I only learn that his sister and Robin are friends.

There's an open spot by the curbside of the first location. As Robin fiddles with the key box, Ben walks up and down the block, snapping a few pictures along the way. I take stock of what could be my business neighbors. Across the street there's a dry cleaner, an ice cream shop, and an insurance agent's office. A few storefronts are boarded up. Still, it's an okay area considering how many businesses shuttered their doors in the last economic recession.

Robin gets the door unlocked and allows me to enter first while she holds the door for Ben to make his way back. The place is stale and dusty in the corners, but I put on my creative lens and try to envision what the space could be. The front area is larger than necessary for intake. There's a room that could be the designated party room, but it's smaller than I thought it would be from the pictures. With a table in here and chairs, I couldn't have a party bigger than eight people. Not bad, but kids tend to travel with a parent or two.

"What are you thinking? Talk me through it," Ben says as I worry my lip when we're moving to the main attraction—the kitchen. He'd been so quiet I could have forgotten he was here if it were not for his hulking size and his footsteps trailing us. "I'm trying to get a sense of what you're looking for, where this is hitting or missing."

"Right." I pause before entering the kitchen and turn back to face the front. I give him the abbreviated version of everything I noticed that comes short of my vision.

"Okay, those are concerns I had too." He types into his phone.

We continue and join Robin in the kitchen. She rattles off highlights. "Newly renovated everything. Stoves, cabinets, countertops. It's—"

"Incredible," I finish. There's a countertop in the center of the kitchen—it's much too big to be classified as an island—that's rectangular shaped. There are two outlets on the long sides, one on each of the short. Plenty for plugging in induction burners.

"This was a teaching kitchen. They sold kitchen and household appliances out front, hence the huge space. Back here they held cooking classes."

"Do you think it's possible to make the room out there bigger?" I ask, my brain fishing for solutions now that I've laid my eyes upon this marvel of a kitchen. Near the oven, Ben is snapping more pictures. Since he's taking on this task, it frees me up to focus on the visit and not worry about documenting everything.

"Maybe," Robin says, as if she's having trouble picturing it. I am too.

We decide to walk the short distance to the next store because it's only a few blocks over, and with the one-way streets, it would take about as long to drive—longer if we didn't luck out with parking again. This one sits between a physical therapy building and a restaurant.

Inside, the front waiting area is decent, with empty glass cases separating it from the employee area.

"Used to be a bakery," Robin says.

"This is about the size front area I envisioned," I say for Ben's benefit. It's just big enough for me to facilitate intake before continuing to the kitchen.

"Since the room up here is so tight, your party room is attached to the kitchen." Robin leads us to the back and flicks on the light.

"Oh," says Ben. The fact that he's uttered a word before I can give my opinion is a testament to how poor this kitchen looks, especially compared with the one we just saw.

"Needs some updates, yes, but I think it wouldn't be as extensive as it looks. Plus, this would save you nearly $10K a year, and in basically the same area."

Maybe it wouldn't require extensive remodeling to get my business up and going, but I'd probably spend the first year juggling contractors as I attacked the list already building in my head. Add more cabinets for storage. Replace the rollable table made of steel with a permanent fixture. Replace the old ovens with more modern ones.

In the car on the way to the next neighborhood, Robin pitches the bright side of embracing renovations. It's the best way to get the place of my dreams, she claims. The thing is, I'd be willing to choose a store that doesn't match my dreams exactly, as long as it fills my head with new ones.

We sweep through the next two quickly, having found a rhythm. The selling agent meets us on these two. As Robin chats with him, I verbalize my likes and dislikes for Ben. Overall, they're both average. I could make it work. The locations aren't my favorite, though. Neither seems to get much traffic.

Robin drops us off outside my condo. She puts her hazard lights on as we hustle out. A truck too big to pass honks, annoyed. Robin shouts out the window that she'll be in touch with new finds before continuing down the street at a pointedly leisurely speed.

Ben and I stand on the sidewalk facing each other, and I assume neither of us is quite sure what our dynamic is now. Ben commits to the mentor-mentee relationship and asks, "Do you need to debrief or anything?"

I shake my head. "I know I had a lot of cons, but this trip was much better than the three previous ones with my first Realtor."

His pleased nod doesn't contain the smugness I expected. "I'd say the first one we saw is still in the running?"

"I can't eliminate something with that kitchen so easily."

"Understandable," Ben says. We shift so a person walking their large Labrador can maneuver around us. Penelope and I usually see them around this time. "I'll send you the photos from that one, then, and delete the rest."

I thank him and hurry upstairs to Pen, who's surely impatiently waiting for her afternoon walk.

# CHAPTER
# TWENTY-ONE

Pilar is laughing with the bartender when I arrive at the restaurant she picked out in Humboldt Park. She planned this happy hour for us mentees to commemorate the halfway point for our mentorship. Only six weeks left until we give our presentations and the board decides which five businesses to award additional $50K grants.

She hops up when she sees me and points to a circular high-top still open in the bar area. "Let's get this table so we can have space when Vic and Yaz get here."

We get settled and I scan the specials menu.

"I didn't see you at the office all week," Pilar says. "Where you been?"

"Getting work done," I say, my arching brows emphasizing that point.

Pilar raises a hand to her chest. "Excuse me, we get work done at the office."

"Some, yes." Only the work that doesn't require my full attention. It's more fun working at the office space with Pilar, but it's roughly 50 percent as productive as when I'm isolated in my home office.

Pilar's cell phone grabs her attention. Her face lights up as she types out a response.

"My partner just got back in town," she explains. Her phone vibrates again. "She's going to stop by on her way home. We don't live far from here."

Meeting the partner of my potential soul mate. Nice.

"I'll let you know if I get old-locked-in married-couple vibes."

Our waiter brings us glasses of water, and Pilar immediately takes a generous sip. "We're both going through a change season. It's weird. I can recognize that both our lives are changing vastly, and sometimes it's like I'm watching it all play out from the Sears Tower, waiting to see how our new lives will fit together."

"I've felt like that before," I say. "With friends."

Pilar sighs her relief at my understanding. "Yes. Gia got promoted to a new job position last year, and there's so much traveling. I never considered myself to be clingy, but I got used to her presence in our tiny-ass apartment. And she's arguably the worst long-distancer. Getting her on the phone is a miracle." She ruminates on that with a little head shake. "Anyway, what about you? Are you seeing anyone?"

"In a way, a few," I mumble and take a sip of my own drink. "Mostly this guy Elliot. He's my dog's vet and he's really sweet."

Pilar smiles. "Black women deserve sweet guys. If they're doomed to fall for a guy, that is."

"Since we're so new, it's not *how* will our new selves fit together, it's do we fit in the first place, as we are. You know?"

"Girl." She grabs my forearm, the warmth of her hand searing the feel of its outline on my skin. "Yes. With Gia, it's scary to think maybe one day it'll stop working. But in the same vein, I can talk myself off the worry ledge because I'm certain she's someone who'll be in my life forever. In what capacity, that might change. We've evolved so much over the past four years already. But when I imagine my future family, it's always a village of people, and Gia is one of my people."

I love the idea of gathering your people. In a way, I've already started the process, and Met might be sending me more. It could be Pilar, who is easy to talk to and fun to be around. What would it mean if Pilar's partner, the jet-setting Gia, is my fourth match?

Victor and Yaz arrive, so we put in appetizer and drink orders. They're in high spirits after getting hired to decorate a new client's entire home. The client is a former colleague of Ben's. Ben recommended Victor and Yazmin, and after meeting with the client and sharing their portfolio and ideas, they signed the contract to make it official just yesterday.

"It's going to be a lot of work," Yaz says, signing and voicing at the same time. "But we want to get it done before presentations."

"Is six weeks enough time?" Pilar asks the question into her phone so that the text populates. Yaz and Vic read the screen.

Victor bounces his head in a noncommittal nod and reaches for his phone.

"I think we can do it," Yaz says. "Our website is almost done, and we've made plenty of original pieces for the online store relaunch."

Victor shakes his head, holding up his phone for us to see what he typed there. Ben thinks we should double our inventory.

Yaz rolls her eyes and signs, *"Whatever."* I grin with appreciation of her annoyance. "Victor and Ben are best friends now," she tells us.

Victor doesn't deny it. Instead, he swipes on his phone to show us a gorgeous, dark-wood-framed mirror. He zooms in to show us the intricate carvings on the wood.

*"You two made this?"* I ask, indicating him and Yaz.

Yaz shakes her head, lips pursed.

*"I made it with Ben,"* Victor says. He catches Yaz's unimpressed facial expression and pokes her cheek, making her dimple reappear as she smiles.

"It is one of my favorite pieces in our new collection," she admits.

I didn't know Ben was crafty. My ignorance is entirely my fault, since I spent most of the first half of the mentorship not trying to know him and, above all, not allowing him to know me. But seeing my fellow mentees forge relationships with him makes the stark contrast of our lack of one needle at me. I'm not sure if the feeling is caused by a perceived upper hand they have at earning the extra funding, or if I feel like I'm missing out on something.

After a while, Gia arrives. Her wavy hair is cut short, only a couple of inches long. The chestnut-blonde color perfectly complements her light-brown skin. Vic and Yaz are having a signed side conversation, but I'm watching as Pilar and Gia reunite. Pilar's visible comfort being in Gia's arms. Gia's tenderness as she pulls back from the hug and cradles Pilar's face in her hands. I divert my eyes as they exchange soft whispered words.

After they've shared their moment, Pilar introduces Gia to the three of us.

"I'm not staying," Gia says. "I have to go wash the airport off of me. Just wanted to see my love and meet the people she's been talking about for the past month."

While Pilar repeats what she says into her captioning app, Gia's eyes clock me. I widen my smile a bit, but it feels weighted with unwarranted guilt. I break eye contact and reach for my phone. I hadn't heard anything, but it's possible the alert jingle was lost under the music playing in the restaurant. There's a picture from Clara at my condo with Penelope and a text from Elliot checking in, but absolutely nothing from Met.

# CHAPTER
# TWENTY-TWO

The Thursday before my party, Robin sends me two commercial properties available for lease. One has been on the market for a while, and the other recently returned to the market after the tenant had to back out of the lease agreement. I'm on a video call with Elise and Corinne, discussing the grocery list for the cabin, as I click through the photos of each property.

"Tee, I think you're frozen," Elise says.

I blink and turn back to face my phone.

"Oh, you're back now."

My phone wasn't frozen, but my body was at the sight of property number two. "One sec, I need to send an email." I reply to Robin and Ben, begging her to get me in to see it before I leave the city for the weekend. I'd planned to take tomorrow off for party prep, but if I have an opportunity to see this place before someone else snatches it up, I'm taking it.

Robin, the goddess that she is, responds within the hour saying we're confirmed for 10:00 a.m. I spend the night packing my weekend bag and Penelope's essentials for her stay with our neighbor.

The next morning, I meet Robin and Ben at the site. Robin texted me a few minutes ago that she's already inside with the owner's broker.

I glance down the block as I reach for the door handle but stop short when I see Ben approaching, apparently finishing his observations.

"Looks good," I say. I'm already familiar with this area. There's a creamery I frequent with Clara whenever she's on deadline for an article. I've gotten food delivered from a few of the restaurants on this block as well. It's Friday morning, and some of the businesses aren't yet open, but the street still has a lively energy.

Ben nods, reaching to open the door for us. "Shared lot space—that can't be beat."

Robin lets the selling agent, Kevin, give me the rundown on the place. Light shines in through the front glass panels, the cardboard that previously covered them placed neatly in the corner. The power of natural lighting. It makes even Ben, currently frowning at a hole in the wall, appear optimistic.

"The owner will repair that," Kevin says, noticing Ben's disapproval.

Other than a few other surface repairs, the front is a great size. There are two private bathrooms and a small room with glass windows looking out into the front area. It's too small for a party room but perfect for an office. Since I don't plan on double-booking private parties, the entire front area can be for party use. With cute decor and tables that can be configured to match the party size, I can transform this space. I could commission Devin to paint a mural on one of the walls, something with the shop's name in it that's eye catching enough to serve as the perfect trendy photo op.

We continue to the kitchen. It's not as shiny as the first one we saw together, but it's still in good shape. By the time Kevin finishes pointing out the renovations, I've already composed a list of modifications I'd want to make.

I turn to Ben, ready to list them off, but he holds up a finger and focuses on typing into his phone. My phone vibrates in my hand seconds later with a text from him.

Watch buying signals on this one, it says.

I look up, and sure enough, Kevin is observing us closely. Ben can tell I like this place a lot, and if Kevin can as well, there goes our negotiating power. I round the kitchen once more, keeping my face contemplative as I allow my mind to color the space with possibility.

Kevin locks the doors while Robin, Ben, and I walk toward my parked car. Once we're far enough away, I face Robin.

"I want this one," I say.

She nods, her confidence matching my determination. "Now, I go to work."

~

Deciding to have my party an hour's drive outside the city naturally cuts down the number of attendees. Still, enough people have told me they plan on staying overnight that I'm expecting a full cabin. More people are in need of a weekend escape than I'd previously assumed. I carpool with Clara, Elise, and Devin. We leave early so we can stop by the grocery store and stock the kitchen. Cory drives too, bringing along Corinne, her brother, Lito, and his girlfriend, Maeve. Lito and Maeve recently finished their spring semester at Rochester Institute of Technology and will be road-tripping around the country all summer. For the next week, they'll be in Chicago.

Along with the core group, Chris is coming with his boyfriend, Mitchell. Elliot will be there, of course. And three days ago, Pilar successfully convinced Victor and Yazmin to come, if only for a few hours tomorrow as we do outside activities on the lake. It's a spacious cabin, with eleven beds and a large living room, so there should be plenty of room for all of us.

As soon as we get there, Elise claims a room to share with Devin. I'm in the primary bedroom suite, the only bedroom downstairs. Although Elliot is coming tonight, I plan on sharing the room and the massive California king bed with Clara.

I'm surveying the mostly wooden and stone living room aesthetic when Elise approaches, holding a bag.

"I need your height," she says. From the bag she retrieves, and unrolls, a laminated banner. The words "I'm Free, Bitches" are printed in an arc above a large picture of *The Emancipation of Mimi* album cover, my face photoshopped over Mariah Carey's. The border is composed of every embarrassing picture of me that Elise has accumulated over the past decade. I stare at this masterpiece, open-mouthed. "Don't fight me on hanging this, Tee, I swear," Elise says.

I tear my eyes away from it, surprised she thought there was any chance I wouldn't embrace it. I give her a tight hug, then take the Sticky Tack from her and help hang it above the mantel.

By seven thirty, everyone has made it except Pilar. Elliot is on the couch talking with Chris and Mitchell. They keep leaning toward each other to speak, trying to be heard over the music. It's so loud the bass echoes in my chest. Lito and Maeve dance while conversing in the center of the living room, their signed conversation not deterred by the music at all.

Two drinks and several shots in, Devin decides to make the tacos we'd bought for tomorrow's dinner. Elise is now playing sous-chef. As I grab a bag of popcorn and pour some into a bowl, Elise sidles up to me.

"Elliot seems comfortable with us. That's a good quality," she says.

"It helps that he has a friend. And that you haven't interrogated him."

"Yet."

My phone vibrates in my hand. It's been attached to me in case anyone runs into trouble trying to find the cabin. Plus, I can't hear the doorbell over the music.

"Pilar's here," I relay.

"This is bold of you. Bringing two matches together. Met must be proud."

"It's low stakes. We're just having fun, that's all."

I leave the conversation to open the door for Pilar. She climbs the stairs with a duffel bag on one shoulder and a gift bag in her opposite hand. She holds the bag out for me.

"Happy birthday-slash-quitting."

"I said no gifts."

"I know. I ignored you."

I push the tissue paper aside and dig into the bag. The first container I pull out is for a hair masque. I recognize the labeling immediately as the local sibling-owned brand we went to see. Also in the bag is the most beautiful black-to-teal ombré braiding hair I've ever seen.

"Thank you for ignoring me," I say.

As I start to close the door, another car pulls up, its headlights making me stop short. I mentally run through the list of people I'm expecting tonight as I wait for whoever is in the car to get out. With Pilar's arrival, I'm ready to abandon my phone and enjoy the first night of partying. I'm sure Elise is already pouring Pilar's welcome shot of tequila.

When the car is switched off and the interior light illuminates, revealing a familiar shape, I still doubt my eyes until Ben opens the door and steps out. For a second, I genuinely don't understand why he's here. Then I reason, though Ben rarely says anything in our mentee group chat beyond his coworking office hours, he's very much there. I sent the invite to the chat at large. I expected him to ignore it like he does everything else there that doesn't concern him.

"What?" I step onto the porch as I shout this to make sure he hears me. "The great Benoit? To what do I owe the pleasure?"

"No shit," Pilar says, stepping back outside with me. "I couldn't even get Victor and Yaz to come until tomorrow."

"I'm due at my parents' house this weekend, so I figured I'd stop by for a bit before heading there."

"Oh right, your niece's birthday party," Pilar says.

There it goes, that needling feeling again. But unlike before, this has nothing to do with the mentorship. I can't blame it on my fear of missing out on a possible advantage. I follow Pilar and Ben into the cabin as she asks him what gift he settled on for his niece, then bemoans his academic toy choice.

Similar to how Pilar made a snap assessment and decided we would be mentee allies, she also positioned herself with Ben. From my few observations of them together, she's become his fist-bumping, easy-to-get-along-with friend. It's peculiar. As expected, Elise approaches them with three shots in each of her hands. Pilar and Ben take one each. Elise keeps one, and the rest are unloaded to Clara, Elliot, and Chris.

Corinne comes down from the large staircase that connects to the living room holding a small tote bag, pulling my attention away from Pilar and Ben's relationship and how I can't figure out if I'm envious, and if so, of which one.

She cuts the music and stands on a chair that wobbles a little from one wooden leg being a tad shorter than the other three. Cory gravitates to her side, placing a bracing hand on the back of the chair. Corinne hangs the short straps of the tote on her shoulder so she can sign and speak simultaneously.

"We're playing a game!" she announces.

I walk forward. "No, we're not," I counter.

"Oh yes, we are."

I'm aware of Pilar's excited bounce onto her toes and Ben's instant stiffness even as I'm turning to Elise, who I'm sure is a co-conspirator in this along with Cory. She gestures repeatedly to pay attention to Corinne, who has dismissed me and launched into explaining the activity she's put together.

"It's called Cases and Cuffs," she says.

It involves pairs, attached with dollar-store handcuffs, drinking their way through a six-pack of their beer or wine cooler of choice. Finish your case, be free of your cuffs, and win points. There are also various games we can play to earn points up until the first person finishes their case. This is a bizarre game Corinne has come up with, and I'm sure it's a direct consequence of her attending a PWI.

"Seriously?" I'm at Corinne's side now. "Your idea of a game is to put a room full of Black and Brown people in cuffs?"

Corinne's mouth drops open as she realizes the implications. "I was thinking more like Mary Mary. You know, take the shackles off. So we can dance."

"No," I say, stone-faced. "We cannot dance. And I cannot lift my hands if I'm cuffed to someone else."

"You can if you work together as a team." Corinne points to her temple, eyebrows up. "Plus, this goes with your past life as an auditor. Y'all are like the financial police."

"Mmm, I'd say we're more like financial referees."

"Yeah, definitely referees." Chris backs me up from where he's leaning forward on the couch, awaiting further instructions. I realize then that everyone is waiting for us, and most seem game for shenanigans. I huff and allow Corinne to continue.

With the exception of Lito and Maeve, all the teams will be randomized. Corinne uses an infinity scarf and two sets of handcuffs to attach them by the loops of their jeans instead of their wrists. This way, they can still easily communicate with sign language. The couple tests how far they can separate from each other and then laughs at the tug from their waists that pull them back together.

"This is a totally random pairing," Corinne announces again to everyone. Then she adds in a lower voice for me, "Don't worry, boo, I gotchu."

I make a face. How is that possible when I don't even know myself how I'd like to be got? If I want to win, which I always do, I'd want to be paired with Elise. She'll drink her fair share, and she matches my competitive spirit. If I'm choosing based on who I'd like to be attached to for the next few hours, then it would be Pilar or Elliot.

Corinne pulls out a plastic cup from the bag, already prepped with slips of paper bearing each of our names, and hands it to Cory to hold up for her. Before choosing partners, she reveals another way to earn points—by finding any of the ten fake dollar bills hidden around the house. She's really leaning into this financial auditor theme. Since Corinne hid them, she's disqualified from earning those points. She asks for a volunteer to partner with her who would be fine with not participating in that part of the competition. Of course, Cory volunteers before she can get the whole statement out. I roll my eyes.

If I believed any part of these pairings were actually random, it's disproved when the first names drawn are Elise and Devin. I shake my head at their faux surprised celebration. Next she pairs Chris and Mitchell. Mitchell is relieved beyond reason since this is so obviously preordained. Like countless times at work, I exchange a *something's up* look with Chris.

"Next we have Clara and Pilar," Corinne says. Elliot squints at Clara, his head cocked to the side. I introduced Elliot to a bunch of people at once when he arrived, so this might be the first time he's taken a good look at her.

"We have an odd number," Clara says. "So I'll just be point keeper."

Corinne's head snaps up and surveys the room, her eyes snagging on Ben.

"Or I can do the points," I volunteer.

"No," Corinne sings through gritted teeth. "Here, just . . ." She fumbles with the bag and retrieves a scrap of paper and a pen. She jots down Pilar's, Elliot's, and Ben's names, then rips it in thirds and drops it in the cup Cory holds. "Okay, you pick."

I fish for a slip of paper and pull it out. There's only one unfavorable situation—being paired with Ben—because I'm pretty sure he would drag me down. For one, he's supposed to be going to his parents' house tonight, so I doubt he'll drink more than a couple of cans in our case.

Two, he's had the *I'm too old for this* look on his face since the game was announced.

My heartbeat quickens in anticipation as I scan the paper for a name, find it blank, and flip it over to the other side. Also blank.

"This doesn't—" I start to say before Corinne snatches the paper from me with a nervous laugh.

"Oops, don't know how that got in there, must have been the extras I cut."

I shake my head at her and pick again. She did a convincing job fake-reading blank scraps of paper up until this point. My next draw has a name. I hold up the paper, flashing Elliot an apologetic frown. "Ben."

I 1,000 percent brought this upon myself.

# CHAPTER
# TWENTY-THREE

Fifteen minutes later, we're all paired off and cuffed with our partners.

"'Just having fun' still?" Elise quips in passing, Devin trailing. They hold hands as if the cuffs aren't enough attachment.

I don't drink much beer, and Ben doesn't drink sugary alcoholic beverages, so we compromise and choose hard cider for our case. Writing our names on the box with kindergartner-like focus, I tell Ben my assessment of the situation.

"Finishing the case is worth five points, but every dollar found is worth one point each. If we find the majority, then try to win a few card games, we're in good shape even without getting top points for our case."

"You're very strategic for someone who didn't want to do this." Ben plucks the Sharpie out of my left hand just as I finish the first *a* in my name. He then lifts our conjoined limbs—my right and his left—and replaces the marker in my dominant hand.

I shoot him a half-hearted glare and quickly finish jotting down our names. We take a can each and sit the remainder of our pack in the fridge.

"When do you have to leave?" I ask, plotting. Surely Clara will release us early if he has to go. We'll need to earn as many points as we can before then.

"Not until we break every chain, apparently."

I press my lips together, but a snort of laughter still escapes.

Corinne counts down from ten to commence the start of the competition. Then she turns the music back on, thankfully at half the volume it was at previously.

With some awkwardness figuring out how best to position our cuffed hands, we open our ciders, tap our cans together, then try to take our first drinks, only to realize we're standing too far apart for our linked wrists. Cider nearly sloshes onto my blouse. In our first synchronous movement as a team, we switch our drinks to our free hands and take sips.

Around us, pairs have started to go through the games available for use on the dining table or wander around in search of the hidden dollars. Ben and I stand in the living room, sipping as a means of productivity until I realize I'm more than halfway done with this can already. I swirl it between me and Ben, though I can't hear the empty space over the music.

"We might as well chug the rest of this," I say. He nods and turns the can over into his mouth. I watch as his lips purse to capture the last drops. He waves at me to catch up, so I do.

"This has to be frowned upon in the mentorship program," I say, tossing my emptied can into the recycling bin.

"Strangely, I doubt it. You wouldn't believe the number of happy hours the other mentors arrange for their mentees. I was falling behind before this, so thank you."

We grab new full cans of cider from the fridge, though neither of us rushes to open them. My stomach is already full with the first. Pilar and Elliot intercept us as they leave the table, holding a trivia board game.

"Hey," I say. "So you've met Pilar already. This is Ben."

"The mentor, nice to meet you," Elliot says while throwing me a weighted look.

"Do y'all want to play this with us?" Pilar holds it up and shakes it. "Winner gets a point."

Ben turns to look at me, his head already tentatively nodding.

"Maybe later," I say, tugging Ben with me as I take a few steps toward the stairs. "We'll be back down soon."

"I thought you said we should win a few games?" Ben asks as we're climbing the stairs. Our attached arms are both fully extended, the pinch of my skin urging me to slow down.

"Yes, but dollars first. We can't let the other teams find them all before us. And no board games. They'll take too long and are worth the same as a quick card game."

"Wow. Okay."

I start with the last room down the walkway. The upstairs banister overlooks the living room. I evaluate the competition as we pass. Lito and Maeve seem to be the only other team searching for bonus points still. Everyone else is drinking or trying to arrange games to play. Of them all, only one person is looking up, tracking my movement. Elliot.

I do feel bad about being separated from him. But not enough to tank my game. I'll make it up to him as soon as I'm free of these cuffs and declared the winner.

The room we enter is the largest upstairs room with four bunk beds. I check the pillows and comforters as best I can without ruining the neat dressings. I tug on Ben's wrist until he obliges and kneels on the floor with me so I can check underneath.

"What's stopping us from pouring our beers down a sink when no one is looking?" Ben muses as I finally catch sight of a dollar. It's folded several times and pushed into the corner underneath one of the beds. I try to reach, but not even my arms are long enough to get it while on my hands and knees.

I pause at Ben's question and sit back on my heels to peer at him. "The honor code, I guess. And an innate sense to not waste alcohol."

"I have no qualms about wasting alcohol," Ben says. He sits his can on the floor to pop the top, then takes a long draw. I know I need to keep pace with him, so I open my own and take a gulp. The key is drinking it while it's still cold. Once it gets warm, I can't stop the thought of drinking sweetened pee. I sit the can on the nightstand for safekeeping.

"Lie down," I direct Ben. He hesitates. "I need to scoot under the bed to get that dollar, and I can't do it with you anchoring me." He obliges, and I'm able to push myself with my knees and elbows until I can snag the bill. I do the same in reverse to get out, Ben moving to provide room for me to get up. So eager for the light and the fresh air, I try to lift my head up too soon and hit it on the wooden bed frame.

"Ouch," Ben says in solidarity. I press my lips together and scrunch up my face against the pain, a habit I formed when Grandma would do my hair and slap my arm if I whined too much. Also by habit, I start to reach my right hand to rub my head, only to be thwarted by Ben's attachment. "Sorry," he says and reaches his own hand to my head and rubs circles there.

The door opens and Chris and Mitchell enter. I quickly take over rubbing my tender scalp, pushing Ben's fingers out of the way. We stand, and I hand the dollar to Ben since his pants have pockets and mine do not.

"There probably aren't any more in here—we got to it first," I say.

"We'll see about that," Chris says with the self-assured smirk he wore a lot in the office.

I grab my cider from the nightstand as I leave, drinking more as I go. Six beers wouldn't be this hard to finish between two people if we still had the stamina of college students. And if we hadn't let Elise convince us to take all those welcome shots as people arrived.

Ben and I search the other upstairs bedrooms and come away with two dollars. In the bathroom a dollar is hidden up high on the curtain rods, so Ben's extra height comes in handy. One more from the bathroom, peeking out from under a decorative towel, brings our count to five.

"Should we check how everyone else is doing with their cases?" Ben asks. He's been carrying around his empty second can since we finished our sweep of the third room. I frown at my own half-full can. Ben holds both his can and his free hand up, an offer. I happily swap with him, and he starts picking up the slack for my half-completed effort.

Back downstairs, we take stock of the other pairs' cases. Elise and Devin have four left. They're not even trying. Chris is complaining about the taste of their wine coolers, so I'm pretty sure the three they have left won't be consumed. Two beers remain in Lito and Maeve's box. With Ben finishing my second can for me, we grab our final two. The only other team with an empty box is Pilar and Elliot. They have their last spiked lemonades in hand and are currently in a heated game of Trivial Pursuit with Chris, Mitchell, and Clara.

"How good are you at dominoes?" Ben asks, spotting the tin box on the table.

"It's a numbers and strategy game," I answer.

He nods and grabs the box. Seeking opponents, we drift to the living room and sit with Elise, Devin, Cory, and Corinne. I try to slide into the conversation without fanfare, but Elise doesn't let me get away with it.

"I don't think we've met," she says to Ben while looking at me.

"My bad," I say. "This is Ben, from the mentorship. Ben, these are my friends." I sweep my hand in their direction unceremoniously. Elise's lips part in mock affront.

"I'm her *best* friend," Elise says. "This is my boo, Devin."

"We met at the conference," Corinne says.

Cory simply points to himself with his thumb and says, "Cory."

Ben barely gets the words "Nice to meet you all" out before he's leaning toward me to retrieve his vibrating phone from his pocket. He glances at the screen and winces. "I have to take this." He stands, taking my arm with him.

I turn to my friends. "We have to take this."

The quietest place to take a phone call is outside on the wraparound porch. We leave through the front door and walk around to the back side of the cabin, which faces a large yard bordered by trees.

"Hey, what's going on?" Ben says.

He listens for a bit, his body turned away from me. The night air is a refreshing reprieve from the warmth caused by all the people in the cabin and the alcohol consumption. I crane my neck up to appreciate the clear, star-speckled sky.

"Oh," Ben sighs. "I don't know. It doesn't matter."

Whoever he's on the phone with seems to disagree, from the responding stream of words. Where I stand, the sound is too faint to discern what they're saying. Plus, I'm not actively eavesdropping.

"I'll pick it up when I'm back in town, then." This must be the right thing to say, because I can't hear the caller when they next speak.

"I know you're not, I just . . ." Ben turns and glances at me, and I pretend I don't notice. "I know," he finishes. Giving me nothing. "Yeah, talk later. Love you."

He twitches and freezes. I turn to him as he slowly pulls the phone down from his ear. The call has already been disconnected on the other end. I eye his shocked expression warily. He holds up his last cider.

"I'm cutting myself off," he says.

"Why? We're so close, and it's barely affecting you."

He levels me with his stare. "I just told my ex I loved her. Which is technically true, but it's been six months, so no."

"Yeah, no. Give me that beer and your keys—you're trashed."

He lets out a self-deprecating laugh, and we make our way back inside. When he tries to head back to our vacated spots on the couch, I stop short.

"Um, I need to pee."

Ben's gaze travels up and to the right. "How's that gonna work?"

It works with me getting my pants down with my left hand, since I refuse to have Ben's hand anywhere near undressing me. Then it's my pants around my ankles, right arm outstretched so that Ben is as distanced as possible, facing away from me. I'm pee shy until my bladder can't hold it anymore and releases for a full minute. Then I curse myself for never practicing wiping with my left hand, because as soon as I stand, I swear I feel a drop of pee leaking down my inner thigh, and so I sit back down quickly and grab more tissue.

To make matters worse, I have to shimmy back into my underwear and my tight-ass pants. After silently standing by, his back facing my struggle, Ben says, "Do you just wanna?" And I relent and use my right hand to pull my pants up properly. My elbow bumps into his, but he makes sure his hand stays clear. Then, as I'm washing my hands, excited that the worst is behind us, Ben regretfully announces that now he has to pee. The bright side, Ben points out, is that he gets to aim with his more skilled hand. Yep, I'm definitely seeing the effect of the alcohol now.

We leave the en-suite bathroom silent and sneaky, like we've been up to no good. Our last ciders are on the dresser. I open both of them.

"If we finish, then we get uncuffed, and we never have to do that again."

We bump our cans against each other's, united in our humiliation, and take swigs.

Pilar and Elliot come barging through the open door of the suite. Their arms move freely, detached from each other.

"Y'all finished? You won?" I ask.

Neither of them responds right away. Pilar slaps the back of her hand into Elliot's arm.

"We forfeited. Pilar was about to throw up. And I need to talk with you. Privately."

I lift Ben's and my cuffed wrists. With our biggest competition out of the running, this will be a cakewalk to the finish line for us. "Can it wait? We're almost done." But with the way my stomach churns from the last sip, it's going to take me a while to get through it.

Elliot's gaze remains on the cuffs attaching me to Ben long after we've lowered our arms to our sides. He shakes his head slowly, then lifts his eyes to mine. The urgency there makes me forget the game for a moment.

"Just dump the rest," Pilar says. "We won't snitch."

Whatever Elliot has to tell me, I want to hear it. Right now. I take the few steps required to get back to the bathroom sink, Ben in tow, and overturn my can. The liquid chugs out in uneven sloshes.

"There. I'm finished."

Ben looks at me for a beat, expression unreadable. It takes me right back to the panel, when he doubted everything about my business, about my ability to succeed. He sighs and it ends with his lips upturned, but it feels like a frown impersonating a smile. Then he pours the rest of his cider out too.

"Come on, let's get uncuffed, then," he says.

After Ben and I are declared the (cheating) winners and freed from being each other's tether, Clara starts unlocking everyone else's cuffs. Elliot and I sneak away into my room, closing the door behind us for privacy.

"Are you having fun?" I ask him, taking a seat on the edge of the bed.

Elliot lifts a noncommitted shoulder at first but ultimately nods as he sits beside me. "Pilar is great, but I'd trade her to be your teammate in a second. I told her that too."

I grin. "So that's why you two forfeited. Infighting."

"Nah, I just told Pilar how I missed you. I know we're technically together, under the same roof, but I still miss you. She heard that and demanded I tell you right away."

"I'm glad you did. I think this is another level up, missing each other."

"Speaking of, is impressing your undercover aunt enough to be kept around part of a level I didn't know about?"

I cover my cheeks with my hands. "I'm so sorry. I promise I didn't put her up to that."

Elliot scoots closer to me. "I like you, Tiwanda. When they announced this game, my first thought was: I wouldn't mind being attached to you. Then I realized that's because I already am."

"Oh. Crap." I drop my hands to my lap.

"Yeah." He laughs a bit. "I know you're probably not getting the signals I am, but I want to continue leveling up with you, at whatever pace it takes." His intense gaze roams my face, awaiting my answer.

My eyes narrow as I consider his words. "Did you use your last name on purpose?"

"I didn't plan that, but it was good, right?"

For the first time in my life probably, I giggle.

"I wanted to be attached to you too," I say. And even though it's true (he was my second or third choice!), it still feels like betrayal after Ben was so supportive of my competitive antics.

Elliot interlocks our hands, resting them between us on my thigh. I look down at them for a moment, then back up at his face.

"Is this okay?" he asks.

"I'm getting some signals."

Using our opted-for attachment, I pull myself closer to him. His glossy brown eyes move to my parted lips. With my nod as confirmation of my intentions, he closes the gap between us. Just like he promised, it's at our own pace. Elliot's lush mouth moves against mine in a well-measured caress. His sweet-and-sour breath tickles my nose. I release his hand to hold on to his bicep instead, while my other grips his thigh. All the feelings I've allowed to gather between us since we met come charging forward. Our friendship, his understanding. The safe place he's created within himself for me. He's made me feel good in so many ways, and this is another.

# CHAPTER
# TWENTY-FOUR

The following day is much less chaotic. Ben leaves early to get to his mom's house ahead of his niece's birthday party, but everyone else stays through the afternoon. Victor and Yazmin arrive just in time for canoeing on the lake. It's a relaxing day, partially due to half of us being hungover. In the evening, everyone except those who came in my car and Cory's car leave ahead of Sunday morning's checkout time. The smaller group is a comfort. I make dinner with Clara and finally have a moment to chat with Lito about his post-undergraduate plans come December. Corinne and Elise also enjoy having only our core group, because they finally have the chance to tease me about my three Met matches openly.

Once I get home on Sunday, I only take care of Penelope and lounge around the entire day. My Sunday laziness leaks into Monday, because why conform to the standard business week when I'm self-employed? Plus, I'm regularly checking my email for updates from Robin. Throughout the day she asks questions here and there about my renovation plans and my contract-length preference. So far, we're not in competition with anyone, so I'm hoping the business plans, credit report, and bank account balance information I provided are enough to convince them. Since the property is only on the market because the previous arrangement fell through, Robin hopes she can get the leasing process expedited.

In place of my weekly check-in meeting with Ben, I make plans to meet up with Cousin Vonnie. Then I text Ben to tell him the news.

Me: No need for a check-in meeting this week

Ben: ??

Me: There's nothing to report. If we meet, it'll just be me whining about the wait and catastrophizing.

Ben: Article Link: Five Tips for Getting the Most Out of Your Mentorship

Ben: #4

Penelope must sense my weird mood. Either that, or she missed me this past weekend. For the first time, she puts her little paws on the couch, wanting to come up. I let her snuggle against me while I click on the link. Number four: Don't hesitate to share your doubts with your mentor. They might have been in the same situation themselves, but even if they haven't, part of their role is to be a listening ear.

Me: 😠

Ben: You don't seem busy, so we can hop on a call now.

The alternative is meeting in person at the coworking space tomorrow, so I accept the upgrade. I don't even relocate to my office. With Pen cuddled into my side, her head resting on my torso, I dial Ben's number. He asks about the rest of my cabin weekend, and I ask about his niece's birthday, and then he listens to me complain about everything that has gone wrong and could go wrong for twenty minutes straight.

～

Vonnie meets me at my condo the next afternoon. This is my best attempt at controlling the environment. Backyard family get-together was too busy, retirement dinner too combative. So today, it'll be just the two of us.

"This is a great area," Vonette says as she enters my condo. "You must be paying a grip."

"It's not bad," I say. I only debate for a moment before adding, "Auntie Yvette owns the building. You know she's into real estate." Because what's the point of trying to rebuild a relationship with Vonnie, with my mom's side of the family, if I'm going to feel compelled to not talk about anyone from Dad's side? Yes, it was unfair that neither side did much to get me access to both sides of my family. I lost my mom, and then my dad five years later. You would think they would understand that I needed all the family I could get. Instead, they were focused on keeping me so that they wouldn't lose the remaining piece of the person they'd loved.

"Yvette always had landlord energy," Vonette says as I conclude our quick condo tour. "But at least she's doing some good with it."

I choose to ignore that dig. I grab beverages from the fridge, and we sit on the couch together.

"I'm sorry again about your retirement dinner."

"It's not your doing, so you don't need to apologize."

I pull my pursed lips to the side. Vonette opens her can of sparkling water and pours it into a glass.

"Oh." I stand and go to the built-in shelves beside the fireplace. "I guess I can return this to you." I sit back down, holding the journal out to her.

She reaches out to touch the cover but pulls her hand away without taking it. "No, it's yours. Always been yours, really. I'm sorry I held on to it for longer than necessary."

I sit it on my lap. "What you said about my mom not wanting Grandma to raise me . . . was that true? Is that why you tried for custody?"

Vonette looks at me apologetically and shrugs. "Speculation. When both your mom and dad were alive, I only remember her talking about a care plan once. You were only a few years old, and I can't remember how we got on the subject, but I do remember her saying that I would be the best choice to raise you. Sure, she thought I spoiled you, but she said once if I learned how to say no to you, I'd do fine. That, along with the rocky relationship she had with your grandma at the beginning . . . that's just the inference I've been telling myself all these years. But now I see you. Provided for. Thriving. And Whitney would be so proud."

Moisture gathers in Vonnie's eyes. I rest a hand on her knee.

"If I were raised by you, I probably would've turned out the same." I doubt the validity of that statement as soon as it passes my lips. Who would I have become without the afternoons spent baking with Grandma? Or without Clara to look up to as she forged a unique path for herself?

Vonnie seems to think the same, because she shakes her head. "You'd be different. I'm not saying better or worse, but different."

I sniff, looking down at the journal in my lap. "Before I got this, I would've said I was at peace with losing her, and my dad too. I thought I was done grieving. Now, I think of her all the time."

"Oh, baby." She presses her lips together, trying to reel back her tears. "I don't think it ever goes away. So long as they're gone and we're here."

"I got really good at ignoring it." My voice comes out hoarse. Retrospectively, I can see how my adolescent brain developed ways to help me move forward. My grief was disturbing, so that's all anyone wanted. The counselor, my grandma, teachers, and coaches—they all wanted me to focus on moving forward, the one thing I couldn't stop if I tried. As if time would cure my grief. I believed it would. But losing my parents blasted a gaping hole into the brick wall of protection they'd built around me. When Mom died, Dad tried to cover that hole himself and was conscious of his failure every day. When Dad followed her, I figured out how to patch up the hole on my own. I sought out anything or anyone permanent, anything I could control and decide to keep. It didn't change the fact that the hole was still there. There isn't a thing on earth that could fill it and make it exactly the same as it was before. However, the wall was functional again.

"I ignored it so well, I'm not even aware of all the ways it's influencing me. Like, do I need to build trust before forming connections with people, or am I seeking some impossible sense of permanence?"

"I wish I could tell you. My mom died in my adulthood, and I don't know how differently it would have affected me if it'd happened as early as you had to experience it. But, Tiwanda, you *can* just accept that the influence is there. You don't have to pinpoint it. It's not an ailment you have to diagnose. It's just part of you. And isn't it kind of wonderful that they will always have a presence within you?"

Her insight relieves the pressure sitting heavy on my chest. It's carried away by my deep breaths and by the tears streaming down my face. I don't try to quell them prematurely. My parents, after all the years I've suppressed mourning them, are worth every one. I, from child me to thirty-year-old me, am worth every one.

"I'm sorry I didn't pick you," I say, my guiltiness bubbling to the surface.

Vonnie's eyes squint in confusion, so I explain. "When the judge asked me if I wanted to go live with Grandma and I said yes."

"Oh." She waves a hand. "They'd already made up their mind. You practically already lived there; Wendell was a huge momma's boy. I don't know how to explain it, but . . . I just had to try. You were my baby." She places her hand over mine.

"It's not bad to be wanted. I just hate that it resulted in me losing contact with half of my family."

"As much as it's your grandma's fault, it's mine too. I got too wrapped up in life. Healing from losing my cousin and best friend, feeling like I'd lost you, getting married and eventually divorced. I got complacent with seeing your life play out through Facebook. Not anymore. I'll give your grandma a call. She probably won't answer, but I'll try."

I nod, feeling confident for the first time that a new relationship could grow here. I might not put her and Grandma in the same room for a while, but we have a fighting chance.

~

Robin calls me Thursday morning while I'm online placing an order for essential oils to replenish my personal soapmaking stock.

I scramble to answer the phone and greet her with, "Good news, please."

She laughs. "Were you worried? We didn't have any competition."

Still, I was sure someone else would swoop in before negotiations ceased. Robin gives me the most notable wins, along with a few compromises. It's for a three-year lease. No rent for the first three months, then a flat rate after that. The renovation restrictions are pretty loose.

The foundation has lawyers on retainer for the mentees, so I get my contract sent over for their expertise. They're able to read it over the weekend. After a few clause changes, I have the contract signed by end of business day Tuesday.

Two days later, after the hole in the wall has been repaired, I meet the selling broker at the store—*my* store—where he hands the keys over and allows me to do the honor of unlocking the door and letting us in. He turns off the alarm and gives me instructions on how to change the code. Then he leaves, and I'm left alone to marvel at the fact that I'm standing in what will become my dreams manifested.

Robin couldn't make it to see the culmination of her hard work, too busy running around for other clients. Ben comes by after he concludes a work meeting. When he arrives, holding a grocery bag, I'm in the process of making an exhaustive list of tasks I need to have done before launch. Since my start-up renovations are light, a fall launch might happen after all.

Ben follows me back into the kitchen, where I am midway through typing into my notes: Replace ovens. He puts the plastic bag on the center counter and pulls out a sweaty bottle of champagne. He also pulls out a pack of plastic flutes.

"I didn't know if Pilar or your friends would be here, so I got a pack."

The week leading up to this moment has been so hectic and uncertain, my friends only got basic updates from me. I texted the group when I finalized signing the lease and told them I'd be picking up the keys today, but I didn't consider turning it into a celebration.

"Nope, just us." I pick up the bottle and study the label. "Nice," I say.

"It's my sister's favorite." He fills two flutes and holds his up to eye level.

"To you," he says. "Congrats on finding the perfect spot for your business. Here's wishing you the best of luck and much success."

"Thanks," I say. Before taking a sip, I raise my own glass. "To you too. For helping me with finding this. And for not being as useless a mentor as I thought you'd be."

He guffaws at me, and when he starts to retort, I emphasize, "I said I was wrong."

He accepts this and simply takes a swig from his glass. I take a sip too, the crisp bubbly traveling down smooth. Then I put the glass aside and hitch myself up to sit on the counter.

"Those cabinets"—I point to the right—"will be for the soap supplies. At home, my stuff is crammed under the bathroom sink. This will be much more organized."

"What about the chocolate supplies?"

"Some will need to be kept in the fridge. But stuff like food coloring and molds and the mixing bowls will go over there."

Ben follows my index finger to the cabinets I'm pointing toward and nods. We sip in silence for a moment while I imagine the decor I could add to make this kitchen match the homeyness I'd envisioned. When I finish my flute, Ben asks if I want a refill.

"No, thank you. I drank enough during my party weekend that I'm now sober for the rest of the year. Minus this. Thanks for coming and humoring Corinne's game, by the way."

"It was fun, so no regrets . . . other than slipping up and telling my ex-fiancée I loved her. That resulted in an hour-long call the next day, rehashing everything I thought we'd settled."

I cringe. I had wondered if he'd been able to patch that up. "You were engaged? That's bold," I say.

"What do you mean?"

"You got on one knee, I assume, and professed your love to someone. Asked them to be with you forever. I can't imagine."

"How do you know she didn't propose to me?" I stare at him until he relents. "Fine, I did, on bended knee and everything. She never gave me an ultimatum, but it still felt like the required next step. We'd been together three years; she was thirty-five and wanted children. Is this blurring the line of mentor and mentee too much?"

"That's the question we should've evaluated last weekend when we were cuffed together. Also, I'd challenge I never wanted you as a mentor in the first place. And it's a temporary arrangement."

"Uh-huh."

"Like your engagement."

"All right, we're done here."

He starts to walk away, grabbing the champagne bottle on the way out. Laughing, I hop off the counter and catch his arm before he steps out of the kitchen. "Too far, too far, I'm sorry," I say. He allows me to pull him back. "I want to hear about it, really. It would be helpful."

He gives me a knowing look. "For you and Elliot?"

I lift a shoulder. "Just in general. I've never been in a capital-*R* relationship." Yet here comes Met, trying to ruin my perfect track record. "I'm curious about how they can be successful."

"I might be the wrong person to ask about that, obviously. But from my limited experience and observation, they're only successful when they function within the confines set by those involved."

I frown at him. He takes a gulp of champagne right from the bottle before continuing.

"What I mean is, as soon as one person tries to do more with the relationship than it was designed to do, it collapses. I thought I could just go along with what was expected. Get married, have a child or two. Maya knew I wasn't one hundred percent in it. And she deserved someone who matched her dedication."

I nod, sagely. "I get that. I'd be in the same boat as you if my partner wanted children." I think of Elliot. We haven't discussed many long-term topics, his wants for the future. It feels premature, but I make a mental note to bring it up. I could see him being satisfied with our furry babies, and what better pet parent than a vet?

After wrapping up my list, we leave, and I lock the doors behind me for the first time. In the simple action, I imagine a future when locking up has become a habit after a fulfilling day of work. Though quiet, this is one of the top moments of my life. And, I realize on my drive home, it wasn't shadowed by the absence of my parents like my triumphs usually are. All I feel is happiness, the ever-present "despite" nowhere to be found. Maybe this is healing.

# CHAPTER TWENTY-FIVE

I should probably be more concerned that I've pretty much settled on my Met pick when the fourth one is still at large. But I know how rare the feelings that have grown between me and Elliot are, and I doubt it'll be replicated. Elliot was patient even when I was ready to write him off. Now, I'm pestering him with every animal meme I come across and carving out time to meet up at the dog park during his lunch breaks or for actual lunch on his off days.

It truly does require carving. Now that I have my store for Bathe in Chocolate, everything that was contingent on that step is in motion. I'm having light aesthetic renovations done while figuring out logistical issues and enlisting my friends to help with decorating. Each expense toward equipment or furniture is a reminder of how far the additional $50,000 grant would go to offset starter costs.

Corinne and I make a run to Menards to pick up paint supplies. I show her the grid of nine colors Devin sent me that they think will pair well with what they have planned for the mural. We get a worker to help us with paint-brand recommendations and select two colors. A pale yellow for one of the kitchen walls and an icy-blue shade for the front area.

"When is Devin supposed to paint?" Corinne asks as we survey our roll brush options.

"They said the end of next week," I reply. "Once they're back from Cali." They had to take a short-notice trip back home with their family.

"Have you talked to Elise recently?"

"Texting, mostly. When I called her a few days ago, she was about to head into a rehearsal." She's been busy since our cabin weekend. I assumed she'd started auditioning again, though she hasn't sent me any of the usual audition stories. Corinne's thoughtful expression makes me ask, "Why? What's up?"

"Nothing, I just haven't spoken to her either. Devin stopped by the office earlier this week, though, to talk to Aisha about the volunteering they do with us."

"Oh. Nice," I say even though Corinne's leery expression negates that assumption.

She shakes her head a bit before changing the subject. "Can we check if they have clothing racks? There's not enough closet space for Cory's wardrobe."

I stop her from trying to push the cart to avoid my delighted, open-mouthed gawk. "This is your way of announcing he's moving in with you?"

"No, this is my way of saying we're going to be on top of each other until my lease is up and we can get a bigger place."

"That's a freakier description than completely necessary."

She shakes her head and takes off in the direction of home accessories.

~

After clearing my emails Friday afternoon, I decide to begin my weekend early. The last few days of May have been heating up to the ideal summertime Chi weather, which is reason enough for me to pull out the compressor ice cream maker I bought during a particularly brutal busy season two years ago. Since that night of the impulse purchase, I've only used it three times.

I'm going through my bookmarked recipes and eliminating based on preference or not having the necessary ingredients, when I get a call from Ben. So determined to protect my afternoon off, I almost ignore it. But I sent him the link to my completed website earlier, so he might be calling with feedback.

"Hey, what's up?"

"I have a late birthday-slash-quitting gift for you. Are you at the shop? Can I swing by?"

"I'm at home. You can always swing by with gifts, yes. Even if it is a whopping"—I count the months on my hand—"four months later."

Twenty minutes after we hang up, Ben sidesteps through the door, careful not to bump the doorframe with the massive wooden whatever the hell it is he's carrying. It's a dark wood similar to my mahogany flooring. Penelope leaves her bed to investigate, growling in her cute little way as she scurries over. I pick her up to meet Ben at a more level playing field, just as soon as his hands are free.

"What is this?" I ask as he squats to properly place the carpentry on the ground. It comes up to my knee.

"A chest. The best one I've made—look." He opens the top, revealing medium-size square compartments on one half and larger rectangular compartments on the other. The depth is only about a third of the chest's total height. Ben shows me why when he pulls the handles on the face of the chest. There are two rows of drawers underneath the top level. The middle drawer has more compartments, but the bottom drawer is just open space.

"This would be perfect for my soap supplies."

"I know. You mentioned it was crowded underneath your bathroom sink."

I'm so taken aback by the gesture, the safeguards I have for interacting with Ben at an emotional distance are momentarily disarmed. I shift Penelope between my left arm and side, then run my fingers across the chest's glossy finish.

Ben explains the design in my stunned silence. "The wooden panels I used at the bottom of each level are somewhat permeable, so I added wood-patterned linoleum liners on top of the real wood in case you put oils in here that are prone to leaking."

I finally look up at him and notice the tentative pride contingent on my reception. "Ben, thank you. Is it acceptable to hug your mentor?"

He shakes his head but opens his arms wide enough for me to fit against him and briefly squeeze him tight with my one free arm. I formally introduce him to Penelope, and once he holds her briefly so she can see the world at an even better height, she trots back to her bed.

"Since you're here, can you help me put it up?" I have the perfect place in mind. I lead Ben and my new chest through my bedroom and into the attached bathroom. I open the door to the linen closet and remove the dirty-clothes hamper from beneath the shelves. The chest fits perfectly.

"I didn't know you were into woodworking until I saw the mirror frame you made with Victor," I say as I lead us back into the front. I resume my post in the kitchen with my ice cream maker as Ben stands on the other side of the bar counter.

"It was all I cared about in high school."

"You ever think about doing something with it? Not that my chest isn't something. But maybe, I don't know. Get a show on HGTV and knock down some old cabinets with a mallet."

I'm glad the squinted look he gives me only lasts a fraction of the time it used to linger on his face when I'd say something off the wall. Now, it's quickly replaced with an indulgent smile. "I had a conversation with the shop teacher when I was a senior about career options.

I was always there before school started to continue working on my projects before the first bell, there again during the actual shop period after lunch, then again during my off period at the end of the day. That was the last time I considered 'doing something' with it. But what I am doing is plenty for me."

"Wait, what did your teacher say about career options?"

"Just told me all the avenues he'd tried, a series of failures. Then he decided to teach so he could finally have a paycheck he could count on. I learned then that it's all right to keep your passions as hobbies. Some are meant to stay that way. Sometimes you try to capitalize on a passion and it ruins it. Muddies the process in the dirt that comes along with capitalism."

"Says the venture capitalist."

"Exactly." He counters me with a hard stare. I enrolled in pastry school with the intention of making a living off my passion. The thought of selling experiences to people, teaching them how to make the things that have kept me sane over the years, fills me with joy. I hope that feeling is enough to shelter me from the vicissitudes that come with tying business transactions to it. "I'm not saying it would be that way for you," Ben adds.

"Good. I was about to add that on the list of unhelpful mentor guidance I've been composing to send to the board."

Ben's nose flares, but it's balanced by the mirth in his eyes. Grinning, I turn and start to gather the ingredients I need to whip up this batch of ice cream, referencing the recipe on my tablet.

"Is this chocolate you're making now?"

I hold up the heavy cream and wave my hand toward the appliance on my counter, as if it means anything to him. "Ice cream. I'm attempting to make this honey cashew recipe I found."

"Do you think you'd offer ice-cream-making classes, too, one day?"

"Nah. Gotta keep some passions a hobby, right?" I wink at him.

"Watch it. It sounds like you're learning from me." He actually looks pleased with himself, so I decide not to deny it. "Guess I should get going and let you get to work, or rather, play."

"You can stay if you want. I can teach *you* how to make ice cream, and then you can draw conclusions as to how effective I'll be once I'm teaching classes for real. Since that was a concern of yours. My ability to provide a good enough teaching experience that people return or refer friends."

"I . . . don't think I said that."

"You can start by washing your hands."

This recipe is advertised as "quick and easy," so it doesn't use a custard base and skips the simmering step. I put Ben on whisking duty as I add heavy cream, whole milk, sugar, a bit of salt, and vanilla.

Once we pour our base mixture into the prechilled machine to churn, I set my timer for twenty minutes. Then I shoo Ben back to the other side of the breakfast bar so that I can clean up while we wait. It's how things will work at Bathe in Chocolate. People come in, have fun, make a mess, and then the team and I will handle cleanup as they drive home with their goods and memories. When the timer goes off, I add sweet brown butter cashews in the thickened mixture along with a drizzle of local honey. Then I reset the timer for five additional minutes.

"I think I can relax next week," I tell Ben, picturing my reduced to-do list. "Which means I can meet the team at the office more."

"That reminds me, I have to go out of town on Wednesday. I'll be sending a notice to the team later tonight."

"For how long?"

"A week and a half. I know," he says in response to my widened eyes. "I tried to put it off until after the mentorship period, but it was either now or during presentation week. You're all at a good place, though. And I'll still be reachable."

"Oh, that wasn't panic here." I point to my face. "It was elation."

"Uh-huh. When you need me and I'm all the way across the Atlantic, we'll see."

I can't hide my rueful grin. "Where are you headed?"

"Luxembourg. A business I'm evaluating has an office there."

"Sounds like a nice getaway. I'm going to need one of those when this is all over with. The week leading up to signing the lease for my kitchen, I couldn't sleep through the night."

"Come to Luxembourg with me. It's right next to Germany and Belgium—they must have good chocolate. It can count as a business trip."

"Ha!" He's joking, but I'd love to take a trip to Belgium one day. It's been on my travel list since the Chicago Pastry Forum had a chocolatier from Belgium do a demonstration on uses of chocolate to enhance contemporary plated desserts. I was halfway through the chocolate portion of the semester, and that demonstration tipped me over the edge to my undying loyalty. The timer goes off. "Ready to try what we made?"

I look at him eagerly, brows raised. His smile is slow to match mine, like his thoughts were elsewhere. But he snaps out of whatever it was and joins me in the kitchen again to scoop out some of our soft-serve honey cashew ice cream into a bowl. The rest, I quickly transfer into the storage container that came with the machine and stick it in the freezer to harden. I grab two spoons, handing one to Ben. We dig in simultaneously, then share looks of delight over the bowl.

"So tell me," I say as I hand Ben the bowl to finish it off. "Would you come again or refer to a friend?"

"I don't know—your teaching style is not for the faint of heart."

"I'll be sure to smile more for the children." I contort my face into the most malevolent smile I can pull off, lowering my chin for a touch of creepiness.

"And that will be the last kid's birthday party you do." His words erase my mask and replace it with a genuine smile. He takes another bite.

The way his gaze wanders, I think he's contemplating the flavor profile of the ice cream, but then he asks, "Why don't you want children?"

I frown at the segue. "You first."

"Oh. All right. I don't think I'd be a consistent enough parent."

"That's fair. Mine is kind of the same. Having children is making a promise you can't guarantee, no matter how good your intentions. Anything can happen to you. And then what happens to the child?" *Me, I'm what happens,* I finish inside my head.

"Well, damn." Ben's stricken face is hilarious. He's more moved by this than my creepy smile.

"Also, I just really enjoy kids in small doses. An hour here and there. Maybe a weekend with my younger cousins. I should've led with that reason."

"Yeah. The bleak part could've stayed between you and your therapist."

My laughter comes out unevenly, tangled with the surprise of Ben being purposefully humorous. Perhaps this is what I sensed I was missing, when I was jealous of the easy relationships Ben formed with the other mentees.

"Since we're getting personal," I say, "I need advice."

"You're lucky I haven't left the country yet."

I flash him a shallow scowl before continuing. "Remember we were talking relationships? How do you know if both people have the same design in mind?"

"Talk. Ask them point-blank what they want, and be honest about your wants. See what matches, what can and cannot be compromised. The more honest both people are, the easier it'll be to decide if you should continue the relationship. Or in what capacity. Maya and I decided distant friends would be best, for example."

I nod along with his words. "Maybe you should've been my relationship mentor this whole time. We think the same. My friends don't approach it this logically."

162

"Honestly, I wish I didn't have to be so logical about it. But avoiding logic got me nowhere."

"I wouldn't say nowhere. It got you the experience needed to be able to give me sage advice, so, thank you for your service."

Ben brushes aside my teasing with a quick purse of his lips. "You mentioned no relationships. But no semi-serious dating either?"

I shake my head. "Elliot is the first person I've ever considered doing any of this with." I try not to show on my face just how much I've been freaking out about that. With Unicorn Tobias, I didn't plan out further than expressing my feelings. That alone was a feat for me. Elliot makes me want to try, so much. Every time I've met up with him since my party, I've been tempted to throw my ban against PDA out the window just to make sure that night wasn't a fluke. I focus on taking the empty bowl of ice cream from Ben's hand instead of looking at his face. "I'm aware that for that reason, this might mean more to me than it does to him. So at his next available, I want to touch base with him and see what our status is."

Ben confines his laugh to a few short bursts of air through his nostrils. "Reel in the logic side a bit. It's sounding like you're discussing a corporate meeting."

I roll my eyes, but my lips lift into a smile. "Fine. I want to meet up at his place, make out with him again, and see if we still have that spark. If we do, then I want to try going further."

"Further, like with your words? About intentions?"

"With our body parts, Benoit."

He holds his hands up. "Okay, okay. I get it. Just wanted to clarify. And this would come before or after the relationship design conversation?"

"I'm sensing the logical thing to do would be conversation first, *but* you just told me to reel logic in, so I think you know my answer."

Ben rubs his forehead, his eyes closed for a few moments. "I've never felt like more of an inadequate mentor than right now."

I scoff. "This is what did it?"

"I just hope it all works out, that's all."

"Oh, it will. One way or another." Met guarantees it. And for once, I'm happy to have it on my side as I reach unprecedented levels with the person it has sent me, and that I've in turn chosen.

# CHAPTER TWENTY-SIX

Since Elliot arranged our first date, I take the reins for our second one. Two weeks after laying out my plan with Ben, it's a go. Like me, Elliot has lived in Chicago most of his life. So I figured he probably has the same separation between his daily life and the tourist experience. For out-of-town guests, my city exploration usually peaks somewhere between the Bean and the Museum Campus. When I saw a Groupon for this After-Dark Segway Tour, I snatched it up.

We meet up in a parking lot along the lakefront. The sun is threatening to call it quits for the day but goes out in a burst of color, casting the sky above Lake Michigan with swirls of sherbet orange and pink. Elliot strolls along casually, as if this walk to the meetup point is part of the experience. It is scenic, but if we don't hurry it along, we'll be late. I slide my hand into his as he's suggesting we bring our dogs on a lakefront walk. He cuts his sentence short and looks down at our conjoined hands, then back up to me with squinted eyes and a knowing smirk.

"Don't think I don't notice we're walking faster now."

"I don't know what you're talking about."

"A complete one-eighty. You've become a hand-holding manipulator."

There are five of us for the excursion plus our guide, Evan. He gives us a quick orientation on how to use the Segways, and then we're off. The summer evening wind whips the ends of the long twists I put in my hair last night. But even when we make a stop for Evan to explain the significance behind Buckingham Fountain, I don't tie them back. I love the sensation against my arms and shoulders. It feels true to the city. If I had to describe summertime Chicago to an outsider, this is the feeling I'd try to capture. The wind that's a blend of exhilaration and suffocation, the shimmer of the skyline reverberating in my chest. I swerve and narrowly miss hitting a pole, lost in my reverie. The sound of Elliot's laugh is extinguished by the wind, but I can infer the noise he makes from the wide gape of his mouth and the upward tilt of his chin, even as he keeps his eyes ahead.

When the two-hour tour wraps, we walk back to our cars.

"What are we doing the rest of the night?" Elliot asks as we cross the parking lot.

My lips curve up at the swaggering glint in his eyes I've come to anticipate. "*We* should go to your place. Penelope is with the dog sitter."

He pauses with his grip on the door handle of my car, surveying my face carefully. Satisfied with whatever he's deduced, he pulls it open for me and says, "Bet."

Elliot lives in a South Shore bungalow-style house. He says many of his neighbors are senior citizens who have lived there for decades, thus the quietness on a Friday night. He bought it two years ago after it had undergone a complete renovation with a kitchen that makes my mouth water.

"You can come over to use it anytime," he says as I touch the nobs of the stove.

"And leave all the appliances I've curated at home? No thanks."

He offers me a drink and I choose wine. We sit on the couch together in his living room. My legs, crossed and turned toward him, press against his right leg.

"How's your business going?" Elliot asks.

"It's . . ." I release a huge sigh. "A lot. Every time I cross something off my to-do list, three more things pop up. But I'm having a good time."

Talk of business building makes me think of my last conversation with Ben, and how he'd want me to ask Elliot about defining the relationship *before* I put my wine aside on the coffee table, swing my leg around, and sit on his lap to pick up where we left off at my party. But Ben's not here, and I do what I want!

I abandon the wine on a coaster and look at Elliot with a suppressed smile.

"What?" His face already starts to move to match mine.

I clear the humor from my face and thoughts of this inside joke of sorts with Ben from my mind before continuing.

"I've been thinking about my party. A lot."

"Me too," Elliot says. He sits his wineglass down too. Perfect.

"You were very convincing that night."

"Because I was convinced. *Am* convinced. I do want to be with you, exclusively. But you're setting our pace. You make the call when you feel the same."

I nod as if that'll help convince my brain I'm ready. I want to call it now, declare we're together and relieve him from this waiting game. Because I care about him, and I want him to be happy. But I care about myself too, and in these uncharted waters, I have doubts. Since I've always been a tactile learner, understanding best from trial and error, I commit to my initial plan. Elliot watches me move to straddle him with eager eyes. His hands settle on my waist.

"I think I want that," I say.

"You have time to think," he assures me.

Instead of derailing this with acknowledging the panicky things my brain is doing, I lean down and kiss him. And I remind myself what Met is doing: helping me give people a chance.

His mouth presses against mine with more intensity. His tongue pulls my focus from obsessing over the rightness of this back to the actual moment. I match his vigor, my hands roaming his chest and my tongue meeting his. His low groan resonates in my throat. The growl that follows soon after does not. Elliot breaks away from me, and I follow his gaze to the German shepherd baring his teeth, staring right at me. In one fluid motion, I roll off his lap onto the other side of the couch. Elliot immediately stands and holds out his hand.

"Down," he commands. Kyro obeys. I thought we were cool after our numerous playdates at the dog park. Now, even as he lies down, he eyes me with distrust for mauling his human. "I'm going to put him in the room," Elliot says. He pats his leg twice and starts walking in that direction. Kyro follows but doesn't seem happy about it.

I reach for my purse and retrieve my phone, my hand's muscle memory pulling up the Ask Met chat window while I listen for Elliot's footsteps.

Do I want this? I realize as soon as I press enter that Met is an app, not an untapped portion of my brain. I really should be better at phrasing these questions by now. I quickly send an amendment. Should I want this?

> *Miss Thing.*
> *No matter how you phrase that question, I'm not*
> *going to give you the answer. Try again.*

I groan under my breath, but at least Met is even allowing me a replacement question. No matter its slightly condescending tone.

Is uncertainty bad? It's the best I can do as I hear a door close down the hall and Elliot start to make his way back to me.

He's only a few steps from view as the answer appears. I school my features as close to what I imagine I look like whenever I'm scrolling social media.

*It's not bad. It's just a feeling. You're uncertain your business will succeed, but that doesn't deter you from trying. Plus, with your fourth match coming and the way I've been sending quality matches, it's natural to feel uncertain.*

Damn, Met. Way to remind me. I toss my phone aside as Elliot retakes his seat.

"Sorry about that," he says.

"He's protective of you. It's cute."

He tilts his head and makes an unimpressed expression. "Cock blocks are not cute. Come here." He reaches out to me. I nestle beside him but don't return to my seat in his lap.

"Are you panicking?" he asks.

"What? No." I press a kiss into his neck to support my claim. Though the gesture makes his lips tick, his gaze is unrelenting in its assessment. I rest my head onto his shoulder before saying, "I just want us to work, that's all."

He brushes his lips against my forehead. "I can easily see a future with you."

"Yeah?" I lift my head just in time to catch his solemn nod. *Just bask in his want for you, Tiwanda! Ben is barely your mentor, don't listen to him!* My mouth opens despite my inner turmoil. "So you're looking for something serious?" *Like, soul mate serious?*

"Honestly"—he shifts a bit so we can see each other better—"I'm tired of casual dating. I've always pictured myself settled down by now. I'm tired of going to weddings and not knowing when my own will be. Or who it'll be with." I register the strain of my eyes only when he reaches out to place a reassuring hand over mine. "I'm not saying you have to know you want to marry me right now. I would never settle just for a title. My parents divorced when I was thirteen, so . . . no. I just want you to know I take this seriously, that's all."

I swallow down that momentary urge to bolt. "I always imagined if I ended up with someone for the long haul, our relationship would be strange on the outside." He cocks his head to the side, so I explain more. "A relationship that's so uniquely us, my grandma would call it an unconventional lifestyle."

He chuckles. "I like that. Too many people build their relationships around an ideal marriage and not what works for them. I'd want something more unconventional too. A real partnership, fifty-fifty everything, from decision-making to parenting."

Does that still classify as unconventional these days? I almost miss the last part of what he said until my brain catches up, flagging the word *parenting* for further interrogation.

"You definitely want children?"

"One day. I'm a fourth, so I have to keep the lineage going." He gently takes my chin in his hand. "Your face is doing a thing. It's too soon to talk about this, isn't it?"

I smile in an attempt to stop my face from betraying me. "No, I don't think it's ever too soon to talk about your wants for the future. It doesn't have to mean you want it with the person you're discussing it with."

"It doesn't," he agrees, and laces his fingers with mine. "But in this case . . . I can't help filling you into all my dreams, Tiwanda. Every one of them."

I can't control it; I wince. The picture he's drawing is beautiful. But I don't think my jumble of colors fit inside the lines. They just don't. No matter how neat and possibly satisfying it would be if they did. So I steel myself to give Elliot the transparency he deserves, hoping that maybe my aversion to procreating and cynicism toward marriage won't be deal breakers. That maybe he'll say, "It's okay you don't want to have my namesake baby—we can just name our first dog together Elliot the Fifth instead!"

"I'm not sure if I want children," I say. As soon as the words leave my mouth, I'm surprised by how I framed it like I'm undecided. "Pretty sure," I amend.

"Oh," Elliot says. He visibly deflates.

"Is that . . . a future you could see maybe? Without kids?"

He hums a little as he sits up straighter, really giving it thought. Grabs his wineglass and takes a sip, returns it to the table. His eyes linger on my face, which is hopefully awaiting his answer. "I don't think I can."

"Okay." I clear my throat. "It's okay. This doesn't have to mean anything yet. We can see how things develop."

The flash of teeth as he bites his bottom lip draws my attention to his mouth. Why hadn't I just stuck to my original plan of kissing that mouth?

"Children aren't an optional detour. For me, they're the ultimate level. Ever since I had a concept of family, I imagined myself with kids. In a strong marriage like the ones I saw on TV, but not in my own home. I wouldn't feel complete without it."

"I have to think about it some more. You consistently meet me where I am. I want to see things from your point of view too."

Elliot shakes his head, his lips forming a sad smile. "I don't want to have to persuade my partner into something so life altering. We'd both need to be one thousand percent in."

"Maybe I can get there." I believe every word that's coming out of my mouth. People change their minds all the time about this, so it's not impossible. In this moment, I still don't want kids. But I want Elliot. And he is exactly the type of person I could see myself compromising for, with time.

"I'm sorry, Tiwanda. In this stage of my life, I don't think we're compatible. I want to start a family soon. I crave it. As much as we like each other, we don't want the same things. If we were to keep going on the off chance you change your mind, it would just hurt us both more in the end."

As easily as he claimed to see a future with me, it's just as easy for him to delete it. Apparently, the beautiful picture was created with erasable color pencils. It might smudge a bit upon my removal, but once he colors it in with the next girl, no one will be able to tell the difference. Because I'm expendable, and his ideals for family are not. Maybe that's the correct order of things, but damn, it still hurts.

# CHAPTER TWENTY-SEVEN

I call Elise on Saturday morning, after taking the rest of Friday night to wallow in Elliot's rejection. It shouldn't hurt this bad. I didn't want this situation in the first place. And it's not like I'm in love with him. However, I'm just now realizing that maybe I've become enamored with the idea of him. The idea of Met working for me.

"Are you calling me from your walk of shameless? Tell me everything."

"No, I'm calling you from the walk to my kitchen."

I didn't video-call her, but in the short pause that follows, I can picture her lips pinching up as she ponders my meaning. "So you didn't spend the night with him."

"Nope."

"And now you're in your kitchen?"

"Making chocolate, yeah."

Another pause. "I'm coming over."

In the time it takes for Elise to arrive, I manage to fail at yet another thing. This one adds insult to injury, because someone who is trying to build a career on chocolate should be able to temper it in their sleep. I usually can, which is probably why, despite the temperature displayed on the handle of the spatula, I allowed my dark chocolate to overheat.

I hustle to the freezer with a large plastic bowl and transfer a few cups of ice into it. This will help me cool it down quicker. Then I'll raise it back up to my target temperature. Elise comes just as I finally wrangle this batch into submission. I remove the pot from the heat and let her in. She drops her duffel bag beside the opening to the hallway and follows me to the kitchen.

"You're making chocolate in your pajamas. Elliot is cool, but he can't be worth all this."

I look down, unreasonably surprised to find the aforementioned pajamas. I open my pantry door and grab one of the aprons hanging on the hook. "He isn't," I say as I loop the apron around my neck and tie a clumsy bow around my back. "I was just restless."

Elise nods, biting her lip as she takes a seat at the kitchen bar. "I've been like that, too, lately. Let's see what we're working with." She lifts the paper where I've jotted down my recipes for these two batches. "Caramel apple and gingerbread? Interesting choice for summer."

"I'm trying to think about what seasonal flavors I could have for classes in December other than peppermint."

Because Elise is my best friend and she knows me so well it's almost inconvenient at times, she doesn't ask me about Elliot while I work on my bonbons. Recovering my rhythm, I make the two recipes simultaneously. Gingerbread ganache goes into one molding tray while the other gets a layer of caramel topped with cinnamon apple butter. All the while, Elise regales me with stories from her rehearsals.

Once both molding trays are filled, sealed with a final layer of chocolate, and sat in the fridge to harden, we relocate to the living room. Here, Elise finally circles back to the topic she graciously saved for after I finished with my chocolate.

"What's up with you?" she asks as she joins me on the couch. Penelope trots over and rubs her body against my calf. I lift her onto my lap, where she settles immediately. Her sixth sense for emotional support is becoming apparent.

"What do you mean?"

She gestures toward me. "Your energy is all off, and you still haven't told me what happened with Elliot yesterday."

I sigh. "Suffice to say, he's not an option. Or rather, I'm not an option for him."

Elise wrinkles her nose. "If it's not a match, it probably goes both ways."

"True, but I didn't want to end it without trying. He was the most patient and understanding man I've ever met. Figures I'd manage to get to the bottom of that well."

"You do realize patience and acceptance is a low bar, right?"

"Yet so many can't clear it."

"The bright side," Elise says with a sly grin, "is that Corinne owes me twenty dollars now."

"You bet on me?"

"It was at your party. The edible Clara gave me made me do it. And you had three Met matches there. It was kind of amazing. Like a harem or something." I gawk at the mental image her words inspire. "I'm sorry it didn't work out with Elliot."

I shrug, attempting nonchalance but falling somewhere near despondent. "It's all right." I pet Penelope's warm body, allowing the repetitive motion to soothe me. "I just allowed my expectations to shift. So many years of being uninterested in romance because I'd been so sure it wouldn't happen to me, in that way. And I was fine with that because I have my family, and friends, and you, and that really is plenty. But then with Met, I got curious." I groan.

Elise is unusually quiet. I'd expect her to commiserate or encourage me to set my intentions on what I want. Not that it would work, since I don't know what or who I want. I want someone from the future to come and tell me how it shakes out.

The grim look on Elise's face puts me on alert. "I think your energy is off too?"

She looks over at me, then away. Okay, definitely off, then. I wait for her to talk because I know she will when she's ready. She drops her shoulders and straightens her posture. "I'm moving to LA."

My brain refuses to accept this statement. It twists it a few different ways to find a meaning that fits better, but fails. "Why?"

"I want to audition for more television roles, and that's the place to be. It would also be nice being closer to my family."

*We're family too.* I bite my tongue to hold that thought in. As true as it is for me, of course Elise would want to be near her sisters and parents. If I had them, that's where I would be. I'm rooted to Chicago because of my family. I can understand that. I have to.

"What about Devin? You're going to try long distance?"

Elise shakes her head, a tight movement, though her lips purse into a small smile. "They're moving with me. Found a teaching position for next school year."

My mouth drops open as I regard her. Her tentative happy face persists until I scoff. "When did you decide this?" Elise might not be a planner like me, but she does envision. She figures out what her goals are, envisions the life she'd have once she attains those goals, then takes the necessary steps to get there. That Devin already has a job lined up tells me Elise has known awhile and didn't share it with me. Unless it wasn't originally Elise's idea at all. All those trips to California Devin took suddenly make sense.

"A month, maybe," she says.

"This is Devin's fault." I didn't plan to say that aloud, but it's just the same. Devin is the reason I see a lot less of my best friend. I accepted that. It doesn't compare to how seldom I'll see her if she actually goes through with this move.

"Don't blame Devin. I'm the one who wanted to move; Devin just loved the idea."

Encouraged it, I'm sure. "A year ago, you would've told me you wanted to move. Instead of springing it on me like this, when the decision had already been made."

Elise lifts her arms wide, then lets them drop back down. "Maybe I would've, but now I have a partner to consider."

I nod, a bitter smile on my lips. "Your partner of a year." I hold out my left hand, palm up. Then I do the same with my right hand and say, "Your best friend for nearly a decade. Nice." Roused by my movement, Penelope leaps from my lap and retreats to her bed.

"You really need to let go of the linear concept of time and embrace change," Elise says.

I frown, an overwhelming sense of sadness hitting me at once. The denial and anger swooped in quickest, but they both were powered by how sad I am to be losing proximity to my best friend. Tears spring to my eyes within seconds and fall without hesitation. I swipe them away and stand, escaping to my room.

Phone in hand, I consider calling Cory or Corinne for backup, but I have the feeling neither of them will take the news as hard. It makes me feel weak. This is not losing Elise, I try to convince myself, over and over again.

Elise's claim that I'm somehow change resistant is outrageous. How can someone lose their mom, then their dad, and *not* adapt? I'd say that was me embracing change. My phone chimes with Met's signature tone. I roll my eyes, though part of me is hoping it's a lifeline.

*Met Tip: Have faith not that things will always work out, but that you'll figure out a way forward regardless.*

I stare at the fortune cookie advice for three full seconds after I've finished reading it, and then I chuck my phone into my pillows.

There's a knock on the door, and I call for Elise to come in. She pushes the door open and takes a few steps inside. The whites of her eyes have become pinkish. The sight of it compels me to my feet. Like polar ends of a magnet, we are drawn together into a hug, seeking comfort in each other. My arms wrap around her shoulders and hers around my midsection. She's the best friend I've ever had, and I'd willingly say that to Cory's face.

"I was scared to tell you." Her voice is muffled against my shoulder. I nod, trusting she'll feel the movement, and take one final deep breath before letting go.

Now it's my turn to fear how this will impact our friendship and, on a larger scale, my life. Met says the only way is forward. It's just . . . any path forward I see looks like crap without Elise prominently featured, like she has been the last nine years.

"Does this mean this is our last summertime Chi together?"

"For a bit, yeah. We're leaving early August."

"I don't like this."

"I know."

"I'm still proud of you."

She bumps her shoulder into mine. "I know."

# CHAPTER TWENTY-EIGHT

When my dad died, my family thought it would break me. They didn't say that outright, but I could tell from how they regarded me. Devastated as they were, they still stepped out of their individual grief bubbles to check on me. Clara would pop up in the doorframe of the guest room at Grandma's house that would become my permanent room. Grandma would ask me what I wanted for dinner, when I never previously had a choice as to what she cooked. My other aunts and cousins, who provided a steady stream of company the first weeks, sought me out to share their thoughts about life and afterlife.

But if I'm completely honest, it didn't hurt as much as my mom. And it's not due to incongruities of love or closeness. In the five years after my mom died, my dad didn't date. His entire focus was work and taking care of me. His heartbreak overshadowed my own. With his passing, I felt a complex mix of emotions I spent many sessions discussing with the therapist Auntie Yvette insisted Grandma take me to. The most surprising, amid the expected sadness and anger, was jealousy. Dad had gotten what I wanted, to be with Mom again. So though the doctors said he died of a heart attack, I know a broken heart was the likely culprit.

After Elise goes home the following morning, tension leaves my body. I hadn't even noticed the way my shoulders contracted as I tried to remain upbeat. My reaction to her news wasn't the best, and I spent the rest of the day attempting to remedy it with questions about her plans. But each answer resulted in a stab of annoyance that she'd been keeping all of this between herself and Devin.

In my feelings, I pick up my mom's pregnancy journal from the bookshelf. I don't know why Elise leaving stirs up thoughts of my mom and dad. They're totally different situations. Still, with Elise's absence, I'm free to lean into my melancholic ruminations.

I flip to an entry from my mom's third trimester. When I think of my mom, this is how I most often remember her. Face puffy, unafraid to leave the house in slippers when her feet swelled, a beautiful glow encompassing her even as her body struggled with the changes. I'd sometimes touch her belly and imagine it was me in there. This entry must have been one of those times.

*I can't wait to not be pregnant anymore. Wendell has gotten in the habit of telling me I'm beautiful every day, and honestly it makes me want to hit him over the head. But with a pillow, because he means well. I don't remember it hurting this much the first time around. That's how it gets you. The moment your baby is born and you hold that soft, perfect thing in your arms, a sort of amnesia washes over you. You forget the aches and the gas and feeling like you've lost control of your body. And when you forget, you end up like me, letting your husband convince you to do it all over again.*

*Little Miss Thing is both fascinated and horrified by the process. Every day it's a new question. Doesn't it hurt? Is this just like with me? After watching A Baby Story on television, she even asked me if the baby was breech. I think both of us will be relieved once we get this baby out of me. And then I'm getting my tubes tied.*

She goes on to talk about finally getting the crib set up and the baby shower that Vonette is planning for that weekend. Something about this entry unsettles me. I don't think I lingered on it during the first read. This was the section I'd read the quickest, flipping pages as if it were the climax of a thriller novel. The only thing I'd really taken away from this entry was that my dad was the reason they tried for baby number two. Upon second read, it feels more foreboding. Nothing about this makes me want the future Elliot wants.

I reread it, my eyes catching on something new, yet again. *Little Miss Thing.* It's not like I'd forgotten the name she used to call me—I just hadn't thought about it in such a long time. She only seemed to use it when I was a bundle of energy, bouncing all over the place. Or when I was being inquisitive, pulling at the last strands of her patience. Whenever I heard that moniker along with the answer to whatever question I'd asked, I knew that was the last answer I'd get before she suggested something else for me to do with my time. And her suggestions were never fun.

It's been a long time since I've heard the nickname, but I've seen it recently. Sort of. I reach for my phone and pull up Met. What I'm looking for isn't far up the Ask Met thread. There it is, in reprimand to my silly question posed at Elliot's house. My brain fills with a rush of static. When Corinne experienced this . . . connection of sorts with her best friend, I didn't think too much about it. I accepted it as another inexplicable thing of the divine. It seemed to help her, so I had no reason to question it.

But now it's in my hands, and my heart is surging with the overwhelming sense that Met connects to my mom somehow. My fingers tremble above the screen. Is this something I can just ask for Met's confirmation?

Are you controlled by my mom's spirit?

I wait five full minutes before I accept it won't respond to the question.

Am I imagining a connection to my mom?

Configuring dots appear, and I grip the phone tighter.

*If it exists to you, how can it be imagined?*

# CHAPTER
# TWENTY-NINE

I can't focus. Since I wasted most of my day yesterday with the same inability to stick with one task long enough to get it done, I decide to start today off with making a to-do list. I got as far as getting my notebook from my office before I got distracted by an email requesting another supporting document for my business license application.

Just after 1:00 p.m., I gather the bags of shop decorations I've collected sporadically over the past couple of weeks. Hopefully I'll fare better with a task that's more hands-on. My phone vibrates as I struggle to hold all the bags in one hand and ruffle the top of Penelope's head with the other. The missed call is from Ben, so I give him a call back.

"Welcome back," I say. I figure I should greet him this way since I never responded to the email he sent to the mentee group yesterday alerting us of his return.

"Thanks. Are you close?"

"To . . . ?" As I drag the single syllable out, it dawns on me.

"The office. We have a meeting scheduled for five minutes ago."

Having the ability to compartmentalize would really come in handy right now. With that gift, I wouldn't be such a mess. My mind wouldn't be ricocheting between Met, my mom, and Elise so insistently it creates a cacophony that drowns out any other thoughts.

"I completely forgot. I'm so sorry. Can we hop on a video meeting? Or I can drive there, but I'd be thirty minutes late."

"Are you at the store? I was leaving here after our meeting anyway, so I'll just swing by instead. It'll be good to see what you've done there."

I exhale a sigh of relief that I'll still be able to make my trip to the store, thus not messing up that task as well. I tell Ben I'll meet him there, grab two of the shea-butter-and-fennel bars of soap that have cured long enough, and make a second attempt at getting my bags of decor down to my car.

Ben arrives minutes after I do. His large figure on the other side of the door, waiting to be let in, is a welcome sight. We exchanged several emails over his time away, but I kind of missed having the in-person, subtle-facial-expressions, apathetic-until-proven-not Ben experience.

He looks refreshed as he steps into the store. Even though his travel was work related, there's an air about him that makes the store feel a bit more energized. It brings a smile to my face that he thankfully doesn't notice, since he's focused on the paint job and the tarp shielding one wall from view.

"What's this?" he asks, gesturing to the wall.

"The mural my friend Devin is painting. They don't want me to see it until it's all finished."

"You haven't peeked?" He lifts a corner of the sheet, eyebrows raised at me.

"No, I can be patient." Though the real reason I haven't been tempted is because I don't want anything to do with Devin at the moment. Though Devin's and my respective relationships with Elise are very different, it's hard not to feel like I've been replaced. Because truly, I have been in ways. Devin is now Elise's closest confidant. And they totally give off that "I'm married to my best friend" vibe, so it's just a matter of time before Devin replaces me in that role as well. *Bleh*.

Ben lets the tarp covering fall back into place. "What's wrong?"

I shake my head. "Nothing, I just had *quite* the weekend. Come look at the kitchen. The new counters are in."

He shows an adequate appreciation for my new quartz surfaces, paying special attention to where they meet the wall and noting how well fitted they are. I catch him up on everything else I've done in the past two weeks in several unenthusiastic sentences.

He looks up from the counter and stares at me, eyebrows pinched, for a few seconds. He breaks his scrutinizing to take off his backpack.

"I brought something for you," he says as he unzips the front compartment. He pulls out a clear freezer bag. Inside are several waxy paper bags and a small box.

I squint at him in a good-natured show of curiosity. It's the best moment of getting gifts, an activity I love. He waits for me to get around to finally opening the thing like he has all the time in the world.

I smell what it is when I open the bag but pull out the sole box to confirm it nonetheless.

"You brought chocolate back for me?" I waste no time taking out one of the petits fours and holding it up to Ben to break off half. "Have you tried it yet?"

He shakes his head, and we work together to split it. "I stopped whenever I came across a chocolate shop or bakery. These are from three different places."

Underneath the chocolate icing is a bite-size, two-layer cake. We bring it to our lips at the same time and watch each other's faces for reactions. There's an apricot jam between the layers, with a slight crunch of chopped nuts, maybe almonds? Not bad, Luxembourg.

"Is it good enough?" he asks me.

I nod as I reach for another. "I like it, so it's good enough for me. I'm going to admit something to you that I don't want you to repeat, all right?"

"Oh . . . kay," he says, worried lines forming between his brows.

"I'm not a chocolate snob. Like, at all. I just love it, in so many different ways. If you brought me a TWIX, I would've appreciated it the same."

His face is his signature shade of expressionless as he considers my admission. Then, his head jerks up and to the side. "No. I reject that. Days of making sure I don't leave this bag any place it can melt? You have to recalculate your appreciation."

I grin up at him, shake my head, and turn to walk toward where I placed the bags I brought from my apartment. "Fine. TWIX barely has any real chocolate in it, so your efforts earn fifty percent more appreciation. At least."

"I'll take it."

"I got something for you too," I say. I rummage through the bags until I find the two soap boxes.

He takes them from me and opens the boxes. "You made these?"

"Of course. And my soapmaking chest is now completely stocked."

He lifts the bar to his nose. "I haven't used bar soap since I lived with my mom. She's a bar soap purist."

"It's all natural. This one helps to soothe skin, good for irritation."

"Thanks, I'll try it."

"So what's my appreciation level? Compared to if I got you soap from the store?"

"Come on. No comparison."

I grow warm at the sincere compliment. Then, since he's here and eager to be a useful mentor, I ask for his assistance with hanging the wall decor. He's no help with deciding placement, but once I figure out where I want it, he stands near the stepladder as I hammer the nail in the wall. Then he hands me the picture to hang, telling me when I've gotten it straight. We repeat this a few times around the kitchen, then put up a few in the front area for the walls not covered for the mural.

"Did you pick a launch date yet?" Ben asks when we're back in the kitchen. He's on his phone, checking emails. I've pulled out my tablet and am using my phone as a hot spot to browse seating options around the island. I also need to find some type of booster step I can use for younger kids, since the countertop might be too high for them to create comfortably. I don't know where to start with that.

"I want to do a soft launch on the last weekend in July." That way Elise can be there. "But I don't want to officially launch then, because it'll be the last weeks of summer, and everyone wants to be outside."

"There's no reason why your official launch can't happen later. Second weekend in September maybe? That gives you all of August to adjust as necessary following the soft launch."

I pull out my phone and check the date. It avoids Labor Day weekend, so that's good. I shrug. "Seems good to me."

"What do you have planned for the soft launch?"

I hadn't given it much thought beyond it needing to happen before Elise and Devin move. "Chocolate, probably. That's as far as I got."

Ben gives me a strange look that I immediately question.

"Just surprised you don't have something already planned out for once," he says.

"Yeah, well. The presentation and closing out this mentorship come first."

"I'll start making a list of some things you should consider for launch," he says, taking out his phone to either make said list right this minute, or set a reminder to do so. When he slides his phone back into the side pocket of his backpack after tapping out a short note, I figure it's the latter.

"What types of things?"

"Like a photographer and videographer to get footage you can use for promo. If you'll provide food or drinks. That kind of stuff."

"I hadn't even considered that part of it. Thank you."

I hold up my tablet to show him potential adjustable chairs, with back support but no armrests.

"Maybe something similar but without wheels? Seems risky."

I nod, picturing teens using the chairs for mischief while they wait for their chocolate to harden. Finally, I find one with a stainless steel base and black cushions, without wheels. It will blend in with the kitchen and provide an option for patrons to sit, since making chocolate and soap can be a long process.

Next, I move on to the booster steps. I see a few sturdy-looking individual ones and wonder if I can simply have a few on hand for kids who need it. I flip the tablet around to Ben.

"One wrong step and the poor kid . . ." He makes a clicking noise with his tongue.

I groan. "I'm looking for something like a bandstand, but one that wraps around the island perfectly." It's a terribly specific ask, but that's the only thing I can think of that would be safe for the children to move around and be properly nosy about what their friend is cooking up.

"One you can latch the pieces together, and then unlatch and store when not in use?" Ben asks.

"Yeah, I suppose a latch would be good so it doesn't shift."

"I can make that for you."

I survey him. His work with the chest was amazing. This would probably be child's play for him. "How much would something like that cost?"

"For you? Nothing. No, I take that back. You have to admit I'm a good mentor."

"You're not just a good mentor. You're like, a legit one. Sorry it took me a while to realize how lucky I was to get paired with you."

"I requested you, so not that lucky."

"Really? After that panel? After the bar?" I finish the last part in a whisper.

I'm pretty sure I'm breaking the unspoken agreement we had to never discuss that night, before I left the conference hotel and when I thought it would be my last chance to tell Ben off and make sure he wasn't my soul mate. At the mention of it, Ben appears more thoughtful than embarrassed on my behalf.

"After both of those. Once the board picked you and mentees were up for grabs."

I'm taken aback. I know he said mentors had to agree to their mentees, but I imagined the board initiating the pairing. He grins at my slightly parted lips, waiting for me to respond, but I have nothing to say.

I'm just . . . fond of him. And I'm scrambling trying to figure out when this happened, exactly. Yet another person I like spending time with who will leave me around the end of July. He'll be going back to Philadelphia. Sure, it's not like he'll be unreachable after the official mentoring period ends, but we won't be chatting and hanging out like this anymore.

The grin slips from his face as his eyes implore mine. I wonder if he can see the sadness I'm trying to combat at the thought of this friendship we've built not lasting.

"How did it go with Elliot?" he asks suddenly.

I let out a derisive little laugh, snap the case of my tablet closed, and put it in a bag. "Your advice worked, in that it ruined everything."

His lips turn up again. "That was not my goal."

Honestly, after the bombshell Elise dropped, my failure with Elliot is not as painful as it was initially. Or maybe it's still there but the comparative dismay I feel about Elise overshadows it.

I pack up everything I'm taking home with me. Ben carries all but one of the bags, since I insist on not being empty-handed, and walks me out to my car. I open the back seat for him. After placing the bags behind the driver's seat, he moves back just enough for me to close the door. I lean against the side of the car.

"I'll sketch a few ideas and send you pictures for the riser. It shouldn't take me long. I can get some parts from the ReStore near my mom's house."

"Can I come?"

"Sure. I'll be at my mom's most of the weekend, so sometime then." He takes a step to the left and opens the driver door for me. "You know what, you should come for dinner, and then we'll go afterward."

I frown. "At your mom's house?"

"Yeah, she wanted to have a nice dinner with the family Saturday night, and she loves when we bring people. I've told her about my mentees, and she's been wanting to meet you all since I got here."

The tension in my shoulders dissipates. He's inviting the entire team, not only me. "I love family."

# CHAPTER THIRTY

Clara shakes her head from the kitchen entrance as she cradles Penelope like a baby. The ticking timer on Pen's patience is visible in her furry, annoyed face.

I'm ignoring Clara's disapproval and transferring the chocolates I made earlier this morning into gift boxes for Ben's family. He told me his mom loves peanut butter and toffee, so I did my thing. There's a box specifically catered to her tastes and another with some of my favorites for the rest of his family.

"All those fancy pastries you learned how to make in school and you still show up with a box of chocolates."

I finish boxing them and tie a decorative ribbon around each of the boxes. I'd offered to bring a proper dessert, but Ben insisted his mom was already preparing too much. This is the best gesture I could come up with.

Clara follows me into my bedroom, where I go back and forth between my closet and dresser twice before giving up and texting Pilar to ask what she's wearing. That'll help me figure out how casual I can go. Per usual, Pilar is a quick responder.

Pilar: A T-shirt and underwear.

Okay, that seems a tad more casual than I thought acceptable. Before I can respond, another text comes through.

Pilar: Gia thinks this is you hitting on me LOL.

After a few more exchanges, I confirm Pilar is not going to Ben's mom's house for dinner because she didn't know it was happening. It's not alarming when I think about it, since the only reason he invited me was because it's convenient for our shopping trip. I just assumed he would make it a team event type of thing. I go with a comfortable summer dress and wedge sandals, then leave Clara to bond with Penelope in my absence.

Ben's mom lives near Naperville, a forty-five-minute drive southwest of the city. I text Ben when I arrive, and by the time I've locked my car and walked halfway up the path, he's opening the door for me.

He leads me inside, where his entire immediate family is. When I'm introduced to his mom, Efe, she places her hands on my shoulders and says my name proudly. "Tiwanda. So nice to have you here." She's a handful of inches shorter than me, but with her posture and regal-like command of her home, I'm sure I'll imagine her looming over me in my mind's replay of this meeting.

Ben's dad shares his stature but in a slightly shorter frame. When Ben leads me to meet him, he's hunched over, tending to the chicken roasting in the oven. He says a quick hello, then shoos us out of the kitchen. Ben's siblings are all in the living room. From right to left, he introduces me to each.

"My sister, Oni, and her husband, Akin." Oni has straight shoulder-length hair and an inviting smile. "My brother Jacqui. He also works in business." Jacqui looks the most like Ben, just a leaner build. "And Nehikhare, the youngest of us."

"Call me Nehi," he says just as the unmistakable jingle of Met wreaking havoc sounds. My smile freezes on my face.

"Nice to meet you all. Excuse me, I have to take this. I'll just be a minute."

Ben points me in the direction of privacy. I hear him asking about the whereabouts of his niece and nephew as I retreat to the open office space connected to the foyer. That was for Nehi, right? I'd met the four of them so quickly. What if Met was operating on a lag?

Messy, I type into the Ask Met box.

*That isn't a question.*

"I know," I say to myself, through gritted teeth. "I just wanted to *comment* on how rude this is."

I tamp down my agitation enough to formulate a useful question.

*Is this a viable match, or are you messing with me?*

Because, *really*. If Nehi is a throwaway, please, Met, take pity on me now and let me off the hook.

*Has Met given you any bad matches so far? Why go out with a dud?*

*I thought I'm supposed to be asking the questions.*

I'm not surprised when there's no reply to that.

I return to the living room with Ben's siblings. From my seat on the couch with Jacqui, I try to subtly take in Nehi sitting in an armchair. I can't immediately place his looks as aligning more strongly with either of his parents, so maybe it's a grandparent who passed along his almost sculpture-like features. His hair is short, sponge curls on top with a fade. Tiny gold hoops adorn his ears.

"The Bulls are out, so I really don't care," Jacqui says, redirecting my attention to the conversation at hand.

The television is tuned into ESPN. His brothers are debating the potential outcome of the NBA championship series and which players are performing the best in the postseason. I haven't caught all the games, but when I'm home, I usually have one on in the background as I work or cook. Nehi defends his positioning with stats and specific game references. When he's done, no one can refute him.

"What do you do?" Ben's brother-in-law, Akin, asks me.

Nehi sucks his teeth. "Ben told us she's an entrepreneur already; don't go giving her the third degree too." He turns to me. "I get this from him every time we're in the same room."

"I'm just curious!" Akin defends himself. "Every time I see you, you have a different job."

The middle brother, Jacqui, mumbles "True" under his breath.

"Anyway," Akin continues, "I meant, what's your business?"

I explain the premise behind Bathe in Chocolate as briefly as I can.

"People pay for that?"

"Guess we'll see."

"They will," Ben says, reappearing. I shoot him a thankful smile for backing me up, but I'd already decided not to waste my time convincing people my idea is worthwhile. I'll just show them.

A young boy, maybe seven or eight years old, runs into the room. A younger girl follows at his heels. "Uncle Nee, can we go outside and play basketball? Nana said we can."

Nehi exchanges silent approval with his sister, Oni, and then stands. Jacqui hops up too. "I want my HORSE rematch."

"Mind if I join?" I ask.

Nehi tilts his head. "You ball?"

I respond by standing up. He's the shortest brother, and I'm nearly as tall as him barefoot. He makes a big show of eyeing me up and down, then nods once and leads the way. Ben stays behind but wishes me luck.

The community basketball court is two blocks away. The kids run ahead of us but stop at the intersections to wait for the adults to catch up so we can cross the street together. This wasn't the activity I had in mind when I'd chosen my outfit. But I haven't played basketball in so long, and I miss it. I used to shoot around every so often with my little cousins, but since they're now more interested in video games and phones, the activity has been sidelined.

The kids spend a good twenty minutes double dribbling, throwing the ball as far up as their puny arms will allow, and running around before they're tired and want to go to the swings at the playground beside the court. Their uncles allow it, and then we begin our game of HORSE. This, I can do just fine in my shoes of choice.

Jacqui calls out "Ladies first," though Nehi was ready to shoot for it. I start with a simple shot from the free throw line, since it's known to trip up even professional players. It's muscle memory for me, so I sink the shot easily. Nehi follows with a soft swish. Jacqui puts a little too much power behind his shot, and it deflects off the back part of the rim. That's an *H* for him.

We go on, taking turns with who picks the shot that the other two must match. When Jacqui gets eliminated, missing five shots to spell *HORSE*, I'm at *HORS*, and Nehi is at *HOR*.

"Tiwanda will be joining you soon," Nehi says cockily.

It's my turn to pick the spot, so I take the ball from him and go to the corner three-point shot he missed on the opposite side a few letters ago. I sink it. He doesn't seem insecure as he goes to replicate it, but it still swirls in, then bounces out.

"Are you serious?" he yells, gathering up the rebound and bouncing it hard against the concrete with two hands. "I was robbed."

"Stop complaining and shoot your shot, *Nee*." I put an emphasis on the nickname his niece calls him.

We go a few rounds of perfect shooting. I try to get him caught up in basic midrange shots, but his cockiness is buffeted by his consistency. I even try another corner shot, but he doesn't miss it a third time. Finally, he goes for a half-court shot on his turn. He's forfeited his pick twice before trying this Hail Mary. This time, the ball goes in with a resounding swish. He's celebrating before I even get the ball to take my turn and try to make it myself. I launch the ball in the direction of the hoop, stumbling a bit as I land. It doinks off the backboard.

Nehi launches into another round of celebration. The kids join in, mostly because they were ready to go home ten jump shots ago. He doesn't stop his showboating until we make it back to the house.

"You weren't half-bad," Nehi says as we walk into the foyer. "Better competition than this one." He slaps the back of his hand against his brother's arm.

"Oh good," Efe says as we walk farther into the house. "One of you help me with this cake."

"I told her to let me bring a cake from the bakery," Oni says as she ushers her kids upstairs to freshen up.

I'm sure Efe was speaking to her sons, but I volunteer. I use the guest bathroom quickly and join her in the kitchen. She's currently focused on the pan full of plantains frying over the fire when I join her.

"Ah. Thank you." She nods to the oven mitts. The Bundt cake inside looks and smells perfect. The golden-brown color is a satisfying sight.

"It's an apple-cinnamon cake," Efe explains. "My first American friend taught me to make it. Now whenever my church has an event it's, 'Efe, are you going to bring that cake?' Usually I top it with a caramel glaze, but it won't make much difference."

"I can whip it up if you want. Shouldn't take long."

She tells me where to find the pot, brown sugar, butter, and whipping cream. I come across chopped pecans in the pantry, and she gives me the go-ahead to add them to the glaze.

"Going to school for baking is fanciful, no?" she asks when I explain how I picked up these skills.

"Very," I agree.

"But now you're making it a business—impressive. I always tell Benoit, 'You make good furniture, why not go sell it?' But it's always, 'No, Mama, it's my art.' Pfft."

195

As I laugh with her, I catch sight of Ben in the dining room setting the table with his niece and nephew. It's mostly an open floor plan, so each word of our conversation is easily heard. He scowls in our direction but dismisses it with a shake of his head as he refocuses on his task.

We all get settled around the dining room table. Dinner consists of the roasted chicken and peppers Ben's dad was doting on, with rice and yellow curry sauce. The plantains Efe made are delicious. I'm seated between Ben and Nehi, who calls me "runner-up" at every opportunity.

"Tiwanda," Ben's dad addresses me in his gruff yet trustworthy voice. "Tell us, is Ben a good mentor?"

I'm midchew, so I can't respond immediately. Ben's siblings pounce on the opening.

"I knew it," Nehi says.

"Ben gives Dr. Doom a run for his money," Jacqui says. "Always expecting the worst."

"He's *preparing* for the worst. It's different." Oni defends him. "Though, I was surprised he signed up for this."

"He's good," I say, after finally emptying my mouth. Most of the faces staring back at me are unconvinced. "All of the other mentees love him."

Peripherally, I'm aware of how sharply Ben turns his head to me. Efe begins speaking before I can try to catch the initial expression there, before he undoubtedly covers it up with something impenetrable.

"Of course he's good, I'm his mother."

"She's a professor and mentors young academics." Nehi leans toward me as he supplies this information.

"Our children are very different," Ben's dad says. "When we moved here from Benin in '91, Benoit was five and Oni four. Their first years of life were in a country going through many changes. Then we lived with my brother and his wife in South Chicago until we could get our own place."

Efe nods along. "Back then, there weren't many of us. We found community in church and with other West Africans. Now the Beninese community is bustling. It's incredible."

"So yes, maybe Benoit is a bit jaded and Oni worries too much for her own good," says Ben's dad. Oni frowns at this. "Jacqui and Nehikhare were born here, and their optimism and lousy French prove it."

"I can hold a conversation," Nehi protests, then says something in French to drive home his point. His dad just shakes his head and takes another bite of rice.

I shrug. "Sounded good to me."

Nehi smiles and adds another string of musical words, adapting a lower and—dare I say—suggestive tone.

"All right," Ben says. His next words are in French and lack the romantic quality of Nehi's. Yet, for an unknown reason I should probably try to unpack later, his brisk delivery does it more for me. I shift in my seat and pop another plantain into my mouth. No one volunteers a translation, and the conversation switches back to English with nothing more than a raised eyebrow from Efe.

After dinner, Ben's niece pulls me upstairs to play. Oni tries to get me out of it, but I don't mind. I'd think the kids lived here by the number of toys they have in their wooden chest pushed into the corner. We play until I catch the time and realize Ben and I have two hours to get to the ReStore before it closes.

I go downstairs in search of Ben and hear his voice immediately from the kitchen among the sound of running water and the clack of dishes. I start to round the wall and enter when I hear my name and stop on reflex.

"Tiwanda," Efe says. "She's gorgeous. And smart! And knows her way around the kitchen."

Ben grunts what I think is agreement. Or vainly hope it is.

"How old is she?"

"Thirty, I think."

He thinks? He was just at my thirtieth birthday-slash-quitting party—he better know.

"You should set her up with Nehi. They get on well."

What sounds like a plastic dish hits the ground. "Mama." Ben pauses a bit, and I can imagine he's casting a look around to see if anyone is nearby to overhear. I take a step back, farther away from the entrance, and bump into the table. A small carved statue sways, and I reach to steady it.

Ben continues, "I can't just pass people along."

"She's not yours to pass. You are friends, no? Business acquaintances?"

"No. I mean, yes. But Nehi? Come on, you know he doesn't have his life together enough for her."

"Tiwanda could be just what he needs."

Ben changes the subject. I wait for them to exchange several sentences on this new topic before appearing at the entryway, in a way I hope comes across as casual.

"Hey." Efe brightens at my appearance. Ben dims. "Are we still going to the ReStore? It closes in two hours."

Efe calls Nehi from the living room to replace Ben in the kitchen so we can get over to the store. Ben drives Jacqui's truck and turns on the music, saving us from having to speak. I don't know what's on his mind, but it's nice to be silent after so much time spent talking to people. My energy is shot, yet I'm so fulfilled. After basketball with Ben's brothers, it felt natural being around his family.

Ben knows his way around the ReStore. He goes straight to the aisle that has long pieces of shelved plywood.

"I'm thinking something like this. The depth is enough that it'll support a good deal of weight. I can use steel for the frame and then figure out how to make the stands."

"Should we use a darker wood to match the kitchen?"

"Whatever plywood we get, I can cover it with linoleum. You can go simple with black, or maybe a pattern. I'll email you a website."

We load the plywood onto our dolly and go to check out. Though he tries to thwart me, I pay for it. It's the least I can do with him putting in all this free labor. We assure a worker we can handle loading it in the truck ourselves, then leave with our haul. With the disappearing sun, it's become a few degrees cooler outside.

"This would've been the perfect time to play basketball," I say, thinking of how the sun blinded us at some angles earlier.

Ben glances at me and lowers the tailgate so we can access the bed of the truck. He puts the first piece of plywood in. Since the dolly blocks me, I go on the same side as Ben and pass the next pieces to him.

"Nehi said you were better competition than Jac."

"I see why Jacqui wanted a rematch so bad. Nehi is a terrible person to lose to."

"Why do you think I didn't go? He has a short-guy complex."

I laugh, because it's something only a tall family would say about a man who's at least six one. We're both silent as we get the rest of the wood in the truck bed arranged so that it won't slide too much on the drive home. As Ben closes the tailgate he says, "Maybe Nehi . . ." He turns to face me, and whatever he was about to say dies on his lips. Though he's taken care to clear his face of expression, I can tell something is troubling him. Concern tugs at me, and I take a half step toward him. Presumptuous of me to assume my proximity would bring comfort, but he starts again.

"Maybe you and Nehi might want to hang out." He can't even hold eye contact with me through the duration of that sentence. His eyes skitter midway, but he wills them back to mine by the end. My heart drops at the suggestion. When he'd so immediately rejected the idea to his mom, I'd felt . . . I don't know, protected? Or maybe it's just that I'd hoped there was another reason, beyond his brother's immaturity, why he felt strongly against the idea.

You know what? *No.*

I take another step, wedging myself in the tight space between him and the dolly, my side pressing against the back of the truck. His head and shoulders flinch back a bit, but he holds his ground and my gaze.

"You'd want that?" I ask.

He stares at me impassively. I watch closely for the answer, because I have an inkling it'll show even if not verbally confirmed. My shoulder twitches up along with my eyebrows, imploring any response from him. A couple rolls by us with their cart, and still he doesn't break. I'm about to give up and return our dolly when it happens. It's the slightest squint of his eyes. According to my Ben records, that's a signal of his objection. Vindicated, I nod. His eyes dip to my lips, so quick I could have missed it if I weren't so attuned.

Benoit, who I once wrote off as nothing more than a thorn in my side, a Met match I couldn't get rid of, now stands in front of me as someone I voluntarily spent my Saturday with. What I'd classified as merely an aesthetic-level attraction might have morphed into . . . I'm almost scared if I name it, I'll chase it away.

I take a half step forward until my chest presses against his. My sandals give me extra height, so when I angle my face up to his, his lips are barely an inch away. Unlike before, his response comes quickly. He brings his lips to mine, a short brush, then pulls away. That's enough for me to realize something is here. The slight sensation traveled into the pit of my diaphragm. Desire drives me to kiss him again, but I only catch his bottom lip. I think I've lost him, that he'll step away, but then he lowers his head. This time, he presses his lips against mine fully.

When I open my mouth to his, he moves even closer. I almost lose my balance, but he reaches around me and grabs on to the tailgate, shifting us so that my back presses securely against the truck. His body is like a wall, closing us off into our own private alcove. His free hand moves up to the side of my neck, and he leverages his thumb on the underside of my chin to tilt my head up. The gentle pressure on that sensitive patch of skin might be the most intimate touch I've ever experienced.

A gentle breeze helps to keep the heat building between us at bay. I lick at his lips. He becomes bold enough to release the truck and settle his hand at my waist. I arch my hips up into his, and at the contact, a car horn blares. We break apart. I peek over Ben's shoulder to confirm the honk wasn't meant for us. But no, it definitely was. Across the row, there's a young guy laughing behind his steering wheel while the lady in the passenger seat swats at his arm.

"I'll go return the dolly," Ben says. He unlocks the door for me to enter before wheeling it away.

I kissed Ben. *In public.* And I didn't throw up. Thinking about it now makes me a little nauseated, but in the moment? I didn't give two shits about the setting. Neither of us initiates discussing what happened on the ride back to his parents' house. I try to convince myself I'm avoiding it because I haven't figured out what it meant to me, but really I'm nervous that talking about it will ruin the possibility I feel, just like it did with Elliot. I unbuckle my seat belt before he's even parked the truck, beyond ready to make my escape.

But he doesn't seem eager to pick it apart either. He tells me he'll get the plywood out later with his brothers' help. I go back inside to say goodbye to each of his family members. His mom invites me to stay longer to watch a movie, but I use the long drive home as an excuse. She walks me to the door along with Ben, inadvertently providing a buffer. I hug them both, trying my best to keep the two embraces identical.

Efe says I'm welcome back anytime, and I beam at her, my penchant for holding on to people I've connected with stirring within me. She leans her head back into the house and calls out Nehi's name. After raising four children, she's perfected the volume and tone required to get them moving. He's at the door with us in no time.

"Give Tiwanda your number in case she wants to join us for dinner when Ben isn't in town."

At this request from Efe, Nehi's eyes immediately slide toward Ben. As do mine. When Ben doesn't show an ounce of objection, just continues looking passively at me, Nehi haltingly says, "Yeah, sure," and rattles off his number.

"I'll be in touch about the riser," Ben says. The formal cadence of his voice shrivels any hope that whatever thoughts he has locked away bask our kiss in a positive light.

# CHAPTER
# THIRTY-ONE

Me: Did you see that game winner??

Me: This is Tiwanda btw

Nehi: Jac owes me lunch with that win

Me: And I'm sure you won't let him forget it

Nehi: Not in this lifetime

It's the night after dinner with Ben's family. Of course, watching game seven of the NBA Finals, cuddled on my couch with Penelope, made me think of them. I wondered if they were sitting around the living room together again, critiquing players' performances. Or maybe since tomorrow's a weekday, they watched separately in their individual homes. Wherever Nehi was, he was sure to be showboating. Since I had the means, and a bold streak triggered by Ben's reshuttered walls, I put Nehi's number to use.

Our brief exchange is trivial, but something about it feels right. It's counterintuitive to tie more strings to Ben, what with his impending rejection and all. Still, it brings me comfort doing the little I can to keep the people I want in my life. Maybe I can't stop Elise from moving, nor Ben from putting distance between us, but I can send a text to Nehi and kick-start a line of communication.

My phone vibrates on my belly, making me jump and Penelope reposition with passive-aggressive circling in place.

Nehi: I have a job interview Friday

Nehi: I have a rule not to tell the fam until I get an offer because, well you've seen how they are. But I want this one a lot, and since you don't have a job either it feels like you're the right person to tell.

Me: Excuse me, I have a job! Kind of.

Me: I think it's brave of you to change jobs often. Restarting is . . . a lot.

Nehi: You want to go somewhere with me?

~

I meet Nehi in Bronzeville two days later, a neighborhood on the South Side. Grandma's family used to live here when she was young, and whenever we're in the car driving through the area, I'm treated to a bit of history from her childhood point of view. She says her mother, who owned a hair salon, met Louis Armstrong at a dance hall. She always points out where the old theater used to be, and how jealous she was when her parents left her in the care of her older brother to attend the play.

Bronzeville in the present isn't the same as it was in its heyday, but events like today's summer festival are aimed at bringing some of that magic back. I meet Nehi at a booth near the entrance that's stocked with an array of visitor guides, foldable maps of the neighborhood, and flyers for upcoming events. We grab a map and take pictures of the flyers we don't want to tote around. From the main stage, a local jazz band showers the lounging audience and booth hoppers with vibrant tunes. I make us stop at a handcrafted jewelry stand and an essential-oil booth. Nehi zeroes in on a shaved-ice stand because he's burning up in his nonsensical chinos and polo shirt.

"This is a random place to want to meet up, but I love summer festivals, so good pick."

Nehi bobs his head up and down as he surveys the remaining booths we've yet to pass. We're soon served our shaved-ice cups and continue along our route. There's a dedicated section for informational booths. Many have community resources, like the one from the Chicago Public Library. I'm mostly focused on my pineapple-mango shaved ice, but Nehi steers us toward one booth in particular.

Two people sit under a purple tent, manning the cloth-covered table crammed with pamphlets and trinkets for kids. With no other festivalgoers at their booth, they're attuned to our approach and greet us immediately.

"Hi, we're A Welcome Home, and we provide resources and pro bono lawyers for immigrants. I'm Becca. I'm a paralegal."

"I'm Mark, and I'm not."

Through their amusement, they jointly explain Mark's role of outreach and resource coordinator.

"I'm Nehi. I actually have an interview with you all later this week. Saw the booth here and figured I'd stop by."

I fill my gaping mouth with another spoonful of shaved ice while Nehi slips into easy conversation with Becca and Mark. He's lucked out because Mark says he'll be one of the staff members interviewing him. It's not until after Nehi finishes sharing an abbreviated story of his family's immigration experience that they realize I never introduced myself, expert nod-alonger that I am. I plug Corinne's nonprofit and grab a card to pass along, since it seems like a good fit for collaboration. Nehi deftly excuses us under the guise of an unfulfilled promise to buy me a turkey leg. Then we're off, Nehi successfully positioned at the forefront of the job candidates.

"Sounded like y'all could have talked for an hour," I say once we're far enough away and *not* heading toward the food truck selling turkey legs.

"Don't want to run out of things to say in the interview. Thanks for being my wingman."

"Your unsuspecting wingman." I pull at his sleeve. "Explains your outfit of choice. What position are you interviewing for?"

"General aid. It comes with a lot of variety. I could be sitting at booths like that a year from now."

"If you are, I'll come bring you shaved ice."

As the meandering crowd thickens with the after-work rush, we leave the booth area and sit on the bleachers near the main stage. It's mostly empty, between the folks who brought their own chairs and the steady sunlight blazing on the metal seats. I balance on the edge, careful not to let my bare skin make contact.

"What's up with you and my brother?" The question comes with no preamble.

I tilt the mostly liquid remains of my shaved-ice cup into my mouth while chancing a quick assessing glance at Nehi before responding. "You think something's up?"

"It's not obvious, but my brother is obvious. You know what I mean?"

"Not at all. Ben is the opposite of obvious."

"You only think that because you didn't grow up making it your life's mission to learn how to push his buttons."

Nehi has the clear advantage on that. I'm mainly going off how Ben can kiss me senseless one moment and then say, "I'll be in touch about some wood, but definitely not mine!" the next. And then nothing, blatant nothing, the next.

"What should I watch for, then, if you're a Ben expert?" I'll add his advice to my compact dictionary of Ben's subtle face tells.

"Biggest thing that tipped me off was his annoyance with me and Mama whenever you were involved. He's only covertly annoyed with things he cares about but doesn't want to care about. But never mind that. Ben will answer anything you ask him. If he hesitates, just tell him to be open. He has to be reminded sometimes, especially if it's something he's still working out in his head."

Nehi's simple suggestion tugs the light-bulb switch in my mind. In not forcing Ben to talk about us immediately, I gave him the perfect opportunity to retreat into that brain of his. We really do think too much alike.

"Thanks for selling out your brother's secrets," I say.

"I told you, it's my lifelong mission. Emphasis on the lifelong."

~

"It's ready," Elise says after I answer her phone call. I'm at home, trying to design a package menu for potential customers. There's excitement and pride in Elise's voice, so I know instantly she could only be referring to the mural. I've missed this voice. I spent the past few days reaching for my phone to hit her line, only to decide against it. I resolved to rely on myself because Elise would be gone soon. Like a runner preparing for a marathon, I have to condition myself for such a feat.

On the lookout, Elise stops me as I approach the door to my shop and tells me to close my eyes. I oblige and allow her to take Penelope's carry case from me and lead me the few remaining steps to the entrance. Devin comes up to my other side.

"Are you ready?" they ask. I nod. "Okay, you can look."

I open my eyes to the most breathtaking wall I've ever seen. It's got **Bathe in Chocolate** in large, swooping lettering. The first two words are painted in light blue, and *Chocolate* is painted in a glossy brown. Around it, there's a collage of color. There are groups of people, heterogeneous enough to be assumed friends, making soap. Other groups I assume represent families based on the varying heights of parents versus children. Even the smaller space fillers are cool: a stack of bars of soap, a tin tub with bubbles spilling out of it, boxes and boxes of chocolate bonbons, a person climbing into a chocolate-spewing fountain. It's only when I'm scanning it from top to bottom, focusing more on the easter eggs, that I notice the group of friends painted the largest. I take a step closer. It's not a super detailed rendition. There aren't any facial features. But when I see the skin tones, hairstyles, and comparative body sizes, there's no doubt. Devin drew us. Elise between the two of us, along with Cory and Corinne.

I turn to face Devin with tears pooling in my eyes. Elise stands beside them, nodding emphatically. I wrap my arms around Devin in an embrace. "I love it," I say.

"I'm glad," Devin's stifled reply reverberates against my shoulder.

"And I'm sorry I blamed you for Elise leaving."

"What?"

I release Devin and hug Elise next, painfully aware that there's only a limited amount of time left to do this. It suddenly feels very foolish that I spent the past week avoiding reaching out to her in the moments I normally would. Whatever preliminary detachment scheme my brain is employing, I'll have to actively push back against it. Because this is not me losing Elise. This is Elise getting one step closer to her dreams.

We take pictures of the wall, then pose in front of it. It's every bit as Instagram worthy as I hoped it would be. Afterward, we go to lunch at a nearby restaurant, sitting in the patio area where Pen is allowed. When the topic of their California plans comes up, I don't even flinch. At least not outwardly. That's progress.

When I get home to check my email, I see Devin has sent me the invoice for the mural. My eyes narrow at the bold-font $0.00 with a note: Opening gift. I know Elise coached them to not try this in person because she knows I would've refused it. But here in my solitude I take a deep breath and accept that people care about me and have the right to show that in their way.

~

There's plenty to keep me preoccupied and not thinking of Ben. The chairs I order are delivered, along with my other supplies. The cabinet inventory is nearly complete. Pilar comes over to my condo to practice our presentations and tighten them where needed, since the pitch event is this Saturday. So no, I'm not thinking of Ben. Not thinking about how every email or text I've gotten from him makes my heart drum in my chest, and then ache from the effort once I see it's related to my riser. Not thinking of our final one-on-one meeting scheduled for tomorrow. And definitely not thinking about that kiss.

I'm not thinking so intently that when I go to raid the refrigerator for snacks, I drop several containers of random goods I've accumulated over the past week. Some of the containers pop open, including a thin ganache I'd made for molten chocolate cakes. My tile floor looks like a slasher movie set. I wave Pilar off from helping me clean up my mess. Instead, she runs through her presentation again. Without me in the living room, watching and taking feedback notes, she gets through it much smoother.

"We should order food," I say once everything is cleaned up. The knees of my sweatpants have ganache on them, as well as my shirt somehow. "Let me just change and take Pen for a quick walk."

Penelope's head pops up from her bed at the mention of walking, and she begins to stretch in preparation.

"I'll find some options," Pilar volunteers.

I change and treat my clothes with some stain-removal spray, dropping them into the empty washing machine to launder with my next load. Then I go to put on my tennis shoes near the door. When Penelope's tinkling collar doesn't sound the moment I take her leash out of the basket, I look to her bed. Empty.

"Come on, Pen." I rarely have to convince her to come to me once I have her leash in hand. When she doesn't obey, I ask Pilar, "Where's Penelope?"

"I thought she followed you," Pilar says.

Finally, I hear her collar, but it's not moving toward me. I follow the sound to the kitchen. In the moment I spot her, she's sticking her head under the cabinet to get at the baseboard. Successful in her quest, she begins to chew.

"What do you have?"

My voice is loud enough to scare her backward, dropping half of what's in her mouth. It's a bonbon I made days ago, my take on buckeyes. It consists of peanut butter, which she loves, but also dark chocolate. A choked shriek sounds from my throat as I hurry to Penelope. I scoop her up and dig my fingers into her mouth, trying to prevent her from swallowing. I'm too late. The only thing on my fingers is saliva and a trace of peanut butter.

How is this happening? A container of chocolates fell, but I threw all of them into the trash. Or so I thought. Maybe I was so focused on cleaning up all the syrupy ganache that I missed that one. Maybe I missed more.

"How many did you eat?" I ask Pen. She looks back at me impassively, then tries to wriggle away.

Pilar joins me in the kitchen, worry straining her eyes.

"She never comes in here," I say.

"What kind was it?"

"Bittersweet. Sixty-three percent. She at least ate half of one. Maybe more, I don't know. Shit." I stare at Penelope as if she will offer up the information I need.

"I think you should take her . . ."

"I know, I know." It's just that I haven't exactly had a chance to find a new vet. I thought I had months until I would need one. It's still within regular hours, but I send Elliot a text anyway. Then I quickly gather up the essentials and hustle out of the door. Pilar insists on driving so I can monitor Penelope along the way.

The receptionist is expecting us and calls out for Sue. It's the same vet tech who did Penelope's initial checkup. Though she's tender with both me and Pen, her familiar face serves to intensify my shame. Sue leads us to a room immediately. I gesture for Pilar to follow us back when she hovers in the waiting area. It'll be nice to have a friend, and a buffer once Elliot is involved. I sit Pen on the paper-covered bed.

"Dr. Pace is just wrapping up," Sue says. She gently smooths the fur down Penelope's back as the dog looks around the bright room with distrust. "No symptoms yet, so you probably caught it quick enough."

Elliot knocks twice and enters the room in a rush. "Hey, Tiwanda, P." His eyes are on mine for just a second before he goes to Penelope. "How much was consumed?"

"I don't know," I say helplessly. I try to describe the size of the bon-bon with my fingers. "Half of that, but only the shell is chocolate. If I missed cleaning up more than that one, she could've . . . I don't know."

"Any symptoms? Vomiting? Thirst? Anxiousness?"

I shake my head. "She wasn't anxious until we stepped in here." Understandable, because my anxiety also ratcheted up a notch upon arrival.

"All right. I'm going to induce vomiting. Time is of the essence when it comes to poisoning, so good job getting her here quickly."

My diaphragm squeezes the last bit of air out. Despite this being entirely my fault, Elliot has made me feel like I've done something right.

With Sue's help, Elliot inserts an IV into Penelope's leg to administer the medication. In minutes, Pen begins to stir. They have a bowl waiting and gently direct her to expel the contents of her stomach there. I'm sitting in a chair watching it unfold, which Sue suggested undoubtedly so I'm out of the way. Pilar hasn't moved from her corner since it all started.

With gloved hands, they sift through the vomit. Pilar makes a gagging noise from her corner, which makes Elliot scoff. Next, they give Penelope a bit of activated charcoal to prevent her body from absorbing toxins from the chocolate. Then, they're done. Pen is lying down on the bed, looking like a sad lump of fur. Elliot takes his gloves off and pets her.

"Just continue to monitor her, and text me if you're worried," he says.

"She's going to be all right," says Sue. She gives Pen's head one last gingerly stroke before leaving us.

Pilar pushes off from the wall. "I feel sick, so I'm going to get some water before I, too, need the vom bowl. Nice seeing you again, E."

"You too, P."

Once Pilar is at the door and Elliot's back is to her, she gives me an exaggerated wink.

"Thank you," I say. I figure it's a good place to start. Though my gratefulness will truly be shown when I have to pay for this visit, minus whatever Pen's health insurance covers.

"It's what I'm here for," Elliot says. He rises and goes to the sink to wash his hands.

"And sorry that I had to come to you like this. I'll stop procrastinating and find Pen a new vet."

Elliot's head turns abruptly. "Why would you do that?"

I know I'm not imagining the awkwardness between us. The only time it receded was when everyone's focus was on Penelope. How could it not be awkward? This was the place we first met, after all. Shall we continue gathering here for Pen's checkups or, God forbid, other emergencies, so I can get a good look at how my potential soul mate is getting along without me?

"So you won't have to see me?" It turns into a question, though I'd intended it as a statement.

He takes a couple of paper towels and dries his hands before responding. "Tiwanda, I still want to see you. I still like you. That doesn't go away over a week. I suspect it won't, ever."

I reciprocate his sentiments. Elliot is kind, gentle, and caring. There's so much to like about him. It's hard not to feel like something is wrong with me because I can't fit with him like I'd aspired to. With time, I imagine he'd make me want to give him everything he wants. The marriage, the children, stepsibling dogs. But at what cost to my own wants? All of this uncertainty makes me want to not make a decision at all. Reject Met, even if that means rejecting its connection to my mom.

"Well, good." I scoop up Penelope and nudge my shoulder into Elliot's. "Because it would be a pain in the ass finding another vet."

# CHAPTER
# THIRTY-TWO

Though Penelope exhibits no signs of distress in the morning, I email Ben asking if we can have our final meeting remotely due to a family emergency. The wording, though accurate, was maybe too broad. He calls me within the hour.

"How is your family? We can reschedule if you're not up to it," he says.

I immediately start brainstorming which of my already-deceased family members I can lie about, but I suppress the urge. Ben is my friend and he deserves the truth, even if I was trying to be slick and use any excuse to avoid seeing him.

"It's Penelope; she's hanging in there. Just got her paws on some chocolate, so I'm monitoring her."

"Oh shit. That's dangerous."

"Yeah, but I got her to the vet in time. Elliot. He's her vet. Anyway, I really don't want to let her out of my sight right now."

"I understand." There's a beat of silence. "How about I come to you, then?"

I frown at the phone as if his face is there. Are we ready to do this? To mutually get out of our heads and lay our cards on the table for comparison? "Would you be coming as my mentor or the man who made out with me last weekend?"

He coughs a bit. "Fair, we're long overdue to discuss that. It'll be both, then."

Ben arrives with much fanfare from Pen, who rises from her bed to greet him at the door, placing her little paws on his shins. He picks her up, and she indulgently allows him to fluff the fur on her head a few times before she's returned to the floor. She trots back to her spot, not interested enough to follow us around.

"That's the most excitement she's shown since the incident," I say.

Ben looks rather pleased with himself, as if I hadn't taught him the cheat codes for Pen's approval. I lead him to my office. My presentation is already pulled up on my laptop. If only one successful thing comes out of this, it better be his reinforcement that I'm good to go.

We each take a chair. Instead of doing a full run-through, I just click through the slides and tell him what I plan to expand upon for each. Both of our gazes are careful not to stray far from the computer screen. He gives me a few notes along the way, mostly moving information around for a better flow. Overall, it's in good shape. I shut my laptop, agreeing to make the changes later.

Then I turn to Ben, our knees colliding from my adjustment. I roll my chair backward a bit as he tries to scoot the borrowed dining table chair away. Ben's wearing dark-blue dress pants and a short-sleeve button-up. The soft peach color was made for his deep-brown skin tone.

"Our second order of business . . . ," I start, since my mind seems to already be heading in that direction. It's not until I speak that I realize Ben seems to have been just as distracted. His chin lifts as he forces his gaze back to my face. I can't fault him, since I put on my favorite form-fitting biker shorts and a wide-collared shirt that hangs off my shoulder with distracting him in mind. Or tempting him. Can't make it easy for him to turn me down.

Truthfully, I don't know if he's who Met would want me to pick. In an alternate dimension, it would be Elliot, and the idea of having a family with him would be too sweet to hope for. Or I could be meant to join the vision Pilar shared with me of building a village. Ben's mom seems to think Nehi and I are a good match, and she's the expert on her children.

Ben has become a friend but, I've been shocked to discover, one whose touch inspires unfriendly thoughts. I've spent all my recent days actively not thinking about him only for the suppressed thoughts to catch up to me in bed, when I have no distractions to deter them. This intense attraction is so rare for me, I don't want to ignore it. I want to excavate it for every ounce of pleasure I can.

"Right," Ben says. "You should know, my behavior last weekend was in no way appropriate for a mentor."

"Kind of figured it wasn't on your list of duties."

He's undeterred by my flippant tone. "I think it's important we're transparent about this. Do you feel like I took advantage of you?"

"Before or after I pushed my tongue into your mouth?" I shift in my chair as my words cause him to startle, his eyes darting to and quickly away from my lips. "Ben, I get why you feel the need to do this. But honestly, the conversation should be with someone *not you*. Our mentor liaison, probably." I knew this role existed, I just didn't have any reason to use them before.

"Oh. True. I'll tell Lisa to contact you." He pulls out his phone to make a note.

I place my hand on his knee to bring his attention back to me. "Maybe hold off on that? I'd like to add a few more things on the list to discuss with her."

"That's not funny."

I lean back into my chair and survey him. His face isn't as impassive as I'm sure he hopes it is. With time, I think, I could get as good at reading him as Nehi is. "You know what I've been thinking since Saturday, in the days you've only emailed me about business bull?" He asks *What?* in the way his eyes shift up a bit, then back to mine. I continue as if he'd spoken it aloud. "What would we have done if that car didn't honk at us, if we weren't in a very public parking lot at all? Like we are now."

He swallows, and it's gratifying to see the instant effect my words have on him. And it's not a tease—it's an offering.

"Tiwanda." When he says my name, his lids fall shut. It doesn't work to contain his lust. He wants me as much as I want him. It leaks out through his strained voice. "I'm trying to do the appropriate thing here."

"We can take it back, then. Not literally, obviously," I add at his skeptical brows. I could never forget the feel of his lips against mine. Or his body pressed so close it felt like shelter. "Symbolically. It doesn't have to mean anything."

"Right."

If I hadn't gotten intel from Nehi, I would have accepted this with a nod and walked him to the door. But armed with Nehi's brotherly insight, I understand this isn't clear enough, neither for me nor Ben. Me and the conclusions I draw from whatever information is available if it means protecting myself from future hurt. Ben and his muted expressions, withholding judgment until he deems the information adequate. Neither of us is at our best without having the full picture.

"Did it mean something?" I ask.

"It's your call."

I ignore his avoidance of the question for now because actually, I do want to figure out my own call first. I like Ben. Maybe more than like, since I've liked a lot of people who never inspired me to affix my face to theirs in the middle of a parking lot. Whatever has stealthily built between us is unique, that's for sure.

"If we said it didn't mean anything, I would be pretending."

I hadn't noticed the tension in Ben's shoulders until he releases it. "That's true for me as well."

"Okay great. Now that we have an understanding, I need you to not do this." I move my flexed hand in a large circle encompassing his body.

"Do what?"

"You're giving me fragments. Can you be open with me?"

"I've been open."

"When we're talking about business or your life, yes. But right now, talking about us, this isn't you open. I've seen you. Talk to me for real."

He nods through a deep breath that I hope will release even more of his will to hold his unrefined perceptions in. "I didn't expect it would mean much to you. I know how much you liked Elliot, so I convinced myself that I somehow coerced you. You said you wanted things with him you don't typically want with people. How can I compete with that? It felt like the breaking-up period with my ex lasted months. I thought it would finally end when I got the last of my things out of her condo. But it didn't, not until I realized I'd developed feelings for you. So yes, it meant something. Not that I know what to do about it."

I never considered it a competition between my Met matches. They all stood on their own. His mention of Elliot catches me off guard, because although Elliot and I had something, it's clear to me now that so did Ben and I. I've made a genuine connection with all my matches. But in typical Tiwanda fashion, it took me a while to recognize it with Ben, especially after I'd eliminated him in my head. Still, the potential of us lurked in the background, waiting for me to notice. The path forward is murky for me too, though. For all I know, there's a roadblock awaiting me once again.

"I know what's wrong," I say with sudden conviction. "We don't know what to do because we still don't have enough information. This calls for further research."

A compliant smile ghosts his lips. "How do we do that?"

"Easy. Picking up where we left off."

I rise to my feet and hold my hand out to him. He stares at my hopeful outreach attempt for at least five seconds before loosely grasping my hand as he stands. I lead him to my bedroom, each step notching up the electric feel of anticipation.

"I think it went something like this?" I close the distance between us, mirroring our positions from the ReStore parking lot. He nods and cradles my face in his hands. When his eyes survey mine, I try to project enough certainty for the both of us. It must work, because he lowers his head to capture my lips. I'm relieved by the rush of feelings, as if it were a perfectly functioning faucet just waiting for the handle to be raised.

We restart, but this time we don't stop. We get out of our own heads and chase whatever sensation feels right. My hands sliding below Ben's collar, his grazing my curves and settling on my generous derriere. We desperately contend with clothing in our attempt to explore each other, until we separate with breathless clarity that it's not enough. Ben's steady, heated gaze gets me stripping my clothes off down to my undergarments. I press a quick kiss to his jaw, then get settled against the elaborate pillow arrangement propped on the headboard. When I slide my hand down my body, he begins undressing. His movements are deliberate. Buttons freed one at a time, the slow unhooking of his belt. Each layer he removes feels like a declaration.

Then my bed dips with the weight of him. Ben lies on his side and leans over me, the soft planes of his abdomen searing my skin, and presses kisses in seemingly no predetermined pathway. He moves from my neck to my sternum to my shoulder. At my nod, he replaces my hand with his own and covers my mouth in a possessive kiss. He's unrelenting until I fall apart, as if my release is an agreement. Just in case it is, I take my time coaxing one out of him as well.

# CHAPTER
# THIRTY-THREE

So it's Ben? I type into the Ask Met screen.

*You tell me.*

I could probably count on one hand how many of these Ask Met answers actually proved timely and helpful. Most were just vague or deflections. That could also be blamed on my tactless questioning. Having it at my daily disposal might have made me just a tad bit wasteful. I posed questions knowing that regardless of whether or not they yielded tangible guidance, I could try again the next day.

So when Met follows its useless answer with the message, *You have three days remaining for this feature*, my eyes bulge. Not even a week's notice, Met? Rude. Hello, Kettle, call me Pot.

Three days, three questions. I have to make them count.

Friday:

Why did you pick these four matches?

*They all complement you in different ways.*

Saturday:

How will I know if I picked my soul mate?

*I presume your soul will feel mated.*

And if it doesn't? If I'm not capable of that feeling?
(That was a nonanswer. I deserve another question!)

*Souls aren't bound by what we think we know of ourselves. You should know that by now.*

The business pitch event is Saturday evening. My mentee group, along with two other groups based in the Chicago area, will present in the conference room of a swanky downtown hotel. The board of the grant program will be there, of course, and their judgment will decide who is awarded the extra grant money. Other entrepreneurs and interested parties will also attend, including faculty and students from Kellogg business school, since the program will be partnering with EMBERS starting the next round.

Even though we were kind of lab rats with the structure, I'm glad to be a part of this first round. I hope the program lasts for many decades, infusing the Chicago economy with more businesses owned by people of color.

I park at Cory's South Loop apartment garage, a friend perk I won't have for much longer since his lease is up in a week. From there, I take a rideshare to the venue. It seems like the least stressful option. I don't want rush-hour downtown traffic to put me in a sour mood before possibly the most important presentation of my life.

I'm the first one of my mentee group to arrive, not including Ben, who's standing near the center of the room with someone I recognize from the mentor list and another I don't. Waiters come by with platters of hors d'oeuvres, and the three of them pause their conversation to snag a few.

The best thing about tonight is that now I can reduce my interactions with Ben to only when we want to talk to each other. Not when we're obligated to have business-related check-ins. Like an algebraic equation with sets of like terms, it simplifies things. Especially since in my post-coital haze, I persuaded Ben to let what happened between us breathe for a bit. No rushing to analyze it for meaning, no serious talks about the future. I just want it to *be* for a while. Be something that occurred, something special I enjoyed, something I might want to do again.

I spot Terry, the mentor from Cleveland, as I'm on my way to the refreshments table. That diverts me for a bit, as we catch up on how placing my first supply order went. They get pulled away by another mentor, and I continue on to get a glass of water, stopping with two waiters for something similar to a tiny egg roll and an avocado sushi roll.

As I'm filling my water glass, Pilar teeters up to me, shrugging into her blazer. It's a pop of golden against the navy blue of her dress. I reach out and lay down her collar. As I wait for her to pour a glass of water for herself and dab at her forehead with one of the little square napkins piled on the table, I grab another sushi roll from the same waiter. She smiles as I take two of the little plates this time. "Just keep them coming," I say.

"You can eat right now?" Pilar asks, incredulous. "I feel sick."

"Why?" Though her outfit is on point, there is an unusual uneasiness about her.

She drops her chin and stares at me, then lifts her hand to the large projection screen at the front of the room. "Exhibit one." Then she sweeps her hand to the local news camera in the back of the room. "Exhibit two. And exhibit three is all these damn people."

I wave a dismissive hand. "We practiced for this. You know your material. This is all a show anyway. Most of these people don't have a say. This is for EMBERS to show off what we've been up to these past months. We just have to play along so we can collect our paper." I lift my hand and rub my thumb across the pads of my other fingers.

She blinks at me, then slowly starts to nod in agreement. "Your cynicism is actually helpful sometimes. Come on, let's find our table."

Victor and Yazmin have arrived and are seated with the sign language interpreters. One interpreter holds a printed paper in her hands and nods as Yazmin explains something. I gather they're prepping for the presentation from the context and the handful of signs I catch.

Tactfully seated so that Ben won't be beside me, I ask Pilar about her Sunday plans to distract her. Her shoulders relax in slow increments as she tells me about the activities that'll help her decompress. It involves going shopping for a new houseplant and a couples massage, courtesy of Gia.

When someone comes onstage to announce cocktail hour is ending soon, Ben makes his way over to our table. He makes eye contact with each of us in turn as he says, "Time to show them all what I already know."

His intimate gaze on me turns his words of encouragement into a tease that makes my chest warm. I turn to my water glass instead, acting completely normal and relaxed.

"What's wrong? Is something in your water?" Pilar asks. She picks it up to observe it closer.

I hurriedly take it from her and take a sip before she draws more attention to me. My eyes betray me and slide over to Ben, catching the upturn of his lips, though his focus is squarely on the stage. I follow suit. The second interpreter is now in place while the first speaker comes to join him.

There's a quick introduction and overview of the EMBERS Foundation's mission, and then we jump right into the pitches. Ten businesses, five to eight minutes each. Pilar checks off each business on the program with a purple pen as they present.

I'm the first of our group to go up. By the time I travel from our table to the stage, the tech team has my slide deck at the ready. I start with my short pitch—an appeal to the common experience of searching for a unique group activity. Then I touch on my background and how the idea for Bathe in Chocolate was born. Despite the many hours of work I've put in, I sum up the entire mentorship in a minute flat. Having pictures of my store helps describe it better than any words could.

Seven minutes later, I'm all done. Victor and Yazmin silently applaud me as I rejoin them at our table. Pilar squeezes my arm, then checks my name off the list with gusto. Ben gives me a single nod. There are two other businesses before Pilar is up.

At her turn, Pilar stands confidently in her three-inch heels and strides to the stage. She does phenomenally. Her only stumble, missing a talking point on one slide and having to thread it into the information for the next one, is recovered so well I'm sure I only noticed it because I've heard her run through the presentation so many times. She even works in some jokes that land successfully. Victor and Yazmin are the second-to-last presentation and do similarly well. The best part is the pictures of the full home interior decoration project they finished in time, which has the entire audience salivating. And hopefully copying down their contact information from the final slide.

It ends with quick recognition for the Chicago mentor team. The waitstaff starts prepping the side tables with flutes of champagne and wine to encourage more mixing. Before anyone can leave, the mentees and mentors are called onstage for a group picture, and then the board members are called to join us. It takes two pitch presentations' worth of time to get those done.

Elise, Devin, Corinne, and Cory are all gathered at Cory's apartment, waiting for me to get there, so I only stay for an hour to network. My pitch lures people to approach me, asking more about my future business plans, if I can see this succeeding as a franchise, and other growth opportunities. It's encouraging having so many entrepreneur-minded people engage with me and my business in this way. What started out as an idea is now a full-fledged operation. After filing paperwork, placing supply orders, signing a freaking commercial property lease, it's not until this moment that it hits me.

# CHAPTER
# THIRTY-FOUR

The following week is silent, with respect to the grant finalists decision. I get a handful of calls from people who saw the news segment covering the pitch event. Two of those turn into reservations for group events in the fall. I didn't imagine this would happen before my soft launch and my initial marketing efforts, but I'm officially accepting reservations.

Ben contacts me twice. Once, copied on an email to the mentee group, congratulating us for doing so well on our pitches and informing us that soon he'll be in Philly for a few weeks. He sent me a separate email inquiring about the photographers for my soft launch and assuring me he'll be back in town for it.

Neither of us throws off our clothes and jumps in the other's bed in celebration of no longer being officially tied to our mentor-mentee relationship. We continue along the lines of how our relationship was initially designed to be. I shouldn't have expected different from the man who taught me that theory in the first place. Still, with every communication I can't help but hope his words are laced with a double entendre. That *I'm looking forward to seeing BiC in action* also means he's looking forward to seeing more of *us* in action.

On the weekend, I invite Elise and Corinne to stay overnight. The three of us haven't arranged to do this in a while. It's not until we're all in my kitchen, trying to get dinner together and not bump into each other, that I realize I miss their collective presence.

And since I've been withholding for over a week, I tell them about Ben. Then I tell them all the things about my Met experience I hadn't shared with them. I needed to work through Met on my own, and they understand that. When I tell them there's no love story at the end of this journey, they don't accept this as readily.

"That doesn't make sense," Elise says as we sit around the dining room table to eat. "New and improved Met dealt you a better hand. All bops, no skips. There must be something in one of these relationships you formed."

"Let's see." I hold up my hand and add fingers as I say, "I have a good friend, a distant friend with benefits pending, a vet for Pen, and a basketball buddy." I wiggle my four standing fingers. "That's a pretty good severance package."

"A vet," Corinne huffs. "You lost me good money."

"Yeah, well. Sorry I'm a waste of a romantic partner."

"Don't say that," Elise says as Corinne snorts. "You're not less, or a diminished archetype. You're Tiwanda. The one meant for you will see that." Elise squeezes my forearm.

"Did Met say anything helpful?" Corinne asks.

I bite the inside of my lip, my mind instantly going to my final Ask Met question. I'd spent all of last Sunday trying to think of something foolproof, but nothing I came up with fit the bill. In the panic of the last hours until the clock would run out and I wouldn't get to even ask a foolish question, I typed out, So this is it? You drop four perfectly acceptable people into my life and then take off?

*No amount of time would be enough, but you're ready. You always have been.*

That was the last I'd heard from Met. It's still on my phone, but my question line has dried up, and it hasn't offered any tips. It would probably let me delete it at this point, but I haven't attempted it because I revisit the Ask Met thread more often than I'd like to admit.

"A better question," I say, to deter myself from reaching for my phone and seeing the words already imprinted upon my mind. "When are we going to California to visit Elise and Devin?"

"I was thinking we'd give them about a month before we descend on them? That should be enough time," Corinne says.

"Literally I would welcome you on day one," says Elise. "You could sleep in the living room on a pallet."

It's silent for a moment as we chew. I'm determined to keep my somber tragedizing to myself. Thankfully, Corinne has my back.

"Ugh, this sucks. You better become a huge freaking star."

"I know," Elise says. "But I have to try."

My phone vibrates on the table, and I recognize the shape of the name *Benoit Sabi* in my peripheral before I even look directly at my screen to read it. The dates he planned to be in Philly start tomorrow, so I didn't expect to hear from him until he was settled. I hold it up to Elise and Corinne before swiping to answer it. Then I stand and walk away from the dining table, into the living room.

"Hey. Can I come over?" Ben asks.

My brain spends the first seconds after that question conjuring up a list of why he might want to come over. To talk about us? To *not* talk about us? But then I remember I have company, so his intentions are moot.

"Elise and Corinne are here," I tell him. "You can stop by for a minute, though, if you wanted to talk."

"Oh." The one syllable is apathetic, which I take to mean he's considering. "No, it's all right. Enjoy your friends. I was mainly calling because the finalists were selected. It hasn't been publicized yet, but they told the mentors."

"Okay?"

Just as I know he paused to allow me the chance to tell him if I want the inside scoop, he knows my inquisitive "okay" is the go-ahead.

"I'm sorry, Tiwanda."

I don't hear much after that. They didn't pick me. Maybe he tells me why and tries to assuage the feeling of shortcoming that trounces me. I do catch that Pilar was chosen, so that's a bit of good news. Still, it does nothing to patch up the blow he delivered.

"Okay," I say again.

"Do you want to talk about it?"

"Not really." I hiccup a laugh. "I can't change their decision, so what is there to discuss? At least I got $15K out of it."

"Maybe the—" he starts, surely attempting to offer another route for me to get grant money or other avenues of success.

"I'm going to be all right, Ben. You don't have to coddle me. And you didn't have to break the news to me, but thank you for doing it. It would've sucked to read this in an email."

I hang up with him and turn toward Elise and Corinne, who are wearing carefully tuned looks of commiseration on their faces. Despite the crushing disappointment, a deep gratefulness for them surges in my chest. Elise, with her affinity for seeing only multiple routes that lead to the same goalpost. Corinne, who felt this same sting only months before. I can't be in better hands.

# CHAPTER THIRTY-FIVE

Bathe in Chocolate is complete. After filling a barren spot on the wall with a mirror, I go around taking pictures. The kitchen is bright and inviting. With its new counters and updated appliances, it looks modern and fresh. The fire department cleared me for a maximum occupancy of twenty-two back here, which works since it's greater than my expected class capacity.

The front area needed the brunt of the work, design-wise. Along with the tables I bought, which will be crucial for parties, I also have a love seat sofa and several armchairs that bring a cozy vibe to the space. Against the wall shared with the office, I put a glass case I found from a secondhand furniture shop. In a few weeks' time, it'll be stocked with Bathe in Chocolate merchandise available for purchase. Directly in front of it is a high table that will serve as the place to ensure everyone has signed a waiver before heading back to the kitchen. And of course there's the mural, which makes me smile every time I enter.

The interns I hired, Layla and Dena, arrive at the kitchen for our final training day. I've saved the most intensive for the last of the three. The first day, we all attended a workshop together about guiding cooking classes with children. The second day, we were in the kitchen doing a test run of making bonbons. Today, we're focusing on soap. Neither Layla nor Dena has experience with it, but they did watch the YouTube video I sent them demonstrating cold-process soapmaking in preparation.

We get right to work. In the real classes, I'll have more options for additives available for the attendants. Now, I pull out only the ingredients we need.

Our trio gets along well. Dena is around my age, but Layla just turned twenty-one. Despite the age difference, we have a good rapport. It helps that Layla and Dena already know each other well from school. Layla is enthusiastic and has an endless supply of special-event ideas. Dena loves working with children and comes up with the most bizarre ganache filling flavors that actually taste good. It makes me look forward to the classes all three of us will run together.

We place our finished bars on the soap-drying stand. They'll sit there for a few days to further solidify. Then I'll take them out of the molds and leave them for a month as the last traces of lye are cured. For future classes, I'll send participants home with their soap in a silicone mold they get to keep, a takeaway bag with some branded mementos, and most importantly, a little card that reminds them of the final steps they must follow before using their soap.

To celebrate the end of training, I treat my interns to lunch at the Thai restaurant down the block. We order spicy food and martinis and express disbelief that our soft launch is this weekend.

"Everything will be low stakes," I tell them. "It'll just be my family and friends."

"Teaching people you know is harder," Dena says. "I tried to do a cooking-class-type thing for my aunt and uncle's anniversary, and I felt like I needed to hand my degree from Jon Wills back."

Layla nods in agreement. "Whenever I try to bake something with my cousins, I end up taking over. They're disasters in the kitchen."

I shake my head ruefully and take a sip of my apple martini. The word *disaster* doesn't bring up images of messy counters and ruined pastries, as I'm sure Layla intended. Instead, I picture Vonnie and Grandma getting into it again, this time with chocolate at their disposal for splattering. I picture it being awkward with Elliot, since Pilar convinced me to still invite him, and stiff and formal with Ben.

Whatever. It's just practice and a chance to get photos for Bathe in Chocolate's online presence. Surely, I'll be way too busy running my first class to be bothered with feelings.

~

Saturday evening, my interns and I meet an hour before the soft launch for prep work. We arrange seven sets of equipment around the center counter. Six induction burners are plugged into the outlets. Along with the actual stove, it should be enough to prevent bottlenecking. We work swiftly to get all the ingredients measured out according to my notes. In the front area, I use a table for drinks, a charcuterie board, and a fruit tray. Done with the tasks a half hour before go time, my team of three is pumped up. I love how invested Dena and Layla have become in such a short time of involvement. They're both interested in leading some of the chocolate classes, and I think they'll be poised to take the reins sooner rather than later.

"I got something for us," I tell them. I go to the storage closet that holds aprons for chocolate making and protective gear for soapmaking. I grab the bag I stashed in the corner and pull out three special aprons, each monogrammed with Bathe in Chocolate's logo and our respective names.

"Now we're legit," Dena says.

The photographer arrives first, soon followed by the interpreter. I'm telling the interpreter what she can expect for the night when Ben arrives with Nehi, who's still on a high from getting the job at A

Welcome Home, and Efe. Dena holds open the door for them to enter. I'm so excited to see Efe that I belatedly realize Ben and Nehi each hold parts of the risers Ben made for me. Dena leads them to the storage room, since we won't be needing them for tonight.

"I'll let you know when Victor and Yazmin get here," I tell the interpreter before excusing myself to greet Efe.

"I'm glad you could come," I say.

"After those chocolates you made for me, I had to learn how," she replies.

Corinne, Cory, Elise, and Devin show up together. None of them have seen the completed store yet, so they explore the space excitedly. Layla eventually shepherds them to the waiver-signing table.

Elliot arrives alone and before Pilar, who I planned to use as my shield. I take a deep breath as he walks in the door and remind myself I can set the tone. I greet him with a hug and offer to show him around the store.

"I'm impressed," he says as we leave the kitchen area to return to where everyone is mingling. "Thank you for inviting me. I'm glad I get to see the end result."

"Of course," I say as if it weren't Pilar's initiative.

Speaking of Pilar. "E.!" She comes up to us. I notice Layla and Dena have started using clipboards to bring the waiver forms around to people. "You're partnering with me," Pilar tells Elliot.

Victor and Yazmin also arrived in the short time I was in the kitchen with Elliot. They're chatting in a group with Corinne and Cory, along with the interpreter. The photographer flits around on the fringes, clicking away. As I'm taking stock of the growing group, my eyes catch on Ben, the tallest here. He's already looking my way and doesn't divert his gaze when I catch him. His mom is nearby speaking with Cousin Vonnie. I don't see any plus-one with Vonnie, though I told her it was okay to bring one. I thought she might like to bring her boyfriend or some other backup. I start to head their way, but as soon as I do, the door opens and Grandma and Clara enter. Since Efe and Vonnie are deep in conversation, I go to them instead.

I skip over a formal greeting and ask, "Clara, do you mind partnering with Ben's brother tonight?"

"As long as he's okay with doing most of the work, it's cool with me."

"How is she going to do that when she's supposed to be my partner?" Grandma asks.

"Don't worry," I say. A vindictive little grin touches my lips as I take my opportunity to finally get back at her for the disruption she caused at Vonnie's dinner. "I have a partner for you."

Everyone is in their places around the kitchen, hands freshly scrubbed, aprons and hairnets on. The pairs fit comfortably around the center counter. The interpreter is across from Vic and Yaz at the moment but has a chair out of the way for when she's not needed. I stand at the head of the table to introduce myself and the team. Dena and Layla stand at the ready on opposite sides of the kitchen.

"Hi." I beam at them. "You all know me as Tiwanda, but for the next few hours, you can call me by the name you know or 'Chef.'"

"Okay, Chef!" Elise calls out. She's so excited for me, I can only laugh at her interruption.

Corinne whoops and starts clapping, and in no time the entire congregation joins in. My smile stretches even wider. I lift my hands to gently cut them off, then finish my introduction.

"I've envisioned this moment before, over a year ago. It's amazing to think that back then, I didn't have half of the picture because I hadn't met all of you yet." I look at Ben, who supported my business just as fiercely as he pinpointed its weaknesses during the panel. And my fellow mentees, Pilar, Yazmin, and Victor, who understand this whirlwind process better than anyone. Then Elliot, who sweetened this journey in such an unexpected way. "You all came into my life when I needed you the most, and I'm so grateful you're here. And my OGs. My family, and my friends who've become family, your belief in me is sometimes frightening, but I wouldn't be here without it. In times like this, when I'm so happy it makes me sad that my parents aren't here to witness it, I'm comforted by your existence. Because I learned early that life takes and takes some more. But every time I see your faces or hear your voices, I'm reminded that first and foremost, life gives."

I make a distressed noise as I fan my hands in front of my watering eyes. To quell the tears, I have to look away from Grandma and Vonnie, who are both wiping their own cheeks.

"We want to say a few words too," Grandma says, bringing my attention back to her.

*We?* I panic for a moment, thinking they're going to go around in a circle and each say something nice about me until I'm reduced to a puddle. But Grandma nods her head at Vonnie alone.

"It's a shame your mother and father didn't get the full benefit of you," Grandma says. "They didn't get the opportunity to see the foundation they laid at work. But trust me, we know better than anyone how proud they would be."

"Families fill in gaps. All kinds, but particularly gaps in information," Vonnie says. "If your mom were here, she'd give you space to do your thing but would watch you in awe the whole night."

Grandma nods. "Wendell would have sung your praises to anyone who would listen."

"We haven't done a great job at working together to give you the complete picture you deserve, but we vow to do our best from here on out. Looking at you, I see the sweet girl who endured such loss, the woman you are now, and so much I missed between. Proud doesn't begin to cover it."

I can't carry on with the class without going to hug them both. Swallowing against the thickness building in my throat, I say, "Let's make some chocolate."

As I begin to explain what we'll be making, Layla hands me two small boxes of chocolates we preserved from our training days. I take the lid off each and send them around in opposite directions. As they circle their way back to me, I explain what they're seeing.

"The box on the right has a dark-chocolate shell, while the one on the left is milk chocolate. Both are filled with a rich ganache that we'll be making shortly." I give a brief overview of the process; then I let them decide with their partners what kind of chocolate—dark, milk, or white—they want to use.

Dena, Layla, and I distribute the premeasured containers of chocolate based on their selections for the ganache filling, along with heavy whipping cream. The last pair to make up their mind, of course, is Grandma and Vonnie. I stroll over to them as Dena and Layla help the rest of the pairs use the induction burners.

"Anything I can help with?" I ask them.

"You've done enough," Grandma says under her breath before taking a sip from her plastic wine cup.

"We'll be doing a dark-chocolate center," Vonnie says triumphantly.

My eyes slide over to Grandma, who I know prefers milk chocolate. "How about fifty-six percent? That makes a tasty ganache."

They agree to the semisweet compromise, and I let out a relieved breath as I return to the head of the table to give further instruction. They might have some home training after all. Their joint speech wasn't empty words; the action of them working together backs it up.

Once mostly everyone has their base ganache mixture, my co-chefs bring out the two organizing trays of potential add-ins and put them on either side of the counter. This is my favorite part. They get to be creative and come up with flavor combinations, and I become more like a teacher managing a classroom of students working on different projects. I circle the table, checking in on everyone and offering my opinions. Similarly, Dena takes whatever ingredients a pair is leaning toward and adds one or two more to elevate it. Layla is helping the Cories troubleshoot why their ganache isn't as thick as it should be at this stage.

"Tiwanda, try this," Efe says.

I take a tasting spoon from the container on the counter and dip it into their bowl. Ben watches, uncertainty in his pinched lips.

"Okay . . ." I nod. They used chopped honey-roasted pecans and cardamom. "Try adding a pinch of salt," I say. Salt will bring out the flavor of the cardamom a bit more. "I think a bit of nutmeg would be good in this too." Before I can move away, Ben stops me.

"How's it going?" he says. The kitchen is loud enough with flavor discussions, off-topic chats, and laughter that it feels as private a moment as any.

"Good, I think." I look around at the group. They all are fully invested in perfecting their fillings. Clara is surprisingly pulling her weight, sprinkling in dried fruit bits as Nehi stirs. Pilar and Elliot high-five each other, tasting spoons in hand. "Everyone seems to be following."

"I meant for you."

"Oh. I'm glad I have help." I nod to Dena and Layla, hard at work, probably putting out little fires I haven't a clue about. Without them, I wouldn't have the capacity to run a class of this size with this level of customization.

"We'll debrief later. But in case you don't know, you're doing great, Chef."

I want to stand with him and talk about how private-party bookings have started to steadily stream in for the fall due to the continued publicity following the completion of the grant program, but I'm summoned by Elise and Devin to try their ganache. I give him a grin that doesn't reveal how warm his familiar mix of business and encouragement makes me, and continue my rounds.

# CHAPTER
# THIRTY-SIX

"Now that you've made the inside of your bonbons, it's time to handle the outside," I tell my class after they've transferred their ganache fillings into the fridge to thicken as we move on to the shell. While I give them a demonstration on tempering with the seeding method, emphasizing the importance of heating and cooling to attain that shiny coat, Layla brings out the molds, and Dena arranges the decorative options.

While the water is heating to a boil, those who want to add a bit of color to the tops of their bonbons do so. Victor and Yazmin make a colorful splattered design with cocoa-butter paint. Efe and Ben dust each hole in their mold with gold dust. Armed with their chocolate of choice, each pair positions their metal bowl over the pot of boiling water.

It's all hands on deck then. Dena and Layla assume responsibility for two pairs each, and I monitor three. We remind them of the goal temperatures and assure them they're capable when they grow anxious.

My pairs are Efe and Ben, Grandma and Vonnie, and Nehi and Clara. Efe's letting Ben do the heavy lifting for this part as she speaks with Grandma. I hear Grandma say, "I practically had to force her to quit so she could claim her blessings, mhmm," and resist butting into the conversation. Vonnie is patiently stirring, waiting for their batch to reach the desired temperature. Clara nibbles on morsels of chocolate that are supposed to be used when it's time to lower the temperature, the same thing she does when we're at my condo and I'm making chocolate. But when Nehi removes the pot from the heat, she redirects the chocolate to the right place.

I drift to Ben's side. "Hanging in there?"

He breaks his concentration on the candy spatula thermometer's reading to side-eye me. "You've seen my work in the kitchen already. I can keep up." He looks back at the temperature displayed in the handle, and his bravado wavers. "Oh shoot, it's too high."

"It's fine, it's fine." I grab a couple of pot holders and lift the metal bowl from the pot, sitting it beside his induction burner. "Continue stirring—I'm adding more chocolate."

Ben is back on track once the temperature starts to fall, and I circle the table to check on my friends. As pairs begin calling out that they're done with tempering, we have parchment paper at the ready to test it. If the test drop comes out of the fridge shiny and snaps cleanly in half, they're good to go.

They use ladles or a piping bag to fill all the holes in the mold, tap the side to get rid of any air bubbles, and then pour the excess back into the bowl, leaving only the dome of the shell. They place their molding trays in the fridge, swapping them out with their ganache mixtures. The ganache goes in piping bags. Once the shells have hardened enough, they take the molds out and begin filling each cavity with ganache. They're covered with the base layer of chocolate, scraped clean, and sat in the fridge for hardening.

Pair by pair, people finish. Their excitement over having successfully created reminds me of my first-ever batch. If I get this exhilarated feeling every time I finish teaching a class, I'll never tire of this job.

My friends and family drink wine, gab, and take pictures with each other while we wait for the chocolates to harden enough. I check in with Dena and Layla, and they're enjoying this as much as I am.

Finally, my timer goes off for the chocolates. We place boxes branded with the Bathe in Chocolate logo, paper candy holders, and ribbons on the counter. One person from each pair goes to retrieve their chocolates. Then the kitchen is filled with clacks as they tap the counter to get the bonbons to release from the plastic molds.

They're eager to try their creations. Pilar exclaims, clearly pleased with how their batch turned out. Elliot offers me one to try. It has a kick of cayenne pepper and is balanced with the perfect amount of sweetness. As everyone boxes their chocolates, they also exchange with other groups, tasting the fruits of their labor.

Before anyone leaves, the photographer takes a group photo of us in the kitchen as well as in front of the mural. No one seems to be in a rush to go home, so they hang around chatting with each other for a bit. I want to hang out and revel in this moment with my loved ones, but I also want to leave them to their devices and join Dena and Layla in the kitchen to clean.

Vonnie, who was in conversation with Clara, notices me available for once and approaches.

"I can't tell you how much it means to be here, witnessing you kick off the next chapter of your life."

I nod. "It means a lot to me too."

She gently shakes her head. "Bearing witness to your life is my duty. I owe your mom this, and I've failed her for so long."

I take her hand and squeeze. "We found our way back to each other, so it's not a failure. Just a work in progress."

She wraps me in a hug so comforting it brings the sting of tears to my eyes.

"I'm going to say bye to your grandma before I take off," Vonnie says.

I watch in awe as she heads over willingly and an exchange resembling a cordial goodbye takes place. I pull my eyes away from them and make my rounds to say preemptive farewells to my friends so I can assist with the cleanup. Layla and Dena must be just as exhausted as I am.

Victor, Yazmin, Pilar, Ben, and I finally get a chance to group up and celebrate Pilar getting the additional grant money. Victor and Yazmin also snagged a few big projects from the presentation-night networking. I thank Elliot for coming again, and he leaves with Pilar, Victor, and Yazmin. Ben goes to collect his mom and brother, while I push my way into my circle of friends.

Elise, Devin, Corinne, and Cory shift to make room for me. I love that we can be configured into various combinations and it still works. Not all friend groups have that flexibility. It's a precious thing that won't be lost with Elise and Devin moving, but it won't be at my daily disposal. My options have quickly whittled down to: hang out with Cory, hang out with Corinne, or—a two-for-one third-wheel special—hang out with them both.

"This is it for a while, huh?"

"Temporarily," Elise says. We both know it isn't a promise, but a hope that one day our diverging paths will meet up again and we'll live in the same city. I hug each of them tightly before they leave. When we still aren't satisfied, we huddle together in a group and grasp on to each other for a long moment. Finally, they take off. Met might have allowed me to form quick bonds with new people, but it'll never be quite like what I had with Elise, Cory, Corinne, and Devin. And that's okay. This era didn't last forever, or even for as many years as I would have chosen, if given the power. But it existed and can never be taken away. I'm learning that's enough.

Ben, Nehi, and their mom are still across the room speaking with Grandma and Clara. Efe and Grandma must have struck up an easy camaraderie working next to each other in the kitchen. I thank Efe again for coming, and thank Ben for, well, everything.

"Are you sure you don't need a hand cleaning up?" Ben asks.

"I got it," I say. "Dena and Layla are probably already halfway done."

His response takes a while to get out as he seems to be shuffling through options before settling on, "I'll be in touch about the official opening."

There's no logic to support the pang of regret I feel at his practical words. Efe gives me a warm hug, and the three of them are gone.

Grandma and Clara don't take no for an answer and start gathering the leftover snacks and drinks from the table. We return to the kitchen with our hands full. Dena is washing dishes while Layla rids the counters of all the ingredients and supplies left out. I grab the broom out of the closet and start sweeping. The action is monotonous enough that my mind is free to reminisce on the night. I don't know if any class full of strangers will top this, but that makes me all the more grateful that I was able to kick off this venture with so many people who are rooting for my success. Including Ben, who months ago I would have never considered as being part of this circle.

Ben. I picture his face, so focused on the task of tempering chocolate. It's not so dissimilar from the focus he gave me in bed. I like it, in both situations.

"Honey, I think that spot is clean," Grandma says.

I startle. "Right, just tired." I get my feet moving again.

I still feel Grandma's eyes on me, though. And as if she's read my mind, she says, "Tiwanda, tell me about Efe's son, this Ben guy."

I exchange a look with Clara.

"What do you mean? He's the one I told you about—my mentor," I hedge.

"You didn't tell me he looked like that."

A gasp of laughter comes from Layla while she wipes down the counter. Grandma and I have the same taste in men, awesome. I bob my head, neither confirming nor denying my attraction, and continue sweeping the floor.

"Remember I told you about the first time Wendell brought your mom around? At the party, how they circled each other almost as if uninterested but not quite? Wendell, poor thing, tracking your mom with his eyes from across the room?"

"Yeah," I say, though I don't follow why we're now talking about my mom and dad. "The reason you decided you didn't like her."

"Yes, but that's beside the point. I saw you and that Ben tonight, and it was like I was back at that party. It's like a mirror, how the two of you interact."

Her words take my breath away, and I grip the broom handle as a sharp heat flares behind my breastbone. Before I can form a thought, a chime sounds. It's not from my phone, but the security camera tablet signaling the doorbell. Still in a stupor, I lean the broom against a counter and go to check the video feed. There, at the locked door, is Ben.

"I'll get that," I say.

"You better," Grandma answers.

The small changes Ben makes when he sees me approaching—the straightening of his tilted head, the inhale that puffs his chest, his eyes becoming slightly more alert—they all fire off signals in me. Signals to act. Fight or flight. Fight for what I want, or run from the possibility of being hurt in a way I've never experienced before.

I let him in.

"Did you forget something?" I ask.

"No, and yes."

"Okay . . ." I glance behind him. "Where's your family?"

"Waiting for me in the car." He laughs a bit, then shakes his head and searches my eyes. He takes a deep breath, and it's like he's fortifying himself, drawing strength from my returning gaze. "Mama told us in the car, 'I really like Tiwanda.'" He takes on her Beninese accent. "'I think you should try with her, Nehikhare. It's worth a shot.' And I told them both he can't. I told them I think I'm already falling for you, that I want you for myself."

"Oh, cool." I'm so shell-shocked I let the conversation templates filed in my brain take over while I scramble. "What did she say to that?"

"She slapped me against the arm and said, 'What are we doing here in the car driving away, then?' I didn't have a good answer to that. Only that I won't push you on this if you don't want to turn the night we shared into more than what it is."

My feet seem to move of their own accord. I stop when I've almost closed the distance.

"What about design? We're trying to do much more than what our relationship was set out to be. You said you weren't interested in having your way with me, remember?"

He cradles my neck and jaw in his hands. "So redesign with me."

"I'm not moving from Chicago," I point out.

He shrugs. "I'll go between Philly and here for now."

"I'm never sharing a bathroom with you."

"No, I'm not sharing one with you. I saw how much clutter you had from your soap supplies."

I consider the rest of my characteristics that I assumed meant I wouldn't fare well in a relationship. But I see now I'll do just fine in the right one.

"More things might come up."

"So we stay flexible, keep our designer's cap on."

I tilt my chin up and his lips meet mine, and I register the withdrawal my body has been going through these past weeks. He tastes like dark chocolate and nutmeg, and as our lips caress each other's, the certainty I was searching for claims me. I don't second-guess myself or reach for my phone to see if Met has anything to say. I say, and I trust myself to follow wherever my heart leads. Young me was right. I am owed happiness.

~

Apparently, Met does have something to say.

The notification comes after the Bathe in Chocolate kitchen is thoroughly cleaned and locked up for the night. I'm in my car, hand on the gear lever, when the noise stops me cold. I turn on my car's interior lights and flash my headlights at Clara, who's waiting so I'm not left as the lone car in the lot.

*Met Tip: There isn't only one.*

My heart pounds in my chest like I'm in a horror movie.

*There weren't any wrong choices here. Only right ones, in various ways. The power always lay in your ability to make the decision. The power lies in your ability to keep deciding.*

I inflate my lungs with a slow inhale. The exhale comes out in uneven puffs.

*One last question for the road?*

The app populates the Ask Met thread on its own. Clara beeps at me. When I look up, she holds up her thumb, then flips it down, eyebrows raised in question. I hold up a finger, take a steadying breath, and begin typing. The question comes to me easily.

*How am I supposed to go on again like normal, without you for a second time?*

*You weren't completely without me the first time, Miss Thing. This was just your reminder.*

My throat aches from the tears I refuse to shed. I've had enough of emotions for one night. A chill travels down my spine, and I shake my shoulders against the fleeting sensation.

*Thank Met by leaving a rating!*

The outlines of five stars spiral onto my screen, accompanied by the shimmery tone that signaled each of my Met matches. I press the fourth one. There are a few improvements I could think of off the top of my head, so this is more than fair.

*Share Met with a friend?*

*Aha.* The offer Corinne received that kick-started this ordeal. Lights flash at me again, and I lift my head. Clara moves her hand in a circular motion, the signal for *hurry up*. If I weren't being rushed right now, I'd probably rethink this decision. I'd probably err on the side of caution and not pass along this chain text message–esque app from hell. As it is, I am being rushed. And I did promise to follow my heart.

# ACKNOWLEDGMENTS

Wow, writing during a pandemic is not a fun time! In sign language interpreting, we have this phrase we use—"source language intrusion." It's basically when your English messes up your ASL rendering, or vice versa. All throughout the early drafts of this, I spotted what I referred to as "source trauma intrusion." The reality of the heartbreaking pandemic leaked into a book meant to be an escape. Thankfully, I have a great team who helped me turn it around.

A huge thank-you to Alicia Clancy, whose sharp eye helped me rid this novel of those intrusions. Working with you is easy. I'm continually amazed at your speed and connectedness with my vision, even when I don't have it nailed down myself.

Samantha Fabien, I love having you as my agent. Thank you for your constant support and for bringing together such an amazing #TeamSamantha. Thank you to the entire Root Literary team. Your support and guidance are much appreciated. Team Samantha—I've said it once and I'll say it again, I can't wait to have rows of your books on my bookshelf. We're just getting started, and I'm so excited for our futures!

Thank you to the entire APub team! Working with you all to bring *Have We Met?* and *The Moment We Met* out into the world was smoother than I ever dreamed of. Nicole and the editorial production team, Kristin and publicity, the marketing team . . . thank you all so much! Special thanks to Michelle for coming in and helping *HWM* find its readers! Emily, thanks for providing cultural research reads for both of my book babies. Thank you, Jen, Haley, Robin, Jill, Claire, and the entire editorial production team for this book. You all are not only great at English, but you make sure I don't sound like a broken record.

Thank you for killing it back-to-back with illustrating gorgeous covers that capture my characters, Tyler Mishá Barnett. Thanks, Philip Pascuzzo, for sharing your talent of cover design with us.

Casey, we met twice to try to wrestle all my ideas into something that resembled a plot. You know my struggle firsthand. Thank you for being wonderful at what you do and helping me find the bones of this story! Thanks, Shauna, for knowing so much about soap. My OG CP Gaby—thank you for being on the other end of my long, despairing text threads. I'm so glad we met and kept each other all these years.

My family—I'm sure you see pieces of us throughout this novel. I was able to figure out what Tiwanda was missing mainly by considering everything I have with you all. Thank you for not only filling the gaps, but overflowing them. Love you all!

Thank you to my friends, [copy & paste from first book haha]. Keisha and Joclyn, thank you for being not only my friends, but also my sisters. I promise to publicly claim you. Cathryn, you're the best. Special shout-out to the Covid Cathys (Joc, Diana, Lindsey, and Briana)! We've gone through some changes together the past year. Thank you for having lives interesting enough for me to procrastinate writing/editing this book in favor of making PowerPoint presentations about your shenanigans.

My writing groups have been the highlight of my past year. Lit Squad—y'all are the source of so much laughter. I love you all. Staircase Scream Queens (or whatever we're calling ourselves at the moment), thank you for the writing sprints that become chatting sprints, and the aggressive accountability. Rooting for us, forever.

Finally, thank you to everyone who read and supported *Have We Met?* and *The Moment We Met*. I had such a wonderful debut experience. So grateful you gave me a chance.

# ABOUT THE AUTHOR

*Photo © 2020 Joclyn Torain*

Camille Baker is the author of *Have We Met?* She earned a bachelor's degree in finance from the Ohio State University. There, she took sign language classes for fun, and during business classes that didn't hold her interest, she wrote stories. After graduating, she completed the Interpreter Training Program at San Antonio College. Camille now resides, interprets, and writes in South Chicago. For more information, visit www.camillebaker.com.